The Penguin Killer

(The Redfern Series Book 1)

By Ste Sharp

"You do something to me... something deep inside"

Tuesday 25th July 1995

Caught By The Fuzz - Supergrass

I could tell he was a copper by the way he leaned on my desk.

'Can I speak to the owner of the shop, mate?' he asked.

His cold blue eyes were made more intense by his John Lennon glasses.

I'd left the front door open so hadn't seen him come in, otherwise I would have swept the Rizlas and Amsterdam's finest into the open top drawer.

'Yes,' I answered and breathed in deeply. I'd only had my three o'clock spliff ten minutes earlier so this sudden appearance had killed my buzz and was making me pink with paranoia. 'It's my shop.' I sat up in an attempt to look professional. 'Red Books.'

'You're the owner?' He pushed off the desk, straightened his tie and looked me up and down.

'Yes,' I replied with a deeper voice. 'Luke Redfern.' I fought to control the wave of irritation surging through me. This guy was only a few years older than me, late twenties maybe, yet he was talking to me like he was my Dad. 'It used to be my Grandad's shop.' I found myself explaining.

'Ah.' He raised his chin and turned to survey the narrow, book-lined corridors which branched away from the front room like a hobbit warren.

I swept my arm across the desk and brushed the weed into the open drawer before he turned back and pulled a laminated badge from his pocket.

'Detective Sergeant Mellor.'

He had to be on that new fast-track police system Dad had talked about: all toffs and spotty teenagers apparently. Even though Dad was on enforced garden leave, he'd been in the police his entire working life, so he knew what he was talking about.

Detective Mellor squinted and asked, 'Where's your Grandfather now?'

'He died,' I said and glanced at Grandad's camera sitting on the shelf by the front door.

The Detective pulled out a small black notepad and wrote as he spoke. 'Previous owner deceased. When?'

'March,' I replied and pictured the flowers at the burial, the photo on his coffin, my Grandad's smile.

'And do you keep records of every book sold?' Mellor asked.

His accent was local, not London, not posh: definitely Brighton.

I swallowed. 'Grandad used to, but…'

Sometimes it felt like I was just looking after the shop for Grandad. If I opened up late or forgot to put new books on the shelves I felt like I was letting him down.

'No records since March 1995.' Mellor captured his words with his pencil.

'Well, we were closed for a bit, obviously,' I said.

'Obviously,' Mellor agreed and held my gaze.

I couldn't break away. His stare bored into me and I felt guilty. Had I broken some stupid business law I had no idea about? This isn't me, I wanted to say. I'm not a bookshop owner, I'm a guitarist… a singer… a songwriter.

Mellor broke eye contact and asked, 'So you took over the shop, when?'

'Well.' I had to think back. 'Early May I guess. He left the shop to me so I moved in but I was still at Uni.'

'Moved in?'

'To the flat above – I own the whole building.' Not that it was much to brag about – three crumbling floors of ancient wood and brick held together by mouldy plaster and Victorian plumbing.

'What were you studying?'

'Photography,' I answered.

Mellor snorted and turned to the rows of books. 'They give degrees away for anything these days. Mind if I take a look around?'

'Yeah, sure,' I replied and tried to suppress another wave of annoyance.

What did he know about art? I thought as he wandered off. He had no idea what went into creating a perfect framed shot or the science behind developing film. He probably thought it was all pissing about and…

Calm down.

I took a deep breath and closed the drawer. I had to control these petty surges of anger. That was one reason I smoked weed: to calm me down. Mum said I should let the anger out, not hold it in but that was easier said than done. Instinctively, I looked up to my acoustic guitar hanging on the wall. Getting lost in a good tune was the best way to relieve the tension but, even though I gigged with my band most weekends, I only liked playing when nobody was in the shop.

I tried to distract myself by flicking through the pages of the NME but the Detective's presence made me restless. I'd recently become addicted to a crossword book my Grandad had stashed away in the desk drawer but even that couldn't hold my attention. What if the Detective wanted to go upstairs? I sat up and craned my neck to see where he had disappeared to. I never worked out how Grandad stopped people nicking books - there were so many dark nooks in the shop.

I pushed up out of the chair to have a look but a shape appeared at the front door and I sat back down.

'Alright,' the customer said and we nodded before he disappeared into the depths of the shop.

I'd seen him before: one of the regulars heading to his favourite shelves. Another shape appeared at the door crowned with a cloud of white hair. It was Isaac, who owned the florist next door.

'Want a tea, Luke?' He asked with a smile.

'Err, yeah that would be great, cheers,' I replied and the cloud blew away.

I liked him. He knew I couldn't leave my shop unattended, plus he employed fit foreign girls.

A clicking sound made me turn to the record player by my side where the needle bumped against the edge. I had been playing *I Should Coco* by Supergrass. Lenny finished ages ago but the heavy chords were still echoing around my head. That's how I am with music. I remember songs perfectly like how some people have photographic memories. And I remember events by the song I was listening to at the time. I used to call it my 'radio head' but my brother took the piss so I stopped.

I flipped the record over and started side B: Strange Ones.

'Right then.' Mellor's tall frame appeared from behind the nearest bookshelf. 'Bigger than it looks, this place.'

'Yeah,' I replied. 'A bit of a Tardis.'

He squinted at me then at the record player. 'A bit retro isn't it?'

'It was my Grandad's,' I explained but held back the details: Nana and Grandad had bought it in the sixties when my Dad left home; two-speed; stereo speakers. 'And I like vinyl,' I said. 'Easier to pick out the song you want. No rewinding.'

'You should get yourself a CD player.'

'Maybe,' I said with a shrug and wondered how I could afford one. When Mum helped me sort the tax forms she said the shop would barely bring in any money, not that it had mattered to Grandad – it had just been his hobby really, something to keep him occupied after Nana died.

'Nice selection of penguin books back there.'

'Yeah, in the alcove room?' I said.

I pointed to the copy of the Bookseller magazine on my desk, trying to be professional again. 'It's their 60th anniversary this year.'

Mellor raised his eyebrows, but clearly wasn't interested. He pulled a green penguin book from the inside pocket of his jacket, handed it to me and asked, 'Can you confirm this book was sold by you?'

I took it and felt the smooth cover with my thumb while my forefinger rubbed the ridged creases of the spine. *The Hollow Man* by John Dickson Carr, number 862. Mystery and crime. I flicked the tea-dark pages from back to front, wafting the old paper spice to my nostrils, and stopped at the first page. Nestled in the top right corner, next to the pencilled name of the original owner, was a red 'R' in a red circle: my Grandad's sign.

'Yep, this was one of ours.' I pointed to the sign and handed the book back. 'Here.' I fished out the hand-made rubber stamp and pressed it on the corner of the Bookseller magazine.

Mellor nodded. 'Okay,' he said and paused as the regular book hunter walked out empty-handed. Mellor looked into the back rooms and asked, 'Is there anyone else in here?'

'Don't know,' I said with a shrug.

His eyes widened. 'Well, can you take a look? This is police business.'

'Right.' I slowly pushed myself out of the chair, trying not to get a head rush, ambled past the Detective and into the warren. I'd been paranoid for weeks I'd lock someone in and meticulously toured the shop every evening before closing up, so I knew the best route to take. In the distance I heard a tinkling bell. Every room was empty, so I toured back to the front room, where Detective Mellor sat perched on the edge of my desk.

'Some old boy brought you a tea,' he said and nodded at the steaming white plastic cup on my desk.

The front door was closed.

As I sat back down, Mellor got off the desk. 'What I'm about to tell you is confidential police business, right?'

'Okay.' I felt my cheeks warm a notch.

'This book.' He patted his jacket. 'Was found at the scene of a crime.'

I nodded and asked, 'What sort of crime?'

'I'm not at liberty to say, but you can assume it's serious or we wouldn't be involved. Detective Inspector Knowles believes the book was left by the perpetrator.'

I blinked and shook my head – something didn't seem right. 'How does your boss know the book was left by this… criminal?'

Mellor straightened his neck, looked out the door then back at me. 'I don't… all I can say is we're following every line of enquiry and I would appreciate your help.'

'Okay,' I said and a small voice in my head told me this was serious. Dad said the police always had an agenda – if they asked questions, there was a reason.

The Detective was whispering now. 'It's highly likely the perpetrator bought this book recently and…'

I shouldn't have had my three-o'clock smoke. Mellor was freaking me out. My cheeks were burning and I found myself staring out the window between the piles of books which hid me from the outside world.

'…I just need to know if you have the date this book was sold, okay? Anything to help with our enquiries.'

'Yeah, sure,' I said.

'I'm busy tomorrow.' Mellor's voice was normal again. 'But I'll come back on Thursday to see what you have.'

'We're closed Thursdays,' I said, still feeling in a daze.

'Okay, I'll pop by about five in the evening. Make sure you're here.'

'Yeah,' I said, not really thinking about it.

I was supposed to be going down the beach with the guys from the band on Thursday: have a few beers and smokes, maybe meet some girls. It was the usual summer thing so I could have easily missed it but my Thursdays were sacred now I was stuck in the shop every day.

'Great.' Mellor's eyes bored into me. 'I'll see you Thursday. Remember – eight six two – The Hollow Man.' He pointed at my desk where he had written the book details on the back of his card. 'And by the way.'

'What?' I focussed on him.

He nodded at my drawer and his voice dropped to a whisper again. 'Next time you want some weed, give me a ring. I've got contacts who can get their hands on the decent stuff.' He winked, opened the front door and left, leaving the tinkling bell echoing in my ears.

Wednesday 26th July 1995

There She Goes – The La's

The day after Detective Mellor's visit was another hot day. It felt like this was going to be our summer – a good week or two of sunshine – and everyone was getting into the summer mood. Girls were wearing their smallest tops, everyone had their legs out, smelt of sun cream and walked slower than usual. But not me. I was stuck in the shop. I could have closed up and gone down the beach but I felt this was my duty after Grandad left the shop to me. Still, after years of a being a free-spirited student, wandering in search of the perfect photograph, the shop was starting to feel claustrophobic.

Like most mornings, I clomped down the steep stairs and thought of Grandad. God knows how he dealt with those steps. The shop still smelt of him: the almond tang and dusty spice of the old books mixed with the freshness of the pine bookshelves. He built everything in this shop with help from Isaac next door.

'It used to be a butcher's,' Dad said when he helped me move in.

'Yeah, I remember.' I pictured the blood-stained tiled floor which had been replaced with reclaimed floor boards. 'What was it before that?'

'I dunno, a greengrocers maybe? I'm sure Dad said it had been joined with next door at one time… but they split it up during the war.'

'Right,' I said, wondering if I could convert it into a recording studio but the rooms were probably too small. 'It was a good idea of Grandad's.'

'Yeah, not exactly a money-maker.' Dad sighed. 'But it kept him busy after Mum died.'

And when I moved in, the ancient building nurtured another new start after death, I thought.

The door at the bottom of the stairs opened into the centre of the shop by the Military History bookshelf where I placed my cup of tea, minus a splash on the floorboards and toured the funnel-shaped back half of the shop. I had a habit of running my fingers along the dry spines of the rows of books as the rooms got narrower. Art. Gardening. Science. Foreign Literature. I opened the tiny blind at the back of the shop, lit a sandalwood joss-stick and headed back: detouring for another blind, past the alcove room of penguin books and back to my tea before entering the square front room of the shop.

I turned the open sign on the glass front door, hooked the door to the wall and threw the post on the desk before collapsing into the worn, brown leather chair to drink my tea. The English Channel was only a few hundred metres away so the fresh, salty air soon invaded the shop. After ten minutes I couldn't smell it anymore, but that first hit was a perfect start to the day, especially in the summer. Distant gulls' shrieks echoed through the morning air and, rarely for me, I closed my eyes and enjoyed the silence.

No music yet.

Eventually my eyes opened to absorb the mish-mash rainbow of spines of the room. This was the wallpaper of my waking day. Claustrophobic maybe but full of memories. When Grandad was here

I would pop in after Uni for a tea and chat, but even without him it had an other-worldly charm which felt relaxing. The shop felt timeless, as though each book had captured their individual moments in time and frozen them for anyone to peer into.

Neighbouring shops opened up one by one and I watched the comings and goings through the gaps between the piles of books in the shop window. Bins rumbling. Doors opening. People walking past. The cute foreign girls working in the florist next door walked past in their summer skirts. I picked up my crossword book and waited for the first customers to arrive and the sound of the bookshop to set in: a library-like silence of people thinking and pages whispering.

A man strolled in soon after nine, with a nod to me, and disappeared into the depths of the shop. In the few months I'd been running the shop I had categorised my customers into groups: browsers; collectors; present-buyers. This guy looked like a total book-geek, mid-thirties, thin, wispy hair, wearing a Star Trek t-shirt. Straight for the Science Fiction section I guessed.

A thought came to me: could he be the criminal the detective had talked about? Detective Mellor was only interested in when that particular book had been bought, but I wondered if I should start making notes of all books sold?

My gaze drifted around the room and fixed on my guitar: strumming a song or two would be good, but I decided to put a record on instead. Something I had heard loads of times before. Music makes the mood. I flipped through the LPs behind the record player: new albums, oldies from my parents and a well-worn selection of my own. They weren't sorted in some ridiculous order – I wasn't a bloody librarian – but the albums I hadn't played for a while were at the back. Back to my A-level days - Inspiral Carpets, the Cure… the La's.

Perfect.

The album started with *Son of a Gun*: a few bars of strummed acoustic guitar and picking, Lee Mavers' vocals hit me and my mind was transferred to another place: listening to records nicked from my brother; sitting cross-legged in my old bedroom in front of the record player with my guitar absorbing the music through the sound hole, up the neck and through the strings to my fingers. I could feel the music: the shapes and colours of the chords. Then I would play it back. A duet.

My body relaxed as the music massaged my mind. Maybe sitting in the shop all day wasn't so bad after all?

A silhouette crossed my door as a new customer walked in. Another guy, same age as the first but dressed for the office. He smiled at me and looked around, then ambled through to the darker rooms.

My eye caught Grandad's camera on the shelf and I wondered if I could take a photo of everyone coming into the shop? There was probably a law against it but some shops in town had CCTV cameras. What was the difference? No, I couldn't use Grandad's camera – I didn't want to spoil the flow of images on the film. I'd have to use the old Polaroid I'd found upstairs, but the flash was hard to control and…

The first man returned with a pile of books and placed them on my desk.

'How much are these?' He sounded polite but stood too close for my liking.

I plucked the books off the desk and checked their spines: all dark blue with white stylised writing. Sci-fi. I gave myself a congratulatory smile as I fingered through the front covers, mentally adding up the prices.

'Three pound fifty please,' I said, making a note to keep all prices rounded up from now on as he handed me a fiver and I fumbled in the cash tin for coins.

'Cheers.' I handed him the change.

The record player clicked so I turned the LP over, set the needle and, when I turned back, the second man was at my desk. The man in the shirt and trousers.

'Hello,' he said with a smile and placed four penguin books on my desk.

His smile reached his eyes, so I shouldn't have felt threatened, but my gaze fixed on the orange and green books. 'Sorry, I didn't mean to make you jump.'

I blinked and shook my head. 'No, it's okay.' I carefully flicked through the books to add up the prices. 'Two pounds.'

'Thanks,' he said and fumbled in his pocket for coins. 'Have you got a bag?'

'Sure.' I pulled a brown paper bag from the wedge impaled on a two-inch spike protruding from the wall behind me and stuffed the books in.

'Brilliant, err.' He held up a white card. 'I don't suppose you could help me?'

I nodded.

'I'm trying to find another penguin book – number two hundred and ten, *A Man Lay Dead* by Ngaio Marsh. If you come across a copy could you let me know?'

The card stayed motionless halfway between us where his hand reached out to me.

I swallowed.

'A penguin book?' I asked and took the card.

'Yes, I collect them you see?' He replied. 'If you could let me know that would be great.' He smiled again and made his way out, gripping onto the paper bag like a boy with a bag of sweets. 'Have a good day.'

I nodded and stared at the empty doorway for a few seconds before turning my gaze to the card in my hand: Andrew Smith, Penguin Books. It even had the little penguin in an orange oval. I breathed a lungful of sea air and waited for my heart to slow down. Had he bought the book the Detective showed me? No, it had to be a co-incidence, he didn't look like a criminal.

I sighed and reached over to turn the record player off. I needed to chill, so I grabbed my guitar, strummed a C-minor and waited for inspiration to flood over me. Would a new song come or would I retreat into the comfort of someone else's song? I've always been able to play a song by ear, which I guess is how I fix songs to memories. Hear it once, play it once on the guitar and that's it – the chords, their shapes and feel have been cut into the vinyl of my mind forever.

My fingers ran along silent strings as I looked out the window. My hand slid up the neck, two fingers pressed and the opening melody of *High and Dry* echoed around the room. A wave of harmony washed over me and I was taken away. I sang without thinking. My fingers pressed and switched positions like well-rehearsed dancers and I was lost. The song morphed into one of my own, with new chords and different melody, as I sang with my eyes closed. The chords slowed to a perfect finish.

When I opened my eyes I nearly dropped my guitar: a woman was standing by the nearest bookshelf.

'Hi,' she said and smiled.

'Shit… oh, I didn't see you there, I…' My heart was racing, as though I'd been woken from a deep sleep.

'Sorry.' She looked like a student, my age. 'I just wanted to buy this,' she said, holding up a book.

How on earth did I miss her coming in? She was gorgeous. Slim, long blonde hair and a cute smile.

'I didn't know anyone was here-' I stammered.

'It sounded good.' She came to the desk and a breeze from the door wafted her cotton dress.

For a second I wondered if she was real.

'Thanks,' I replied and could feel myself blush.

'I didn't recognise it,' she said. 'The song.'

'No, it's one of mine. We play it in my band.'

She nodded and her dark brown eyes glinted. 'Sounds soulful – a bit like the Verve.'

'Thanks,' I laughed and started to ease up. 'That's a compliment. I saw them in London a few weeks ago.'

'I missed it.' She turned the book over in her hands. 'So do you gig then? Your band?'

Her blonde hair reflected the light from the door and I was lost for a moment. I wanted to take a picture of her. Right there, right now.

I finally said, 'Yeah, we're playing this Friday actually – the King's Arms?'

'Oh yeah, I know it. I might come along.' She handed the book to me and, despite every muscle in my body urging me to make physical contact with her, I tried not to touch her fingers.

I flipped the cover open and saw £2 written in the corner next to the red 'R' in its circle.

'Call it a pound,' I said and passed it back.

'Thanks.'

She placed a coin in my palm and a tingle ran down my arm. Her fingers were soft and warm.

'No problem,' I said as she pulled away, leaving my hand stranded mid-air.

'Might see you Friday then.'

'Yeah, that would be great. Cheers.'

'I'll let you get back to playing,' she said and disappeared through the doorway as another sea breeze swayed her dress and left me with her perfume and a frozen image of her smile.

After half a minute of staring at the empty doorway, I turned to the record player, moved the needle to track five and an iconic electric guitar riff filled the room. The tambourine, the acoustic guitar and Lee's haunting voice sang my mood: *There She Goes*...

Then I looked down at the desk and noticed my red stamp was missing.

Thursday 27th July 1995

Staying Out For The Summer - Dodgy

A great photo was taken Thursday morning, but not by me. It captured my vision of my mates in the summer: four lads sitting on a wall bathed in sunlight and surrounded by a David Hockney sky. It was taken somewhere in between the piers. James is the black guy wearing shades on the left, then it's me with the acoustic guitar, looking at the camera, baggy jeans and Converse swinging against the wall, next is Rob pushing his hair out of his eyes, and finally Mike, pouting and pointing to the distance like some cheesy model.

'Cheers mate,' I said as I took the camera back from the obliging tourist.

'We should just set up over there,' Mike said. 'I can't be arsed to walk across those bloody stones.'

'We should get away from the prom,' James said.

Rob added, 'The tide's heading out.'

It was Thursday. Grandad always closed the shop on Thursdays – he said it was the worst day of the week for sales – so I kept his tradition. Plus I needed a day off after working Saturdays. Dad told me Grandad used Thursdays to source more books from the warehouses but I usually found Grandad down the allotment, snoozing in his deckchair. Anyway, I had four boxes of books in the flat waiting to be stamped and priced up and they could wait.

'Look, we've got food, weed and plenty of beers,' I said, gesturing to the left of the Palace Pier. 'It's worth walking a bit just to get away from the chip-eaters.' And it was out of reach of any wandering policemen's noses, I thought.

We strolled over to where tourists and day-trippers sheltered polystyrene trays of fatty chips from dive-bombing gulls and an eruption of giggles made us turn to where a group of sunbathing female students lounged.

Mike looked at me and winked. 'Or we could sit over there? I know one of them, she was on my course.'

Four smiles lit up. We were all single, twenty-one year old lads, fresh from Uni and without a care in the world.

'Mind if we join you, ladies?' Mike headed the vanguard. Typical lead guitarist, always trying to get in the limelight. 'Oh, hi, Rachel, didn't see you there.'

'Hi, Mike. How's it going?' Rachel replied but didn't sound over-friendly, so us three hung back weighing up the situation before sitting down.

One of the other girls looked my way and said, 'Oh, you brought a guitar, brilliant.' She flashed me a smile and a warm confidence filled my chest.

'Yeah.' I sat next to her and kept the guitar on my lap. 'I always bring it down to the beach.'

'That's so Brighton,' she said and flicked her hair back in a way that reminded me of an ex from first year.

Rachel did a quick round of introductions as Rob and James sat down and she asked, 'Is he in your band then, Mike?'

I shot Mike a look. **His** band?

'Yeah,' Mike replied and avoided looking at me. 'He's the other guitarist.'

Always in competition, I thought. 'And the singer.' I tried to sound light-hearted. 'Luckily I'm also the one who writes the songs as well or we wouldn't have anything to play, eh?' I strummed a soft chord and despite, Mike's false smile, everything felt good.

'We've got a gig tomorrow if you want to come,' James said and the girls looked at him, reclining with his head on his bag.

'Sure,' said Rachel. 'Are you from Manchester?'

'Yeah, how'd'ya tell?' James said with a laugh.

James was the only one of us who didn't have to try with girls – they came to him. I saw Mike tense and shuffle round to talk to one of the other girls, while Rob stayed quiet and looked butch and moody, like a stereotypical drummer.

'Give us a song then,' one of the girls said and my stomach told me I had to start with a crowd pleaser, but I went for something else – something to test their tastes.

My fingers formed a G-chord and I sang, 'She says there's ants in the carpet…'

Faces lit up and everyone sang the chorus. *End of a Century* by Blur.

Parklife may have been last year's hit but it was a summer album and Blur were big on the radio, gearing up for their new album, so everyone our age knew their stuff.

I followed it up with *Staying out for the Summer* by Dodgy, and the mood set in. This was where I was most content: in a group of people chilling and loving the music. I wasn't in control, like some people liked to be, but I had a voice. Some might say I was hiding behind the guitar and didn't get to interact with anyone properly but that was missing the point. The emotional impact of singing a song to someone can be stronger than any conversation. A connection is made. It's more than just lyrics and melody. The emotion is shared and fed back to the singer. The vibes lift everyone.

'How about a Pulp song?' One of the girls asked a few beers and smokes later.

Mike was on guitar pulling out a few of his old favourites and he gave *Common People* a fair go. Technically he was good but he focussed too much on style. No one could out-Jarvis Jarvis.

And so the day sped away with itself. We grabbed chips for lunch, Mike talked some of the girls into a swim and Rob lightened up when some other lads joined us. Our group sprawled across the stones in a u-shape of towels and rucksacks facing the sea, with plastic bags bursting with rubbish marking our territory, warning newcomers away. I borrowed some sun-cream, chatted about life after Uni, had a snooze and played more songs.

Beach life.

Before I knew it, it was almost 5 o'clock.

I finished the last few chords of *Live Forever* by Oasis and said, 'Right guys, I've got to head off, sorry.'

A chorus of complaints felt like a crowd chanting 'encore'.

'Just one more song?' Rachel asked from where she lay next to James.

'Sorry, I've got to be somewhere.' I picked up my gear, swung the guitar across my back. 'Another time,' I said and crunched away across the stones.

'Laters, dude!' Rob called out.

'Laters.' James raised a hand, followed by Mike's lazy wave.

It was hard leaving but they'd be heading off soon anyway and I usually needed to spend time on my own after socialising, so was happy for some quiet time: a space for my head to relax.

Detective Mellor was waiting for me when I turned the corner into my alley. He was leaning against the shop door, standing in a triangle of sunlight which lit him up like he was on stage with a few top buttons were open on his shirt. The nervous tapping of his notebook told me he was in a rush. Around him, the shops were drawing in their goods and closing up.

'Hi.' I waved to Shirley in the hairdressers, busy with a client and gave Simon a nod as he pulled down the shutters in the antiques shop.

Poor bloke. I felt sorry for him since his divorce. Shirley had filled me in on all the details of course.

Isaac was clearing away tubs of cut flowers and trays of house plants outside his shop but I couldn't see any of his girls. 'Evening,' he said but was too busy to chat.

I entered Mellor's peripheral vision and his blue eyes fixed on me. 'Good.' He nodded and checked his watch. 'Did you find anything?'

'Yeah, but…' I nodded at the door and fiddled with my keys to open it. I didn't want anyone to overhear.

We stepped inside.

'Well?' Mellor asked as the bell rang and the door clicked shut.

The dusty warmth of the books wrapped around me like a comfort blanket as I hung my guitar on its hook and faced Mellor.

'Okay, so I went through the records and found an entry for April the twenty-eighth.'

Mellor's expression remained stony. 'Show me.'

I shimmied around the desk and pulled the racing-green accounting book out of a drawer. The page was marked by Mellor's card and I found the entry with my finger. 'Here... *The Hollow Man*.'

Mellor leaned in to study the page and said, 'So you kept some records then?'

'To start with.'

I couldn't remember why I had stopped. Boredom probably.

'And there are no other records of the same book?' Mellor asked as he turned the remaining full pages.

'Not this year,' I said and moved round to sit in my chair. 'Could have been bought any time I guess.'

Mellor straightened up and pulled at his collar. 'Listen, I need you to keep an eye on anyone else buying penguin books, okay?'

I nodded and remembered the guy yesterday who worked for Penguin.

'Keep a record of all penguin books sold from now on.' Mellor put his hands on his hips and looked around. 'Physical descriptions of the buyers would be good too.'

'It's serious then?' I asked and Mellor stared at me. 'The crime?' I asked.

Detective Mellor squinted as though weighing up his options, ran a hand through his lank hair and said, 'Yes, the incident was serious.'

I waited but Mellor remained silent as questions built in my mind. Was the person who bought the books dangerous? Was I in danger?

'Listen, I need to know a bit more, okay?' I said. 'This is my shop and...'

Mellor's shoulder slumped. 'Okay. Just don't tell anyone or I'll have you on a charge for dealing weed.'

'What?' I said. 'After you offered to sell it to me?'

Mellor held a palm up. 'Don't push me alright?' His gave me a cold stare and fumbled in his pocket to produce a small plastic bag of green buds and dropped it on my desk.

I wanted to tell him who my Dad was and how he could have him kicked out of the force in an instant, but Dad was out of action while his incident blew over, so I held my tongue.

'Pay for this,' he said. 'Then I'll tell you what's going on.'

'What?' I said with a frown, but picked the bag up, pinched open the seal and smelt the weed.

'It's decent stuff,' Mellor said. 'Normally twenty quid an eighth but let's call it fifteen seeing as you're helping me.'

I tried to think of a way out of it but I reasoned I'd used up a fair bit of weed on the beach, so could do with topping up.

'Alright then.' I pulled the notes from my cash tin. 'So what's going on?'

'The book I showed you,' Mellor said with a contented smile as he slipped the notes into his wallet. 'Was found at a murder scene so, yes, it's pretty serious.'

I swallowed. Nobody got murdered in Brighton, Dad always said that. This wasn't bloody London.

'And to make matters worse,' Mellor continued, 'a book has been found at a new crime scene.'

'Another murder?' I asked and felt the room turn cold.

This was an almost out of body experience: one of the most surreal conversations I'd ever had.

Mellor nodded.

It took me a few seconds to gather my thoughts.

'And you found another penguin book?' I asked.

Mellor nodded again.

'From here?' I asked and looked down the dark corridor to the penguin alcove.

'Same red stamp,' Mellor said. 'Two murders and two penguin books… it has to be the same person.'

-The Black Hole-

When she left, the pain had been beyond words.

He didn't cry for days, then it came flooding out on a Sunday afternoon. Whether it was loss or regret, he couldn't tell, but it felt like a piece of him had shrivelled and died within his chest, leaving an empty hole behind.

When he finally stopped crying and beating the arms of his chair, he focussed on the hole, feeling its burnt edges which pulsed like a heartbeat. Inside, he found a place without emotions. A place where the voices fell silent: the voices that told him he should have tried harder and berated him for not building a better life for her.

The black hole was a place of solitude for him, if he needed it.

He tried to live normally again but after days of aching grief, his energy had been used up and he fell into the black hole. It was wonderful. He felt nothing. No pain. No guilt. No remorse. No anger. No past; just the present. He was alive and dead at the same time.

Then something bad happened. Because of her, but not caused by her. He was simply protecting her even though she wasn't there. An accident. It happened faster than he could think and the black hole had been there for him afterwards: somewhere to hide from the new pain and new guilt. It helped him regain his strength.

In the days that followed, the hole called to him and asked for more. It enticed him. It whispered to him during the quiet moments and sang to him in his dreams. He could feel it growing. Not in size, but in weight as it pulsed and pulled at him.

The only way to make it stop was to be with it: to sit inside and hide in its black light. He wasted many days like this until he realised he had lost his way. His mission had always been to make her happy, so he should continue on that path.

With new resolve he would set out again to complete what had been started.

The words had to be heard and maybe this time someone would listen.

Friday 28th July 1995

Rock'n'roll Star – Oasis

The sound of my distorted guitar reverberated off the purple walls of the back room of the King's Arms, echoing James' deep bass. Both sounds rode the wave of feedback from Mike's guitar and Rob's fading cymbal crash. Despite any hidden nerves, we'd played the first song perfectly and the crowd, which had grown from ten to forty during the song, applauded and whistled when we finished.

The stage was only a foot high but gave me a view across the raucous crowd as their cheers sent a rush, like a drug hit, through every part of my body: energy in my belly, in my thumping heart and in my feet. I felt like I could dance a thousand steps and jump to the moon.

The row of lights a few feet from my face obscured half the crowd during the songs and sometimes I could convince myself we were back in the rehearsal room, but I could always feel the audience, just like I could feel the heat from the red light more than the other colours. They gave me energy.

An hour earlier, watching the first band, the nerves had pulled at my stomach as I'd sipped my beer. The rest of the band were anxious too.

'I just want to get up there, y'know what I mean?' James said.

'We'll be better than this piece of crap that's for sure,' Mike said.

They weren't that bad. Better than we had been when we started out, but my nerves couldn't cope with an argument with Mike, so I didn't respond.

Rob shrugged and muttered, 'The drummer's alright.'

It wasn't the gig that had me nervous, it was the audience. Where was the girl from the shop? I'd been round the entire pub a couple of times and watched everyone who came into the back room like a hawk but there was no sign of her.

Eight songs later, we were up. We knew the songs back to front and could ride any little mistakes, so once we got into it my nerves vanished and I was in my element. Exciting times. Time to perform my songs and blow the crowd away. I could see the other bands laughing behind their beers like we did, but I knew we weren't crap. We drew a larger crowd than the first band and I recognised some of the faces in the crowd. We had fans. Groupies! Or maybe they were just regulars who were here last time we played?

No sign of the girl from the shop though.

After the first song I gave James a wink and could see Mike and Rob were chatting, so I turned to the mic. 'Evening all… we're Beachhead.' Someone whooped in the distance. 'The next song's called *Roamer*.' I turned to Rob and gave him the nod to start as Mike stepped up to his mic.

'Come on then,' he said and looked at me. 'What's the next song?' He had a glint in his eye.

I shook my head and waited a second before speaking in the mic again. '*Roamer*,' I said, gave Rob the nod again and he kicked off with a tribal beat. My guitar slipped in four beats behind James, then the opening lyrics and we were away.

In between verses I watched Mike. What had that been about? Why was he trying to unnerve me or make me cock up to make him look good? Possibly, but he'd never done that before. A chorus came and went, leading into one of Mike's elongated solos. He moved forward and planted a foot on the fold-back speaker by my mic, giving me a perfect view down his guitar neck into the crowd… and straight to the group of girls we'd met on the beach. That was it. He wanted to show me up so he could pull.

Twat.

I felt my cheeks burn and was ready to do something stupid, but I carried on playing. Stay professional, I told myself. And as I played a realisation came to me: Mike saw me as a threat. Mike Stringer, the rich, good-looking, arrogant but damn good lead-guitarist saw *me* as his equal. He was scared of my competition and felt he had to bring me down a level. I smiled. The next chorus sounded better than the first and, when the song finished on a high, I was buzzing more than after the first song and knew this gig was going to be amazing.

But it would be even better if the girl from the shop had been there.

The high after the gig was a more subtle version of the rush after the first song. My body was buzzing – everything has energy – and there was a deep strength in my stomach. Achievement. Success. I did it. We did it. It makes you feel three inches taller and able to take anyone on. Even Mike.

'So what was that all about before the second song?' I asked him while we loaded our gear into his van.

'You what?' Mike feigned innocence but his eyes told me he knew what I was talking about.

'You made us look stupid. Like amateurs. I'd already introduced the song,' I said as James and Rob joined us.

'I didn't hear you mate, sorry,' Mike said and made a move to walk back into the pub.

Maybe it was the beer or the way he dismissed me so easily but the energy in my belly gave me the confidence to follow it up. 'Wait.' I put my hand on his shoulder. 'You knew what you were doing, just to impress a few girls, and it made all of us look stupid.'

Mike shrugged my hand off. 'I was just having a laugh with Rob.' He walked to stand between Rob and James. 'Wasn't I, eh? I'll pay more attention next time boss.' He grinned and made a pretend salute.

I grated my teeth and pictured thumping him in the face, I knew Rob would pull me off him, but I could get at least one decent punch in and… a cool breeze blew through the car park and I took a deep breath. This wasn't about Mike: this was about the girl. My head dropped a notch. 'I just want our gigs to be good,' I said. 'Better than just good, okay? It looks shit to the audience when we're just chatting to each other like schoolkids on our first gig.'

'It shows we're relaxed,' Mike said.

I shrugged and James patted me on the shoulder. 'Look, the gig was great, wasn't it lads?' He said.

Rob nodded. 'One of the best.'

'And we'll get bigger pubs,' James added.

'We'll get some London gigs too,' Rob said.

'Come on, let's lock up the van,' Mike said. 'Get pissed and pull some birds – toni-i-i-ight,' he sang, 'we're all rock and roll stars!' He held a hand out. 'No hard feelings?'

I took a second before shaking his hand. 'I guess I'm just getting used to the changes. The end of Uni and all that… it makes it feel like the band won't go on forever and…'

'Of course it will,' James said. 'Just save all that angst for writing those songs, eh?'

Mike said nothing but I could tell he was holding something back as he locked the van. 'Come on. Those girls won't wait forever.'

Two hours later I was kissing one of the girls from the beach, Sarah, on a sofa in an underground funk club when the girl from the shop walked in.

Don't get me wrong, Sarah was fit and she was all over me. Any other night we would be one drink away from heading back to mine, but there was something about the girl from the shop that had me hooked. The way she moved: her hips and long legs. How her eyes smiled when she spoke with her mates and how her mouth always seemed to be on the cusp of breaking into laughter. It was like she always saw the funny side in everything and was making the most of life… and I wanted to be like that.

Sarah slipped away to the ladies and I looked around the club: James was dancing with Rachel, Rob was at the bar and Mike had disappeared with one of the other girls ages ago. Since clearing the air with Mike, the gig-buzz had crept back into my body and I felt invincible, so I thought why not? I stood up, letting two couples collapse in the sofa, and made a bee-line through the chatters and snoggers for the bar where, if I played it right, I would casually bump into her. I ran my hand through my spiky hair to mess it up a bit and pushed through, ready to order a beer when a warm, soft arm brushed against mine. A tingle ran through me and I turned.

'Hello!' I sounded more drunk than I would have liked.

'Oh, hi,' the girl said, sounding quite sober, and studied my face. 'You having a good night?'

'Yeah.' I beamed. 'You wanna drink?' I pointed at the drinks behind the bar.

'Yes, I know what a drink is,' she replied.

'Beer?' I asked, then thought better of it. 'Cider?' She was smirking. Teasing me. 'Wine?' It was hard to hear over the funky bass line of *Memphis Soul Stew*, and I drew closer to her with each guess. 'Baileys?'

She nodded. 'Go on then. You look like you've had enough though.'

'Yeah.' I nodded. 'Big night. Awesome gig.'

Her face dropped. 'Yeah, sorry about that – I said I would go but my housemate, Claire, threw up just as we were leaving and we had to meet her boyfriend in the Brewers' Arms, so we went straight there-'

I put my hand on her arm. 'Don't worry,' I said. 'You can come to the nex-'

Everything went cold.

Extremely cold.

The sensation of having an ice-cold lager poured over your head and running down your neck, down your front and into your pants is not one you can prepare for.

'Far-qwhaa…' I said as I turned to face a furious-looking Sarah.

'You're a twat,' she said, shoved me in the shoulder and stomped off through the bar crowd which she split like she was Moses.

I turned back to the girl and, cool as anything, she smirked, offered her hand and said, 'I'm Lisa by the way.'

'Luke.' I shook her hand before wiping the beer from my brow. 'I'm Luke.'

'Oi mate,' a guy behind me poked me in the shoulder. 'That was my pint.' I turned and looked up to see a bearded guy resembling a Viking. 'And you're paying for it,' he growled.

Whatever was left of the stage energy had been washed away by the cold beer. I stared up at him and started to move my mouth but nothing came out. I felt a warm hand slip into mine and, with a yank, I was pulled backwards, stumbling through the bar crowd. I managed to keep my feet as we hit the dance floor and a mean brass section ripped open a new song. It sounded like everyone in the club was celebrating my escape.

'I love this tune!' Lisa was already dancing.

I threw a glance over my shoulder but the Viking was nowhere to be seen. We were well hidden in the tightly packed crescent around the DJ and I didn't recognise anyone around us so, hidden in the steaming warmth of the funk pit, I danced. I slipped about in my beer-sodden Converse like Jay K dancing in a tiny box. Lisa laughed as the chorus kicked in.

'Kind of ironic don't you think?' She shouted in my ear.

You can feel it all over…

Stevie Wonder you legend.

And we danced. We stared at each other as we followed the rhythm and the beat. We jostled with our neighbours and copied each other's moves as we felt the beat through our bones. Everything was right in the world.

When Stevie faded, Lisa said, 'We'd better get you out of those wet clothes. Your place isn't far is it?'

I swallowed. No words came, so I nodded.

'Come on then.' She ushered me off the dance floor.

The cool summer, salty air of the beach hit us as we sprang out of the exit and onto the prom. It sobered me up as it blew through my beer-soaked t-shirt. I looked at Lisa, her perfect lips and deep brown eyes reflecting the lights of the buildings behind us. Wow, I thought. And the energy was back.

Saturday 29th July 1995
Badhead – Blur

'You were up early,' Lisa said as she rubbed her eyes and yawned.

'Yeah, I was up at five.' I took her in: the sheet wrapped around her body and one long leg resting on mine. All curves and warmth. She wore my Radiohead t-shirt, which just about covered her hips. 'It was nice to come back to you.'

'Was that when…?'

'Yeah,' I said and gave her a kiss.

I glanced at the alarm clock, eight-thirty already, and knew I'd have to open the shop up soon.

Lisa stretched like a cat: her arms reaching out to claw at a pillow. 'Ah,' she said. 'Any chance of a cuppa then?' And she gave me that smile again.

Ten minutes later, we were leaning against the headboard, eating toast and sipping tea. I'd slipped the Parklife album on the record player in the lounge and skipped it forward to *Badhead*. The horns, the guitar and rhythm were perfect for easing the morning in after a late night.

'Good night last night,' I said and gave Lisa a sideways glance.

'Well, it definitely got better,' she leaned over and kissed my arm. 'It started out pretty crap to be honest. I'm always looking after my housemates.' She sighed. 'Broken hearts and exam stress. I'm not sure how I ended up being the Mum of the house but they always came to me with their problems and worries about grades.'

'But you never had a shoulder to cry on?' I guessed.

'No.' She looked up through the window. 'I didn't need it really.' She looked back at me and gave me a smile. 'I'm made of sterner stuff. It's all over now though… I'll miss them.'

'Yeah, end of an era.' I thought about the guys in the band and realised how lucky it was we had all been at the same Uni. 'What next, eh?'

'Well you're sorted,' Lisa replied.

'How's that then?' I scanned the room - the cracked plaster on the walls, the creaking panel wardrobe and the tiny window staring out over grey rooves.

'Well you are, aren't you?' Lisa sat up and fixed her gaze on me. 'Your Grandad gave you an amazing place: somewhere to live. A place to get an income… I mean you could do it up, make it a bit quirky and bring some decent money in. Your Grandad *gave* that to you.'

'I know, but…'

'But what?'

How could I explain? It never really came out right, that's why I wrote songs. The melody and lyrics always seemed to capture it far better than my half-finished sentences. 'I'm just not sure I'm the right person for it.'

Lisa kept her eyes on me as she sipped her tea. 'You could sell it?'

'No.' That was a crazy idea. 'This was Grandad's place… he made it.' I breathed in deeply. 'And he died here.'

Lisa coughed on her tea. 'What? Here?' She slipped out of the bed. 'In this bed?'

'No.' I suppressed a laugh and sobered when I thought of him. 'He died downstairs in the shop. Collapsed… had a heart attack.'

'Oh.' Lisa crawled back in next to me.

'This is all new.' I pointed at the furniture.

'New?'

'Well, second-hand new, from the market behind the station,' I said. 'Anyway, I guess he left the shop to me because there was no-one else to leave it to. My brother's sorted in London, so Grandad left him his old car. And now I just… well, it's like we said – an end of an era.' I paused. 'I'm not sure if this is what I want next.'

Lisa bit her lip.

'What do you want next?' I asked.

'Oh that's easy.' Her face lit up. 'The lease on the house runs out at the end of August, so I'll dump my gear at my parents' and go travelling.'

'Travelling?'

'Yeah, Australia and maybe Thailand, I'm not sure yet.'

'Cool.' Was all I could muster.

Before Uni I had dreamed about travelling to some far-away places. Photogenic places… historical, like Angkor Wat; Macchu Picchu; the Great Wall of China. Places I could build a decent portfolio of buildings and people. Temples and monks. Street markets and hawkers. Somewhere I could build a style and eventually go freelance. But wasn't that every photography student's dream? And I knew I'd never be able to afford the plane tickets out there.

'Expensive,' I said.

'Doesn't have to be... I can work out there and I saved a bit of my student loan back, so I should be alright.'

I nodded and felt a sinking feeling in my stomach. I had just found the girl of my dreams and she was leaving me already. I reached for the acoustic guitar on the floor and strummed a minor chord. 'So, we've got a month then?' I said.

Lisa's eyes widened and she said nothing.

Was there ever better inspiration for a love song? I could feel the chords forming already and my fingers itched for a pen and paper, but this wasn't the time. I put the guitar back down.

'Come with me,' I said and held a hand out.

'What?' she asked.

'You'll see.' I led her through the flat and down the stairs into the shop.

We wandered through the shelves and Lisa squeezed my hand when she realised where I was taking her.

'Travel and adventure,' I said and gestured at the shelves of brightly coloured lonely planets and rough guides. 'They might be a couple of years out of date but if you find something useful, take one.'

'Thank you,' Lisa said with a look in her eyes that told me I'd done the right thing, and she gave me a warm kiss on the lips.

An hour later, I opened the shop up.

'Here's my number,' Lisa said as she put a slip of paper on my desk. 'For the next few weeks anyway.'

'Yeah,' I said and scratched my head. 'You've got mine?'

She nodded and I moved in for a goodbye hug. We kissed as the sea air rushed through the front door and enveloped us.

This was always an uncomfortable moment, the last few minutes before someone leaves after a night together. Usually it was me leaving because I could never take anyone back to my parents' house but now I had my own place this had happened a few times and, to be honest, I'd been happy when they left.

This time I wanted Lisa to stay and to lounge about and talk crap. Drink tea and have a laugh. I wanted to know more about her and hopefully she felt the same about me.

'You can pop in whenever you want,' I said.

Lisa raised an eyebrow and said, 'I was hoping for something a little more substantial than that, Luke.'

Butterflies rushed around my stomach when she said my name. 'Sure, well, what are you doing tonight?'

'That's more like it!' She pushed away from me. 'But I'm busy.' She stepped backwards through the doorway, keeping her eyes on me.

My brother was coming home tomorrow and I promised my parents I'd go round for Sunday lunch so I would be busy all day. 'Sunday night?' I asked.

Lisa shook her head and took another step back.

'Monday night?' I asked.

She stopped, standing on the street.

'Cinema?' I said.

'Okay,' she said with a nod. 'Call me.' She gave a little wave and walked away leaving me staring at an empty patch of cobbled stones.

It took me a few seconds to break out of the bubble and I found myself wandering around the shop in a daze, checking the shelves, doing the rounds. It was a few minutes before I realised I hadn't had my morning smoke. I'd offered Lisa one last night but she wasn't up for it.

'It messes with your head,' she'd said.

Like alcohol didn't mess with your head? I wanted to say, but I didn't want to start an argument and I was happily drunk at the time.

I ambled back to the front room and collapsed into my chair with a sigh. I loved this chair: it was like slipping on a well-worn pair of jeans that fitted perfectly. I loved chilling in the shop too but I knew today was going to be boring after my night with Lisa. I stared at my guitar and considered writing a song but thought better of it. There was something else I needed to do but couldn't remember… the penguin books! Detective Mellor said I needed to keep a record of what was sold, so I grabbed the Polaroid camera and visited the penguin alcove. It was a tight room, probably ten foot by five before the wall of bookshelves had been added and made it smaller. It was coloured with a swath of orange spines, with the green crime books to one side and a rainbow of the other genres on the third wall.

How am I going to manage this? I thought as I crouched and peered through the viewfinder. My idea was to get the books recorded on a photo so I could physically cross out any books sold.

Then I could check the photo against the shelf the next day to see if I had missed any.

I couldn't get all the books in one shot so I focussed on the green shelves, clicked, the camera flashed and whirred, then pushed out its photo like sticking out a tongue.

'Job done,' I said and wandered back to the front room, wafting the photo dry.

'Luke!' A voice boomed and I jumped.

'Alright, Shirley?'

She ran the hairdressers, three doors down.

'Have you seen the Argus?' She dropped the paper on my desk and stood with fists on hips, like a plump sugar bowl. Shirley had two speaking volumes: shouting for when she had something important to say; or whispering for when she had something *really* important to say. 'Those bloody hooligans been at it again.'

'What?' I shook my head and looked at the headline: GRAFFITTI VANDALS TARGET TOWN HALL.

Shirley's mass of curly hair shook and bounced as she spoke. 'The bloody town hall. Just round the corner. Can you believe it? Your Grandfather would be turning in his grave.'

It was true. Grandad loved that building.

The colour photo under the headline showed a yellow wall with six words sprayed in red: *Keep your electric eye on me.* It felt vaguely familiar but I couldn't place it. The last bit of graffiti had been something about dust and roses, sprayed on a crematorium.

'Must be something to do with the CCTV,' I said, offering my best guess.

Shirley shrugged and took a second to let my comment sink in, then she leaned forward and whispered, 'From what I heard, the police think it's Labour supporters.'

I suppressed a laugh. 'Really?'

'That bloody Tony Blair lot. Maybe your Dad knows something, eh?' Shirley was still whispering. 'Let me know if he tells you, won't ya?'

'Yeah, sure,' I said and nodded as she pulled back.

'A bloody shame,' she was shouting again and snatched up her paper. 'Whatever next, eh?' She paused to breathe, then said, 'So, you seen your Dad recently?'

'Er, no,' I replied and collapsed into my chair. 'Seeing him tomorrow though, so I'll ask him about the graffiti.'

Shirley nodded, then leaned in and whispered, 'Have you heard the latest?'

I felt my back go cold. 'About what?' I asked, worried she knew about the murders. If Shirley knew there was a link to my shop, everybody would bloody well know.

'About Simon?'

I shook my head.

'His wife wants half the shop so it looks like he'll have to sell up.'

'Oh no.' I genuinely felt sorry for the guy.

'And Maria's leaving Isaac's shop.'

'Really?' I gave my stock answer to Shirley's gossip. Usually there wasn't much time for me to say anything else, so I had to keep it short. 'The Spanish one?'

'Yeah.' Shirley nodded. 'I knew you were sweet on her so…' Her voice jumped back up to her normal, loud volume. 'Not that you're worried about that now are you?' She gave me a theatrical wink.

I smiled, not sure what to say.

'Well, she looks lovely – I saw her this morning when she left.' Shirley made her way to the door. 'Young love, eh? See you later!' she said and waddled out.

I could feel myself blushing. It was one thing listening to gossip about other people's lives but another when you realise you *are* the gossip. She would tell everyone now. I stared up through the window, at the blue sky above the rooves of the shops opposite and wondered if that was such a bad thing? I sighed and looked at the photo in my hand. The picture was crisp with most of the titles on the spines readable, so I slipped it under the green book register and rubbed my hands. I was in a constructive mood. What could I do next? Price up some new books? I opened the drawer and remembered the Red Books stamp was missing.

'Damn it,' I hissed and picked up the crossword book.

I flicked to my latest puzzle and checked out the next clue. Eight down: *a reason for doing something*. I stared around the room searching for inspiration… a reason.

'Purpose?' I checked but it didn't fit.

Nine letters.

My gaze drifted out the window and my eyes blurred as I tried to think of a reason for doing something, when a guy in jeans and a t-shirt passed and wandered into the shop. He stopped at my desk and I didn't recognise him until his blue eyes met mine, through his glasses.

'Ah, here he is,' Detective Mellor sounded different out of a suit. Never off duty though, I knew that from my Dad. 'I was nearby, so I thought I'd pop in,' he said.

'Right, hi,' I said, wondering what he wanted. Was he here trying to sell me more weed?

'Listen, I-' Mellor looked sheepish and shot a glance down the hall to the back rooms, 'I thought I should tell you, out of courtesy, before you found out.'

'What?' I sat up in my chair.

'The local papers.' Mellor's voice lowered a notch. 'They've got hold of the murder and they're running with it on Monday.'

'Right,' I said without energy.

'D.I. Knowles managed to hold it back from them for now.' Mellor had a twinkle in his eye and I couldn't tell if he was excited or frightened. 'But we need the papers to help find any witnesses we may have missed.'

'Okay,' I said. 'But how does that affect me?'

'Well.' Mellor leaned forward and lowered his voice. 'It might spur the suspect into buying more books while they still can. So you'll need to have your wits about you. Make sure you write down every book and-'

I held up the Polaroid photo and said, 'Already taken care of. If someone buys a penguin book I'll know about it, okay?'

Mellor nodded and shoved his hand in his jeans pocket. 'Good, good,' he said. 'Right, well you've got my number, so call me if you see anything suspicious, okay?'

'Yeah sure,' I replied and shook my head as he left, still wondering why he had come in.

Surely he hadn't just popped in to warn me about the newspapers? Maybe he had just been passing? No, Mellor didn't seem like the sort of person who wandered or walked around without any purpose. He was too driven.

'Ah,' I said and returned to my crossword to scratch the answer to eight down. 'Motivated.'

Sunday 30th July 1995

Connection – Elastica

Until moving into the flat, my parents' house had been my home for eight straight years. During high school and Uni the house had been the centre of my world: my default location. But home is where your stuff is and most of my gear was in the flat now, so I was no longer drawn to the house. In fact, it was a pain getting there - a bus ride and an uphill walk away. Woodland Drive in Hove, actually, just up from the Goldstone footy ground. Despite the road name, the house didn't sit in a wood but just had a few trees looming over the back of the garden. You could gauge the time of year in any photo from my youth by the state of the trees: bare, blossom or full-leaved.

And here I was again, I thought as I trod the familiar pavement. Back home. It felt different now I'd moved out, yet nothing in the street had changed: the same clean cars in the drives; the same manicured front gardens; the same path leading between flowering shrubs to my parents' front door and same doorbell. I held my finger on it, delaying the last ding as long as possible, and smiled. The door swung open and my Mum stood with her arms open, grinning like she hadn't seen me in twenty years.

'Luke!' she said as she hugged me, pulling me down to her height to give me a kiss, enveloping me in her apron's aroma of potatoes and stuffing.

'Hi Mum, miss me?'

'Of course.' She shut the door behind us. 'The place doesn't feel the same without you here.'

I slipped off my shoes and followed her into the lounge where my feet sunk into a velvety softness. 'Is this a new carpet?' I asked almost in horror and scanned the furniture for changes: the TV cabinet, cream sofas and video shelves were all in place, along with the cupboards full to bursting with LPs and the tape deck with the old turntable on top.

'Yes,' Mum replied matter-of-factly. 'Your father wanted to spruce the place up a bit.'

'Are you selling the house then?' I asked, wondering what else had changed.

I shouldn't have cared but it made me feel uneasy. This house was not supposed to change – it might be a pain to get to, but emotionally I needed it to be a fixed point. My anchor.

'No, no,' Mum said. 'Dad thought it would be a good idea now he has some time on his hands.' She looked away.

'Where is Dad?' I asked.

'With Stephen,' Mum replied. 'In your old room. Cup of tea?'

'Yeah, thanks,' I said and bounded out and up the stairs, then stopped at the top and mouthed, '*Old* room?'

I walked the last few steps tentatively avoiding the two creaky floorboards on the landing as I listened for conversation and pushed my old bedroom door open.

'Jesus!' I shouted at my Dad and brother who greeted me from a vast DIY project of plywood and metal bars scattered across an otherwise empty room.

'Hi, Luke,' they chanted.

'Give us a hand,' Dad said. 'Pass me that screwdriver.'

I stood motionless, hands on hips and squeaked, 'My room...'

Stephen grabbed the screwdriver for Dad. 'Not your room any more, young Skywalker.'

'What?'

'Dad always said he'd turn it into a study when you finally got a life and crawled out of your hovel, didn't you Dad?'

'Pass me the instructions,' Dad said, ignoring the conflict like he always did.

'But,' I whimpered.

'All your stuff's in the garage you wimp,' Stephen said and gave me a punch in the shoulder.

'With your car?' I asked.

Stephen's face sobered. 'Yeah.'

'They're next to my boxes from work,' Dad said without looking up.

'Anyway,' Stephen said. 'You've got that flat now, so you don't need this room.'

'But *your* room is still a bedroom,' I said. 'Because it still has a *bed*.'

Less than five minutes back in my parents' home and my brother and I had reverted into squabbling children. Not that it ever amounted to much thanks to Stephen's quick tongue. Three years older than me and always three steps ahead of me.

'I'm here more often than you are anyway, you loser,' Stephen said. 'And when I'm here I always need a place to kip.'

'There'll be a sofa-bed in here,' Dad said, proving he was listening after all.

My shoulders slumped in defeat.

'Come on,' Stephen said. 'Let's go and check out the stuff in the garage.'

'Don't be long!' Dad called out as we stomped down the stairs. 'Your Mum's been slaving over that roast all morning.'

'Back in a bit,' I shouted to Mum as I grabbed my tea off the sideboard.

We dipped out the back door, across the drive and disappeared through the side door of the double garage. In the dim light I could see a pyramid of boxes piled up on one side and the silhouette of Stephen's car on the other.

'There she is,' I said as the smooth shapes of the car flashed in the flickering pulses of the strip lights as they came to life.

'Yeah,' Stephen said, leaning against a ladder with his arms crossed.

The car was beautiful: a blood red VW Karmann Ghia. 1970. Right-hand drive. Hard top. It looked like the kind of sports car I used to draw when I was a kid: all smooth lines and round headlights.

'I never remember him driving it,' I said and tried to picture Grandad as a young man.

'He had it covered up,' Stephen replied.

'I'm guessing he bought it when Dad left home.' I thought of the record player in the shop. A realisation came to me – that was what Mum and Dad were going through right now. Getting their old lives back. 'Nana and Grandad must have been loaded,' I said. 'He did well when he left the army didn't he? Insurance.' I looked at Stephen who looked like he was sulking. 'It's good to have it, the car.'

'It's not the same as having Grandad here though is it?' Stephen said.

'Of course not...' I said and ran out of words.

'You've got the shop, Red Books,' Stephen said and smiled. 'Grandad always had a good sense of humour... read books. Must be where I get it from.' He forced a smile but it was obvious he was still hurting.

'Look,' I said. 'I never knew why Grandad left me the shop and you the car but-'

'I don't care about the shop,' Stephen cut in. 'Honestly. It's just. Why the car? Do you think Grandad wanted to make me more manly?'

'Because you're gay?' I looked at Stephen but he was avoiding eye contact. I gave a snort. 'You know that never bothered Grandad.' I turned to the pile of boxes and picked through the top one. 'Anyway, your life's sorted in London with your plush pad and a job doing something that's actually interesting. I needed the shop more than you. It gives me something to do.'

Stephen joined me at the boxes, focussing on one full of records. 'Maybe,' he said. 'So, how's the shop doing? Sell much?'

'Same old. How about your job?'

'Yeah, it's good.' He was nodding. 'Saw Jeremy from the Greentones the other day – they're recording at the moment. And

Richard reckons Skimrider have got some new material, so they'll be in soon and should have an album out next year.'

'Cool,' I said. 'Any chance of getting our demo under your boss's nose?'

'You know I can't do that,' Stephen said.

'Can't or won't? You know, we're not as bad as you think,' I said. 'You could have a word with one of the scouts? Send one down next time we have a gig?'

Stephen shrugged and picked out an LP. 'Maybe, I'm only involved in the marketing side, so…'

His voice trailed off and a silence took hold as we picked through the records and books. One of the books had a torn corner, revealing a red R in a circle, reminding me of the shop and recent events.

'Listen, there's something you should know,' I said. 'About the shop. I need to tell Mum and Dad but I'm not sure how–'

'Stephen!' Mum's voice cut me off. 'Luke! Dinner's ready.'

'Come on,' Stephen was already at the door. 'I'm starving!'

It's alright, I thought, I'll tell them later.

The spread on the table was the same as ever: the china plates piled with roast potatoes, the cream-coloured gravy jug and the 70's décor bowls full of steaming veg. Dad stood at the other end of the table carving the chicken. He was like a future version of me: high-forehead and short blond hair, just add a belly and a few wrinkles and it was me.

'I picked out a bottle of white,' he said and nodded at the glasses, so I started pouring.

'I'll be Mum shall I?' Stephen said and started placing the meat on the plates.

Dad looked up but held his tongue.

Then Mum rushed in with a plate of Yorkshire puddings and slipped two on each plate. 'My big boys,' she said with a smile and disappeared back out the door, returning seconds later without her apron.

'Sit down, Linda,' Dad said and Stephen smirked like we always did when our parents used each other's names.

'Okay Brian,' Mum said as she relaxed into her chair.

'Brian...' Stephen started singing in his best Shirley Bassey voice, '...the babe they called Brian.'

'He had arms.' I joined in. 'And legs and hands–'

'And I'll use my hand to slap you round the head in a minute,' Dad said with a fake grimace. 'I should never have introduced you two to Monty Python. Come on, let's eat.'

'What, no grace?' Stephen asked and received another glare from Dad.

'Did you hear about that awful graffiti?' Mum did her best to distract us.

'Er, no,' Stephen said, dutiful to Mum as ever.

'Terrible business,' Mum said. 'Someone's been scrawling all over the town hall and other buildings.'

'Probably just kids,' Stephen said.

'It was in the Argus,' I said. 'Shirley was telling me all about it.'

'Oh,' Dad said. 'Good old Shirley.'

'She thought you might know something about it, from the station?'

Dad wrinkled his nose. 'Haven't been back for a bit, so, no. No news.'

I nodded. 'Great roasties, Mum.'

'So what's going on with your work Dad?' Stephen asked. Dutiful to Mum, I thought, but always happy to annoy Dad. 'Mum says you're on leave while they sort it all out.'

'Stephen, not at the-' Mum started but Dad held his hand up.

'Gardening leave,' he said and gave a false chuckle. 'I wouldn't have minded if I was closer to retirement but I'm still paying off the bloody mortgage. It puts them in an awkward position of course.'

'How?' Stephen asked.

'They can't sweep it under the carpet this time,' Dad said. 'Not like they did with Bernard.'

'And Michael,' Mum added.

'So it's linked then?' I asked, vaguely remembering Dad's friends talking about some conspiracy a few years back at a barbecue.

'Of course it is,' Dad's cheeks had reddened. 'But the truth will out, I'm sure.'

'Yes it will,' Mum said. 'More Yorkshires?' She offered a bowl to me and I scooped one with a spoon.

'No, Luke,' Stephen said. 'Use the fork.'

I shook my head, knowing what was coming.

Stephen put on his Alec Guinness voice, 'Use the fork, Luke.'

Dad groaned and Mum giggled.

'Anyway,' Stephen said. 'You could always sell up.'

'No,' Dad shook his head.

'Luke could get a decent job in London, kip with me for a bit then you two could move into Grandad's old place and run the shop.'

Dad laughed and Mum smiled.

Now was the time, I thought, while everyone was happy.

'Actually, I need to tell you something about the shop,' I said.

'They won't lend you any money,' Stephen said.

'No, it's not that, it's…' the conversation had played out in my head all morning but the words wouldn't come out right, '…there's going to be an article in the paper.'

'Advertising!' Dad said. 'That's a great idea.'

'No, no, it's a story they're covering, linked with the shop,' I said.

'Well,' Dad said. 'Any publicity is good publicity, so-'

'No, Dad.' I cut him off. 'There was a murder.'

Cutlery clinked on plates and all eyes were on me.

'In Brighton?' Dad asked.

'I don't know where, but it's linked to the shop, both of them.'

'Two murders?' Mum's voice raised an octave. 'Linked to the shop?'

'Two!' Dad's eyebrows had become one and I recognised his work face. Cogs were turning. Questions would come, just like when he caught me smoking or the first time I came home drunk. Not when Stephen came out if I remembered correctly.

'How are the murders connected to the shop?' he asked.

'They left books from the shop as calling cards,' I said.

'Definitely from the shop?' he asked.

'Red stamp.'

Dad nodded then asked, 'Who's investigating?'

'Detective Sergeant Mellor, but he mentioned D.I. Knowles?' I said.

'That little turd?' Dad was even redder now. He puffed a few times and shot a glance at Mum. 'Well, I'm sure he'll get the… perpetrator. If he doesn't, he'll cover his tracks that's for sure.'

'You're not a fan then?' Stephen asked.

'Let's just say,' Mum answered for Dad. 'He's got a connection with Dad's disciplinary.'

Stephen nodded, while Dad started eating again, taking his anger out on the roasties.

Mum reached out to touch my arm and said, 'Thanks for telling us, Luke. Just take care okay?'

A couple of hours later I was back in the flat. Dad had driven Stephen to the station, so I grabbed a lift home, which meant I could bring back a couple of boxes from the garage topped with a new selection from Dad's collection: *Sticky Fingers* by the Stones, *Low* by David Bowie and *Ogden's Nut Gone Flake* by the Small Faces.

'You'll get some good inspiration out of that lot,' Dad said as he dropped me off and I wondered why it was we could talk forever about other band's music but never about my own. 'Listen, about those murders,' he said, 'just keep your eyes peeled.'

'Okay.'

'Lock up properly and,' he paused as though fighting over what to say next, 'keep your eye on those detectives, okay?' He had a genuine look of concern in his eyes.

'It's alright, Dad. I'll be fine,' I said and gave him a hug.

'And if any journalists come round, don't tell them too much. Nosy bastards,' he said before driving off.

'Alright. See ya!'

Once I'd lugged the boxes through the shop and up the stairs, I collapsed on the sofa. I had a quick joint to sample Mellor's weed and checked the answer machine. There was a message from James:

'Alright mate? Good night last night. Look, we're off down the beach if you fancy it? Usual spot – about three? Laters...'

'Too late mate,' I said, trying to mimic his accent but sounded more like Frank Sidebottom.

I pulled Lisa's number from my pocket. I stared at it for a second and thought, why not? I dialled carefully as a mixture of excitement and nerves tugged at my chest at the idea of talking to her.

'Hi, is Lisa there?'

'She's not in,' one of her flat mates had answered.

'Oh, is she working?' I asked.

'Dunno.'

'Right, okay, err… can you tell her Luke called and I'll see her at the cinema tomorrow night? Seven o'clock.'

'Okay, bye.'

She hung up, leaving me staring at the phone. I couldn't tell if it was the weed or not being able to speak to Lisa, but I felt empty.

Deflated. I moped around the flat like a lost lamb for the rest of the evening. REM were playing a gig on Radio One, which was alright for a bit, then made a cup of tea, put the Elastica LP on and started going through the boxes.

I added the new LPs to my collection and dug into the treasure underneath. Memories. I hadn't seen some of these things for years and each object seemed to open a new door on times from my distant past: an X-wing fighter sent me back to the garden, chasing my brother; a tape of the Shadows Greatest Hits reminded me of my first guitar lessons and an E.T. money box took me back to a distant Christmas with Nana and Grandad.

I sighed, picked out a new box and started rummaging, but didn't recognise anything. Leather-bound books, an old trophy and some brown files. Were these Stephen's? I opened the top file. It looked official. The sheets of paper inside had a number at the top and looked like they were colour-coded. A name jumped out at me: Eric Redfern. This had to be Dad's work stuff – but this was Grandad's file, from when he died. I guessed the police had files for everything but this was more substantial than I had imagined: medical records; bank details; his Will; autopsy results. What on earth was Dad doing with this?

I saw a photo poking out from between two sheets of paper. Black and white. I pulled it out and saw Grandad lying in the penguin alcove surrounded by scattered books. His mouth was open and you could see where he'd cracked his head.

I shouldn't be seeing this, I thought and I started breathing heavily. The photo went out of focus, but it was too late and I knew that image would stay with me forever.

There was another photo stuck to the back of the first, a full colour shot taken closer to Grandad, showing his upper body and head. He looked peaceful and I couldn't take my eyes off him.

Then I noticed something.

It wasn't obvious at first but the more I stared at it the more I convinced myself.

In the corner of the photo was a strip of bare carpet next to the shelves and a scattering of green and orange books spread around Grandad's head. One book wasn't on the floor and, judging by how the books had fallen, there was no way it could have landed like that. It was tucked in Grandad's armpit, sticking out at an angle. I couldn't see the title but the number was clear: 536.

A cold feeling washed through me and I shuddered as though my body had made the connection before my mind did. It was obvious. The book had been placed on Grandad's body on purpose.

Why hadn't anyone else seen this? I thought as my heart raced. Wasn't it obvious?

Grandad was one of the killer's first victims.

-Hiding-

It had happened again. And again.

He knew it was the wrong thing to do but the book couldn't defend itself, so who else would? Just him. And it had to be heard - it needed to be heard.

It was so much easier than the first time, easier because he knew how strong he was now and he had the black hole to hide in afterwards.

The first time had been a mistake. An accident. The man was older. Weaker. And he had argued. It became physical and he knew what to do, the old soldier, but wasn't quick enough. His death seemed fitting – how many men had the old man killed during the war? Something about seeing him dead at his feet, gave him strength. Power. And the way the books lay about him was artistic. That's what she would have said. All the colours lying in a pattern like a rainbow. One title jumped out at him – *The Good Soldier* – and it seemed appropriate for the dead man, so he tucked it under his arm.

And then he hid in the hole and the idea of leaving the book with the man stayed with him. She would have liked the connection. So he found more books. And when it was safe to come out again, he took one with him, just in case.

He needed it.

The people he killed should have lived. They should have been connected through the book. It was strong enough to bind them together, like in a story in its own right, but now he had to link them using other people's words: the book titles.

It wasn't enough. It had to be the words from the book as well. How long had been spent creating these words? Years of thankless labour and life had been poured into them.

So he started writing the words from the book.

On them.

Monday 31st July 1995

Blue Monday -95 – New Order

When I woke on Monday morning my head was throbbing and my tongue felt rough, like I had a hangover.

After finding the police photo of Grandad lying dead, I'd tried to go to sleep but thoughts buzzed around my head with one question coming back again and again – had Grandad been murdered? My alarm woke me as usual and I automatically carried out my morning ritual but I couldn't get back to sleep afterwards and ended up searching the cupboards for paracetamol.

I turned Radio One on and a familiar drumbeat thumped at me. Fast tempo. Synth keys. Bass. Hadn't Radio One banned eighties music I thought as I turned on the kettle.

How does it feel? Bernard Sumner asked me.

'Pretty shit,' I replied and thumped the radio off button.

I sunk into the sofa and stared at the wall. I felt alone. And scared. Not scared of whoever was out there killing people, although I should have been if I was thinking straight, but scared of what I was about to get pulled into – what my family would be drawn into. Forget the shop, this was about Grandad! I felt like I'd let him down every day since taking over the shop and now that feeling was amplified. It felt like a weight pushing down on me.

I looked at the brown file on my coffee table, hiding the photo within. Why did Dad have the file anyway? It didn't look like the sort of thing the police gave grieving relatives. The last thing Dad wanted was more trouble so I pulled out the photo, took a shot of it with my Polaroid and slipped it in my bag.

I wanted to have a smoke and hide away but I had to keep a clear head. It was time to find Detective Mellor.

The yellow tape gave the place away. That and the flashing blue lights and tower of thick smoke drifting up into the pure blue summer sky. Arson by the look of it.

I had walked from the shop, with its closed sign firmly in place, to the police station and then to this random address the receptionist had given me.

The policewoman standing by the tape kept her eyes on me as I approached and I could hear Detective Mellor talking to two uniforms by the back door of a half-gutted warehouse. He sounded different: older maybe, like he had to posh it up because he had authority.

'I'm here to see Detective Sergeant Mellor,' I said and the policewoman raised an eyebrow. 'I'm Luke Redfern – I've got important information.'

She gave me a look of derision before turning to get him.

'Ah, Mister Redfern,' Mellor said and his eyes narrowed. He looked rough, like he'd been up half the night. 'How can I help you?'

I breathed in sharply. 'I think I've found something.'

'Right,' he said with a condescending smile. 'I'm sure you have.'

I handed him the photo from my bag. 'Have you seen this?' I asked.

Mellor's brow creased as he studied the photo. 'How did you get this?' he said without looking at me.

'It doesn't matter. Do you see what I see?'

I held back from pointing my finger at the book wedged under Grandad's armpit. If Mellor couldn't see it maybe I'd been mistaken.

'It's your Grandad,' he said.

I felt my anger rise. 'Yes, it's my bloody Grandad, who died in his shop surrounded by penguin books.'

'With one book tucked under his arm.' Mellor looked at me. 'Did he do that often? Walk around with books under his arm?'

The question threw me. I pictured Grandad pottering around the shop with a box of books or a clip board and a pencil behind one ear.

'No,' I said. 'And even if he did, he would have dropped it when he fell – he would have tried to grab the wall or something. That's how the other books got pulled onto the floor.' I pointed at the scattering of books. 'Were the other victims found like this?'

Mellor seemed to nod, or maybe he was just thinking? 'There were lots of books,' he said slowly.

'And were the houses broken into?'

'Why?'

'Because I'm sure my Dad said he had to unlock the shop when he found Grandad. He'd been ringing the phone and Shirley had been banging on the door, so…'

Mellor's left eye twitched and he looked away. 'You understand this changes everything? Three murders. That means we're chasing a serial killer.'

I nodded and looked away.

'And I'll need to know how you got this photo.'

'No,' I said, scrambling for a way to protect my Dad. 'You can say you found it… looking through the files of all recent deaths.'

Mellor's blue eyes wandered away. 'I was looking for anything suspicious,' he said, trying out the lie. 'The recent death and connection with the bookshop looked an obvious place to start… Inspector Knowles would like that.'

'Exactly.'

'Right, well, I need you to find the book in the photo if it's still in the shop. Don't touch it – I'll need to test it for prints. And while you're here let's get your fingerprints – the lab geeks are over there.' Mellor pointed at a white van. 'Just tell them I sent you.'

'Okay,' I said and headed for the van.

Serial killer? I thought. It still didn't feel real. It sounded like something from a film, not real life. What had my Grandad done to get caught by a serial killer?

'Detective Mellor needs my fingerprints taken,' I said to a woman in a plastic white overall and followed her into the van where she produced an ink kit and few sheets of paper.

'It'll just take a couple of minutes,' she said.

I remembered doing something like this as a kid when my Dad took us to the station for an open day. This felt different as I rolled each finger in their respective boxes on the sheet of bleached paper. This was official, not fun.

As I filled the boxes with black smudges, a man appeared at the van door in a forensics suit identical to the woman's.

'Where do you want this?' He held up a zip-lock bag containing a flat, hand-sized lump of charred wood.

'Here will do.' The woman pointed to the table.

I finished off the last finger and tried to get a better look at the bag while I wiped the ink off with a wet wipe. It was the size of a book, which had me intrigued, so I slowly filled my details on the form and waited for the woman to turn around. The second she did, I flicked the bag over.

I gasped and she turned back.

'You okay?' she asked.

'Yeah.' I sniffed. 'Just a bit of hay fever.'

She went back to her work.

The other side of the book was unburnt and orange. A penguin fiction book. Was the fire linked to the murders? Mellor would think if he saw this. I scribbled the number on my palm: 995. The title was clear: *Summer Lightning*. What did that mean? It was summer and lightning set off fires, but how did that fit in with the other books the police had found? What did this fire have to do with the murders?

Something caught my eye and stopped my thought process: a familiar shade of red in one of the forensics bags on the table.

'Just leave the form there when you're done,' the officer said and left me alone in the cabin.

I threw a glance over my shoulder then took my chance – I reached into the pile of bags and pulled out the one I recognised.

'My stamp,' I whispered and stuffed it in my pocket.

Just feeling the wooden handle reminded me of Grandad and a resolve set in. I felt an urge to get back to the shop and start working this case out: this was more important than anything else in my life. More important than the shop, that was for sure, so I had to scrap any plans for the day. Whoever was leaving these books had killed my Grandad and I had to do something to help catch them. My Grandad deserved justice.

My mind was set: the police would do their work and I would do mine.

The sun was high when I strolled back through streets flanked by the white cliffs of Victorian buildings, so I kept in the shade where I could. I decided I wouldn't open up the shop when I got back to give me time with the penguin books before going out with Lisa in the evening. There was a riddle here just like the crossword clues I had become addicted to, and I was sure solving it would make sense of what had happened to Grandad. I owed him that didn't I?

I was deep in thought when I passed a newsagent and stopped in my tracks. The news board outside the front door. I had to read it twice to take it in: MURDERER ON THE LOOSE IN BRIGHTON.

'No,' I muttered.

I knew it was going to happen, Mellor had told me. I knew the papers would sensationalise it, but that was when the story involved two strangers. Two far away murders, detached from my life. Unreal.

Fiction. But when I read it now it referred to Grandad and the words struck me deep.

I bought a copy of the paper and rushed back to the shop, through the alleyways and huddles of tourists, past the pubs and shops. I waved at Shirley as I passed, nodded at Simon in the dark depths of his antique's shop and had almost made it to my door when Isaac jumped out of the florists.

'You chose a bad day to shut up shop,' he said and smiled, his cloud of white hair wafting around his head like candy floss.

'Really, why?' I asked, remembering Isaac wasn't like Shirley and I had to actually talk to him to find out what he wanted to tell me. Plus, Grandad had said Isaac had lost his wife a few years back so I felt sorry for him.

'You've had loads of customers today,' he said. 'Knocking at the door.' He nodded at the closed sign. 'Some came asking for you ... looked important.'

I thought of Mellor.

'Wearing suits?' I asked.

'Some.' Isaac nodded. 'And some had notepads.'

'Journalists?' I asked.

'Maybe,' Isaac said with a shrug. 'Anyway, it's not like you to shut up on a Monday... I guess that's young love for you, makes you do all sorts of things.' He gave me a knowing look, which I returned with a confused frown. 'Shirley told me all about your new young lady.' He winked.

'Ah, of course she did.' I peered down the road to look for the tell-tale frizzy hair by the doorway in case she was ear-wigging. 'No, it wasn't anything to do with her, I…' I didn't know what to say.

Grandad had been his friend so I didn't want to upset Isaac, but he had a right to know how the shop was involved in the murders.

'Have you seen the paper today?' I asked and felt for the one in my bag.

'Yes.' His eyebrows raised. 'Seen the headlines. Same old bad news, eh?'

'Yeah,' I replied. 'Well, my shop's involved… nothing to worry about but-'

'Involved with the murders?' Isaac's pink cheeks turned white. 'Oh no.' He seemed distracted. He turned to the nearest flowers in tubs, then back to me. 'Not in a bad way I hope?'

'Well, not in a good way to be honest-' I said but he cut me off again.

'Good, good. I should get some little posies made up. A couple of quid each. Make the most of it, Luke, 'cos you're bound to have loads more customers now.'

He wandered back to his doorway rubbing his chin.

'See you later then,' I said and shook my head. He was always thinking about business, I thought. Maybe that was what I was lacking? I needed more sales to make the shop profitable but the last thing I wanted to do was profit from Grandad's death.

I slipped indoors, locking the door behind me, took a deep breath and leaned against the wall. The dark, comforting space of the bookshop calmed me with its cool and musty air. Home. I dumped my bag, pulled out the paper and the headline stood as stark as on the news board: *Murderer on the loose in Brighton*. There was a generic picture of the Royal Pavilion for some reason and another of bustling shoppers. I skimmed the full article on page 3 but couldn't find anything about the books or my shop, just that police were investigating connections between two recent homicides. Three, I thought, and soberly walked to the penguin alcove. I stared at the carpet where Grandad had been found and the shelf where he had banged his head. Then I ran my fingers along the books, looking for number 536… and found it. *The Good Soldier*. The police must have put it back on the shelf with the other fallen books. I didn't want to touch it, but felt drawn to it. No, I had to leave it. Mellor would come to test it for fingerprints.

I felt useless, so meandered back to my desk.

I needed to do something to organise my thoughts. I pulled out a blank sheet of paper and wrote down the books found at each crime scene:

The Good Soldier: 536.

The Hollow Man: 862.

Mellor never said what the other book was, so I left a gap, followed by the book from the arson, *Summer Lightning*: 995.

What was the link? They were in number order and Grandad had fought during the war, so had been a soldier, but how did *The Hollow Man* link up with the other murder? I didn't know who had been killed so there was no way I could connect the title to the victim. I checked the paper again but there were no names or addresses given, just Brighton.

I sighed and checked the time. Better get some lunch, I thought and have a smoke. I bounded upstairs and saw the answer machine light flashing. I pressed play and my belly tickled with butterflies when I heard Lisa's voice and played it three times in a row. She wanted to meet up earlier than planned to catch a bite to eat first.

I stirred the froth at the bottom of the oversized cup and stared about vacantly. I didn't think I liked coffee but this one tasted alright with the frizzed up milk and chocolate flakes. I glanced at my watch: Lisa was late. Or did I get the time wrong? Definitely the right place: the Italian coffee shop on the corner, she'd said. Five-thirty, for a spot of dinner first. Maybe she had second thoughts? It was the kind of thing she would do. Impulsive. But that's what I liked about her.

I had a good view of the street outside but was bored of people watching now. It was mostly tourists heading back from the beach. I picked up the café's copy of the paper and avoided the murder story: water droughts and hose-pipe bans filled the other pages. I turned to an article about the graffiti Shirley had mentioned. Another building had been sprayed but there was no picture this time. Then I felt a presence beside me. A glimpse of a black skirt told me it was the waitress, so I kept my nose in the paper, not wanting to lose my table.

'Can I get you another drink?' she asked.

No Italian accent, I thought.

'No, I'm alright thanks,' I replied.

'Well we might need the table in a bit,' she said.

I sighed.

'We get busy around six and we need every table,' she explained.

My shoulders sank and I put the paper down. 'Yeah sure, sorry.' I pushed my chair back. 'I was just waiting for- '

I stared at the waitress with my mouth open. With her hair up she looked different: it brought out her cheek bones and gave more light to her eyes.

'Sorry I'm late,' she said with a mischievous smirk.

I shook my head. 'That's alright.' I smiled back.

I knew she was impulsive but I hadn't expected this.

'We were rushed off our feet,' Lisa said as she took the chair next to me. 'Another day over though.' She gave a contented sigh.

'I didn't know you worked here,' I said.

'No,' she said matter-of-factly. 'I never mentioned it.' Her eyes glinted and made me wonder what else she hadn't told me about.

'Do you want a drink then?' I asked.

She raised her eyebrows. 'Not really.'

'Don't blame you,' I said. 'It's pretty crap here.'

She laughed and my worries slipped away like a feather in a breeze.

'Let me get changed and you can treat me to some dinner,' she said and kissed my cheek.

'Okay.' I felt my stomach fill with energetic butterflies.

Tuesday 1st August 1995

Girl From Mars – Ash

'Well, I quite liked it,' I said, handing Lisa her morning cuppa.

'You would – it was such a bloke's film,' she replied. 'Next time it's my choice.'

Chris Evans was giggling away on the radio after another Britpop song and the sun was out again. A soft feeling lifted me: Lisa was already thinking of a next time! But why wouldn't she? We had a good thing here. We were comfortable in each other's company and fancied the pants off each other.

I cuddled up next to her, leaning against the pillows and asked, 'So you still think *Clueless* would have been better?'

'Easily,' she replied. 'I mean what were his gills about? And so much water… I don't think I could face being on the beach today, staring at more sea.'

'Well, there was a clue in the title,' I said, enjoying the conversation – so much better than when someone agrees with everything you say. 'The gills were a bit crazy though, I'll give you that.'

'A bit?' Lisa turned her eyes on me. 'They live *on* the water, not *in* it, yet humans have evolved gills in a few generations? Seriously?'

'That's sci-fi for you – it's not supposed to be perfect it's… escapism,' I said, wondering why I was defending a genre I wasn't keen on.

'How about the *Science* bit of Science Fiction?' Lisa said. 'That's where it links to reality.'

I stared at Lisa and found myself smiling.

'Okay, no more sci-fi, I promise. I just wanted to see what the hype was about – it was a pre-release viewing and-'

Lisa kissed me and the song on Radio One blasted into its chorus: *I remember the time...*

She pulled away she said, 'It was a nice gesture, but I'll get my revenge.'

I had no idea where she was going.

'How exactly?' I asked.

'There's a Hugh Grant film coming out this week and I'm going to make you watch the whole damn thing!'

I shook my head and drank her in. This felt perfect – all mornings should start like this.

A thought came to me and I took her hand. 'Come with me.'

'Why?'

'I want to show you something.'

Lisa gave in and let me lead her to the lounge where she sat on the sofa. I pulled out a maroon photo album and placed it on her lap.

'Open it,' I said.

On the front page was a photo of my Nana and Grandad on the beach. Happy days. In their prime: young, fit and full of energy. Lisa turned the page and I sat next to her to watch her reaction to the first page, filled by four by six inch photos. First, her eyes widened, then she nodded, turned the page, then the next. Slowly, she frowned as she flipped through the pages.

'They're all the same,' she said. 'Sunsets... the West Pier.'

'Sunrises,' I said as she turned to the next page and pointed to a greyed out blur of a rainy sunrise. 'They're not all the same.'

Lisa looked at me. 'So that's where you've been every morning? Taking photos of the sunrise?'

'Yeah, it's a… project.'

'But you finished Uni.'

'It's a personal thing. For Grandad.' I could feel tears forming in my eyes. 'I didn't know what else to do when he died… I tried writing a song but that didn't work, then I found myself on the beach one morning with my camera. He used to walk the prom at sunrise to watch the sea and the birds,' I explained. 'So I took a photo for him. The sunrise he would never see. Then the next morning I found myself at the beach again and again … until it became a habit.'

'Every sunrise since he died?' Lisa asked.

I nodded.

'There are hundreds here,' she said.

'Well, just over a hundred,' I said and took the album back. 'It got a bit tricky with the sun rising earlier each day but… I know, it's stupid really.'

'No.' Lisa kissed my cheek. 'It's definitely not stupid.'

A couple of hours later I was back in my daytime spot – the comfort of my well-worn leather chair – staring out between the piles of books in the window. Watching the world pass by. The front door was shut and the closed sign remained untouched, leaving me alone in my book-lined womb where my mind flitted from happy contentment, thinking about Lisa, to mild panic and anger any time I saw something reminding me of my Grandad. Detective Mellor had phoned to say he would collect the book that morning, so I kept the shop closed, which had been a relief because I'd seen two people knocking at the door and they both looked like journalists. Nobody needed to know the shop was linked to the murder spree everyone was talking about.

I picked up my crossword book and chose a new puzzle.

Newest African Country.

Grandad would have known this one, I thought and I checked the date on the book: 1994. I wouldn't rest until I had the answer so, as one of the few people in Brighton with their own personal library, I trotted in search of the most recent atlas I could find.

Half an hour later, Detective Mellor knocked on the door flanked by two forensic investigators wearing their white all-body suits. I recognised them from the burnt warehouse where they'd taken my fingerprints.

'Well that's subtle!' I hissed at Mellor as I ushered them in and locked the door behind them.

'It doesn't matter,' Mellor replied. 'The papers are releasing more information tonight anyway.'

He gave me a *'nothing I could do'* look and walked to the penguin room. 'This way,' he said, guiding the white twins into my shop.

I followed, breathing in the swimming pool vapours trailing behind the forensics pair, desperate to find out what the papers were going to print.

'Here it is,' Mellor said as I peered over a shoulder to see him point at *The Good Soldier* book. 'Might as well take the two either side as well. Prints and fibres.'

'Right you are.' Came a muffled reply. Plastic bags, powders and brushes appeared and they got to work.

Mellor ushered me back to the front room where he pointed at the red stamp on my desk.

'I thought…' he didn't finish his sentence when he saw my face: the guilt must have been obvious. '…you got it back then? Good.' He said, turning defeat into victory.

I sat down and said nothing.

'Look, your Grandad's death's been officially added to the case,' Mellor said, with more emotion than I'd given him credit for. 'But the papers know but won't print any names for now, okay?'

'Right,' I said but all I could think about was my Dad. I'd been distracted with Lisa last night and never got round to telling him anything about the files I'd found or the photo. 'No names.'

'But the shop will be mentioned,' Mellor said with his eyes fixed on me.

I breathed in deeply and nodded. 'Okay. Should I stay open?'

'No reason not to open today,' Mellor said. 'Once we're happy we've got everything we need… which reminds me.' He pulled a plastic bag from his pocket. 'Can you check the records for this book?' He placed the orange penguin book on my desk: *The Grapes of Wrath*, number 833.

'I'll have a look.' I made a note of the title and number. 'At least I've heard of this one,' I said, feeling a little irked still. Now the shop was going to be dragged into the papers I felt I was due more answers.

'I take it this was from the second murder?' I asked.

'Third,' Mellor replied. 'We're counting your Grandad's death as the first.'

I nodded and held my emotions in check. I needed more information if I was going to find out what had happened to Grandad.

'No obvious link with the other books,' I said.

'Not that I can see,' Mellor said.

His guard was down, so I pushed some more. 'And they were all killed in the same way?'

Mellor looked me in the eyes. 'It looks like it, but they're getting more…' he squinted as he searched for the right word '…violent.' His voice dropped to a whisper. 'To be honest, your Grandad was lucky.'

Lucky? I wanted to shout, but could tell by the tense lines around Mellor's eyes that he had seen something far worse than what I'd seen in Grandad's photos.

'And the killer's getting sloppy, so if-' Mellor stopped when the suits walked in the room, illuminating the shelves with their brilliant white glow.

'All done,' the woman said. 'We'll get these back to the lab and see what we can find.'

'Right then, let me know anything you find,' Mellor replied as they left through the door, then his eyes switched back to me. 'If you find any dates for that book just ring me and leave a message, okay? No need to find me.' He waited for the forensics to get out of earshot. 'Unless you need some weed, right?' He winked and left.

I shut and locked the door, making sure the closed sign was still up. I waited a few seconds, letting my thoughts settle. A pang of guilt in my stomach told me I had to tell Dad about what was going on but I had no idea how I was going to break the news.

'For fuck's sake, just do it,' I said to myself and ran upstairs before I could change my mind.

I rang the home number and got the answer machine.

'Hi Dad… and Mum, it's me… Luke. Pick up if you're there.' I waited a few silent seconds then said, 'I just need to talk to you about what's in the paper. The…' I couldn't bring myself to say *murders*, '…the crimes linked with the shop.' I wasn't sure what else to say, so blurted out something about the photo I'd found and given to Detective Mellor, then hung up.

Back at my desk in the shop, tea in hand, I thought about what Mellor had been saying when the forensics guys came in. The killer was getting sloppy. Making mistakes. The police were closing in, which should have made me happy but it didn't. Whoever murdered my Grandad was still out there, killing other people and all the police had were a few old books.

I pulled out the sheet of paper with my list of books and added the new title. There had to be a pattern. Each book had a number:

536, 862, 833 and 995, but the new book threw out the number sequence – unless the second and third murders were out of order? I stared at the titles:

The Good Soldier

The Hollow Man

The Grapes of Wrath

Summer Lightning

I couldn't see a link.

What about the authors?

Ford Madox Ford

John Dickson Carr

John Steinbeck

P.G. Wodehouse

Types of car? No.

Maybe it would make sense if I knew who the other victims had been? There had to be a link.

I sighed and flicked through the pages of the green ledger, running my finger down each list of titles as I searched for *The Grapes of Wrath*. Nothing. Page after page of random book titles I'd never heard of… then I found something odd.

'Hello,' I muttered and wondered why I hadn't seen it before.

Ten books. All bought on the same day by the same person. Written next to the list, in Grandad's old-school writing, was *"For exhibit"*. I recognised a title: *The Hollow Man*. And the name? Simon, in the antiques shop.

I sat up straight and stared at the wall ahead of me as dozens of questions ran through my head. Was Simon connected? He didn't seem like a violent man, but he was under a lot of pressure with his divorce and having to sell the shop… an anger rose in my chest as I pictured Simon attacking my Grandad in the penguin alcove. Did Simon have a key for the shop? That would explain why the shop was locked when they found Grandad's body. I breathed deeply to calm down. I had to think logically, like Dad, so I pushed the images away until my thoughts boiled down to one question: did Simon still have the ten penguin books in his shop?

There was only one way to find out.

Even though it was sunny and we were in the height of a seaside summer, Simon's shop was like Dracula's lair: full of dark brown furniture and shadowy corners. I could see him sitting motionless in the corner furthest from the door at a mahogany desk which was covered with sheets of paper.

'Hi,' I said in a weak voice, which he didn't register, so I set about scanning the various chests and cabinets for any sign of the penguin books.

Every surface was dust-free or festooned with white lace, yet it felt unclean to me, like centuries of grime had worked into every greasy hinge and worn-out horse-hair stuffed seat. Dining tables were folded against walls to provide height for Victorian vases and tall display cabinets loomed above me, harbouring an array of crystal. Any spare wall space was covered with tiny paintings and my eyes were drawn from detail to detail while the musty smell of wood polish and mildew was starting to give me a headache. I was ready to ask Simon about the books when I spotted a mini bookshelf on legs holding a row of tatty penguin books.

'Oh, hi Luke.' Simon spotted me but stayed at his desk. 'Sorry, I'm trying to piece together something I'm writing… is there anything you need?'

'No,' I said, trying to think of a convincing excuse. 'I just fancied a browse. I'm always passing and never had a look, so…'

He stretched to see what I was looking at. 'Ah, a Penguin Donkey.'

'I beg your pardon?'

'Penguin Donkey,' Simon repeated. 'One of the originals – Isokon. Designed by Egon Riss - the Bauhaus designer.'

I gave a polite nod, wondering how much of what he was saying I should have understood.

'They stopped producing them when the war started of course,' Simon said.

'Of course.' I found myself frowning at the books.

Something wasn't right.

'Don't worry,' Simon said. 'I'm not trying to step on your toes… selling books, I mean.'

'Oh, no,' I said and gave him an appeasing smile. 'Not at all, I… I was just wondering if it would fit in the shop,' I lied. 'But there's not enough room as it is.'

'Tell me about it.' Simon's eyes flicked around the room.

'Yeah.' I focussed on the books again and found my heartrate pick up. I edged away. 'Well, I'd better leave you to it then.'

'Yes.' Simon frowned as he turned back to his work. 'A writer's work is never done.'

'See ya,' I said and shimmied around a set of lethal looking fire irons and back into the sunlight.

I walked straight back to my shop, locked the door behind me and ran upstairs. I was breathing heavily and my t-shirt was sticking to my armpits. I pictured what I'd seen. The books – I counted them twice to make sure - there were only nine on the shelf and *The Hollow Man* wasn't among them.

I didn't know what to do with myself so I walked around the flat, visiting my stash tin to roll a smoke but thought better of it and turned to the kettle instead. A cup of tea would make me feel better, I thought, and noticed the answer machine light flashing. I rushed over and pressed the playback button, hoping to hear Lisa's voice.

'Hi Luke.' It was Rob. 'What are you up to mate? Haven't seen you in days... we're down the beach most afternoons if you're up for it, otherwise... err... rehearsals on Saturday isn't it? See you then.'

The light was still flashing, so I pressed it again. The next message was my Dad and he didn't sound happy.

'Luke, what have you done? Do *not* talk to the police and don't give them anything from that file.' He huffed a few breaths and I could hear Mum talking in the background.

'Listen, we're busy tonight,' he said. 'But I'll pop round tomorrow morning, okay? Just don't let them see that file.'

Wednesday 2nd August 1995

In The Name Of The Father – Black Grape

'I didn't say anything about the file to the Detective, honest,' I said as Dad and I faced off over my dining table like two chess grand masters. 'But I had to give him the photo or he wouldn't have believed me.'

Dad's knuckles were white as he gripped his tea and I worried he would crack the mug. 'You don't think far enough ahead,' he said. 'It's always been the same with you… you make your mind up and that's it. Consequences be damned! Just like your Mum.'

'Come on, that's not fair. It was the right thing to do. It's evidence,' I said, but Dad's eyes were fixed on the open brown file on the table.

He breathed out heavily through his nose.

I knew he was in a tough position – he'd just found out his Dad had been killed and normally I would cut him some slack and comply but I could tell there was something he wasn't telling me. Stephen always had the knack of getting information out of our parents but I was useless, or less trusted, I could never tell which.

'So, why can't the police see the file?' I asked, trying Stephen's direct approach.

Dad looked me in the eyes. 'There are files in there I don't want them to see – especially Knowles, okay?'

'Which ones?'

'It doesn't matter,' Dad said and swept the file into his box of junk. 'You should be more concerned about this.' He pointed at the newspaper he'd brought with him.

Another bold headline designed to scare the masses: SERIAL KILLER STALKS BRIGHTON.

'I've got nothing to be worried about,' I said, but felt the muscles in my neck tense.

Dad gave the *'are you sure?'* look he saved for me then said, 'They come back to the scene, it's a well-known fact.'

I scanned the article but Dad had already told me most of it. That was why he wasn't surprised to find out Grandad had been a victim: he'd already pieced it together from my phone message and the article. But the way he remained emotionless riled me. Detached and logical. He'd already grieved for his Dad, he'd said that, but where was the anger or sense of injustice that I was feeling? Why wasn't he trying everything he could to catch the killer?

I re-read the article to hide my annoyance and to give Dad time to react properly.

'The murderer cut into the skin of the victims?' I asked, realising Dad hadn't mentioned it, and remembered what Mellor had said about Grandad being 'lucky'.

'Not Grandad,' he said with a shake of his head. 'I saw his body remember? Identification.'

I felt a dip in my belly, like when you drop in a lift, and wondered if I'd got it wrong. What if Grandad's death wasn't linked after all?

'How did they do it?' I asked.

'A knife. Lines mostly, on their arms and belly after they died,' Dad said. 'Symbols or letters I'm guessing.'

'Letters? Spelling what?' I asked and stared out the tiny window. 'Anything to do with the books?'

Dad shrugged and said, 'I don't ask too many questions, you know how it is, but Bob said forensics are trying to make sense of the markings.' He shuffled in his seat and finished his tea off. 'Look, I've got to pick up your Mum. Just make sure you keep the shop locked at night, okay?'

'Yeah, sure,' I replied. 'What are you going to tell her?'

He picked up his box. 'Nothing she can't read in the paper. Listen, I was thinking of heading down the allotment on Sunday if you fancy it? I need to go through Dad's shed – clear it out.'

'Okay,' I said, sure Lisa was working on Sunday. 'Sounds good.'

Dad's eyes softened. 'Get the shop opened, eh? That's what Dad would have wanted.'

Several hours later, I was back in my usual routine, sitting in my brown chair, rolling a spliff and waiting for a lull between customers so I could pop out for a smoke. I hadn't been in the mood for listening to records, so brought the radio down for a bit of Radio One. I licked the rizla, rolled, twisted and checked the roach, then put it in my top pocket for later. I was at a loose end. Normally I would write lyrics, fill out crosswords or spend ages analysing the NME, but all of that felt like wasting time now. There had to be something I could do to help catch Grandad's killer.

I found myself drawn to the penguin alcove, where I stared at the rows of books. Orange fiction, blue biographies, green crime… of course! Maybe I could get inspiration from the great detectives? I grabbed the first green book I'd heard of and took it back to my chair.

805. *The Case Book of Sherlock Holmes* by A. Conan Doyle.

I flicked through to find the shortest story and found *The Lion's Mane*. It was told by Holmes himself, which was odd because I thought Watson usually told the stories, but I read on. I sprinted through it, guessing the culprit on the second page, and finished it with a mix of disappointment that I hadn't found anything to help me and satisfaction because I'd solved it myself.

'Excuse me,' a voice said and it took me a second to detach myself from the book and look up at the man at my desk.

My first thought was I was looking at journalist but then I recognised him as the collector who bought penguin books last week – the guy who worked for Penguin.

He placed a pile of six books on my desk and said, 'I was wondering if you'd had any luck locating that book? *A Man Lay Dead?*'

I stared at him, open-mouthed, and must have looked like a complete dope-head, but my mind was racing with thoughts. Dad said the murderer came back to the crime scene and the title fitted with the rest. No, surely this guy was too nice to be a killer.

I sat up straight. 'No, sorry.'

I totted up his books and got halfway through when a thought came to me: if he was the murderer and had bought the tenth book from Simon's shop, I could test him.

'Hold on a sec,' I said and flipped open the green ledger back to the ten books Grandad had sold Simon – the titles had been written down and, sixth in the queue, was *A Man Lay Dead*.

'Why don't you try the antiques shop four doors down? I saw some penguins in there the other day,' I said, watching his reaction. 'That's four pounds.'

Not a flinch.

'Great.' He beamed and passed me a fiver. 'I appreciate that – can't wait to get my hands on a first edition, you know how it is.'

'Yeah.' I nodded and handed him a pound coin, then ripped a paper bag off the nail behind me and slipped the books in. 'Good luck.'

'Thanks, bye.' He walked off with a bouncy stride, like a boy who had found a new sweetshop.

He hadn't twitched or given any sign that he knew about the books in the antiques shop. In fact, he seemed genuinely surprised and grateful, which left me wondering how I would recognise a murderer if I ever found them. I assumed they would be angry or violent, like they were constantly holding back the need to kill. Or maybe there was something in their eyes: their murderous intent. But real life wasn't like that. If a confident killer could hide in public sight, that made them more dangerous than an average criminal.

That was as far as my thoughts got when a new customer appeared at my desk with a selection of books. A thin man in his mid-twenties with long hair. I took the books and studied him with my Sherlock mind while I added up the price. Shirt - office worker. Long nails on right hand – acoustic guitar player. Wave-shaped pendant on necklace – recently returned from travelling abroad. Anxious eyes.

'How much?' He asked and I realised I'd taken ages.

'One pound fifty,' I said, bagged the books and took his money.

As soon as he left I wrote the book titles in the ledger with the notes 'skinny, long-hair' and looked up to see another customer had appeared.

It was constant after that. A slow, but steady, flow of customers. I never had a lunch-time rush, but if I did, this would be it. I barely had enough time to write down the titles before the next customer came to the desk. I was too busy to think about what was happening, but after two o'clock, when the rush had died down, I took a moment to reflect. Most of the customers were carrying a newspaper under their arm.

'Cup of tea?' Isaac popped in with the smile he wore when business was good.

'Yeah, that would be great,' I said. 'Busy day?'

'Yes,' he said and his smile broadened further.

I felt a pang of guilt for not telling him about what had happened to Grandad, they must have been close after all, but I didn't want to worry him what with a serial killer on the loose.

'How about you? Sold many books?' Isaac asked.

'More than yesterday, that's for sure,' I replied.

'That's great,' Isaac said and smiled again. 'We've got to keep the customers coming down here – it's good for all of us.' He looked out the door then back to me. 'Anyway, mustn't keep gassing or I'll turn into Shirley. I'll see you in a minute.'

'Thanks,' I said and Isaac was gone.

After being confined to the desk for so long I felt restless. I visited the alcove again to see how many penguin books remained. I blinked away the images of my Grandad's body and checked the shelves - there were plenty of books but I'd have to stock up before they started looking bare, which meant digging through the boxes of books upstairs.

'Excuse me,' a woman's voice startled me.

I turned to see a lady in a skirt and blouse. She was probably in her mid-thirties but her partly-permed hair, like my Mum, made her look older.

'Yes,' I said and noticed a pad in her hand.

'Are you the owner of the shop? Luke Redfern?'

'Er, yes.' I took a step back but was penned in. I cast a look down the hall to see if there were any customers within earshot.

'I'm from the Brighton Argus, I just wanted to ask you a few questions if that's okay?'

'Well-' I started but she cut me off.

'The police reports say a number of books bought here were used by a…'

'Sorry,' I butted in. 'Do you mind if I close the shop first?'

She frowned and didn't reply but allowed me to brush past her. I made a quick tour of the back rooms, then returned to the front room. I could feel my heart racing as I closed the door, like I'd been caught out somehow and needed to think of a quick lie. Dad didn't want me talking to the press but I had to give her something. What could I say?

'So, Mr Redfern, the books - were they all from your shop?'

'Well, yes,' I said and perched on the edge of my desk.

She made a note, then fixed her eyes on me again. 'What sort of books.'

'Penguin books,' I said automatically.

'All of them?' She asked.

I breathed in sharply. The paper hadn't mentioned they were penguin books. It shouldn't matter, but I'd already said more than I wanted and that made me feel more agitated.

'I believe so,' I said slowly.

She glanced at the papers on my desk and I quickly covered up my shelf photo with the paper.

'Do you have the details of each book?' she asked.

'No, I...' I could feel my cheeks burning and had to get out of this, '...look I'm not sure I can help you. The police would be the best people to talk to.'

I moved to the front door and opened it.

'This is a serious matter, Mr Redfern and your shop is involved. The people of Brighton need to know if-'

'I'm sorry but I have to close now.'

'I really think-' I tried to guide her out, '-please, I need to close now.'

'Okay.' She clipped her pen to her pad.

I felt a tingle of relief but she hadn't moved a step.

'Can you confirm one detail for me?' She asked.

I opened my mouth but she cut me off.

'Was your Grandfather, Eric Redfern, the first victim?'

My eyes narrowed and I bit my lip. The mention of Grandad's name set something steely in me and I stepped forward, put my hand on her shoulder and practically pushed her out the door. 'I'm sorry, I really have to close now.'

'I'll take that as a yes,' she said and stepped out of the shop. 'Thank you Mr Redfern, you have been very helpful.'

I closed the door, flicked the closed sign round and slid down the wall. I hit the floor with a bump and held my head in my hands.

After a few breaths I shouted, 'Fuck!'

What had I done? The papers would print everything Mellor had told me in confidence and they would drag my Grandad's name through the mud, along with the shop. As much as it was good for business I didn't want more vultures skulking around picking at the shelves.

I kept my hands over my eyes, not wanting to return to the real world, listening to the footsteps as tourists trotted past. Each pair of shoes created different notes against the cobbles. Deep steps for hard-soled shoes, I guessed, some flip-flopped and other were higher in pitch. Each had their own tune. A soft padding step caught my attention as it ambled up and stopped at the shop door with a crunch. A knock on the glass followed.

'Go away!' I shouted. 'We're closed.'

'Well, that's a shame,' a familiar voice said through the door and my hands fell away.

'Lisa?'

I climbed to my feet and opened the door.

'I read the paper and thought you might want to get out of here?' She tilted her head and gave me her cute smirk.

'Yes, yes I do,' I replied, cupped her face and gave her a kiss.

'Well, here we go then.' She pulled a long green bag off her shoulder and presented it to me.

'What's that?' I asked.

'A tent,' she said with a little nod. 'Come on. Let's catch a bus and get the hell out of here!'

Thursday 3rd August 1995

Good Vibrations – The Beach Boys

I opened my eyes and saw green shapes dancing. It took me a few seconds to work out where I was, but the smell of warm sleeping bags and the cotton lining of the tent reminded me I was in the countryside and the shapes were the fluttering shadows of leaves in the morning sun.

I rolled onto my side to see Lisa's sleeping face lit perfectly by the diffused light in the tent. A cascade of freckles ran across the bridge of her nose. I felt a swell rise in my chest and let out a contented sigh.

We'd caught a bus outside the Pavilion with my bag of essentials: my festival sleeping bag; a bottle of water; some munchies and my smoking gear. The campsite Lisa knew about was by a pub in the South Downs, so we'd eaten there and spent the rest of the evening drinking pints of Harvey's, which somehow tasted better in a beer garden overlooking the flowing countryside.

'I thought you'd be a lager drinker,' Lisa had said when she got the first round in. 'Too fizzy for me.'

'Yeah definitely,' I said. 'And it doesn't taste of anything.'

'Exactly.' Lisa passed me my pint. 'You want the hops and the malt and-' she stopped when she realised I was staring at her. 'What?'

'Nothing.' I felt awkward and raised my glass. 'Cheers!'

I sipped and drank in the view. Our table was in the perfect spot, with views over the patchwork downs soaking up the last of the sun's warmth.

'Go on then,' Lisa said.

'Go on what?'

'What were you thinking?' she asked and nudged me with her elbow.

'Oh, I… just, well, I don't know much about you,' I said, feeling sheepish. 'I mean, who taught you about beer? Your Dad?'

'No.' Lisa fixed her stare on me. 'Why does it have to be a man who *taught* me about beer? Why can't I just know about beer?"

'I…' I stuttered. 'I don't know, I-'

Lisa shook her head and looked away. She was so hard to judge. Here was me opening up to her and she had gone from cosy cat to ice maiden in a flash. I had to think fast to dig myself out of this one.

'Well I learned about beer from my Dad,' I said. 'Otherwise I wouldn't have touched ale. Everyone said it tasted like warm piss, then Dad took me and Stephen out for a pint and I loved it.'

Lisa turned to me and her eyes softened. 'Alright, so my Dad got me into beer,' she said. 'But my Mum drinks it too. And my sister.'

I felt the mood lighten and said, 'See.'

'What?' Lisa asked.

'I learnt something new already… now I know you've got a sister.'

I don't know how long I watched Lisa sleeping in the tent, but eventually her eyes slowly opened and focussed on me. 'Hello you,' she said.

'Morning,' I replied. 'Another sunny one.'

She frowned. 'And a headache to go with it. How many pints did we have last night?'

'Five or six.' I offered her the bottle of water, which she gulped down. 'Sleep alright?' I asked.

'Apart from that idiot chopping wood half the night, yes thanks.'

'Yeah, what was that all about?' I cuddled up close, breathed in her perfume. 'So, what plans do you have for today, Brown Owl?'

'Well,' she was sounding perkier already. 'Seeing as you don't need to get back to your precious shop today, I thought we'd take a walk.'

I smiled, remembering how Lisa had teased me last night about the shop, calling me a hermit and a vampire, scared of going out in the sun. She'd been right in one thing: it was good to get away from Brighton and get a different perspective.

'Where shall we go then?' I asked.

'I've got a map, so we can follow a path east. Aim for Lewes I guess, then find another pub and catch a bus back.'

An hour later, we were chatting away as we tramped the grass with the sun ahead of us.

'That's what I call instant karma.' Lisa was giggling away.

'Lucky there was no one in the tent,' I said and shook my head. 'The branch tore right through their tent – straight down like a bloody dagger!'

'Teach them for chopping up a branch underneath the tree it came from,' Lisa said. 'It reminds me of a Roald Dahl story.'

We sighed, ending the laughter and entered a calm silence as we climbed a style and through a field of cows who were busy grazing at the far end of the field. Life felt good. Simple and good. All we had to worry about was drink, food and make sure we were on the right path.

'So, what's going on, Luke?' Lisa eventually asked.

'What? With us?' I replied, hoping the conversation wasn't going to get heavy.

'No, with the shop. The journalists and all that. You never talk about it.'

'I… well.'

'I didn't want to mention it last night,' she said. 'And you don't have to talk about it if you don't want to, but my Dad always says walking is good for talking.'

'Okay, sure,' I said. 'But it's not good stuff.'

So I set out explaining what I knew about the murders. I told her what Detective Mellor had told me and how the books had been left on the victims. How I found the photo of my Grandad and worked out he must have been the first victim, but left out how Dad had reacted when I told the police.

'That's horrendous,' Lisa said and squeezed my hand.

'Yeah, pretty heavy, hey?' I squeezed back. 'I thought I'd grieved for him but all this stirred it up again and being in the shop doesn't help.'

'I know,' Lisa said. 'I knew you had to get out of there. Especially when we're having a gorgeous summer and this is just on your doorstep.'

'Yeah.' I breathed in deeply and scanned the countryside: the sand-coloured parched fields and the deep green trees, set against the rich blue sky. 'But I still can't get it out of my head.'

'The picture?' Lisa asked.

'No.' I looked at her. 'The puzzle... the books. It's stupid but it feels like if I solve why each book was left on the victim I can work out who the killer is.'

'It's not as crazy as it sounds,' Lisa said. 'One of my final year courses touched on depression experienced after the death of a relative. Grief follows a pattern... denial, yearning, anger, depression.'

'Wait a minute.' I stopped to face Lisa. 'What did you study again?'

'Psychology,' she replied with a shrug and pulled my hand to keep us walking.

'And what did you get?'

'A first, if that matters, but look, it sounds like you're searching for answers.'

'Of course I am,' I said. 'Anything to help the police out.'

'Sure, but I think it's deeper than that,' Lisa said. 'Now you know what happened to your Grandad, you wish you could have done something to stop it.'

I nodded, not sure what to say. Having seen the police photo of Grandad had made his death far more real to me.

Lisa continued. 'So it sounds like you're stuck between anger and yearning.'

'Sounds about right,' I said.

I'd been flitting between emotions and never felt at ease. Trapped. Helpless. But now I recognised it, my stomach felt less tense.

'You know what?' I said.

'What?'

'Your Dad's right – walking is good for talking.'

On the bus back to Brighton another discussion came back from the night before.

'Okay, another example… Leftfield, *Leftism*,' I said. '*Inspection* is **not** the best track – the best song's *Open Up*. Track ten. And how about *Definitely Maybe*? Track eight is *Cigarettes and Alcohol*.'

'A good tune,' Lisa said.

'But *Live Forever* is the best track, everyone knows that.'

'That's just an example,' Lisa replied. 'I'm telling you, my theory still holds. The best song on any *classic* album is always number eight.'

'No way, *Sergeant Pepper's* would be *Within You Without You*.'

'There's always going to be an exception,' Lisa said and glanced out the window as the bus turned a corner, 'but on the old LPs-'

'Vinyl.'

'-yes, vinyl. They had to have a good song to open side B with,' she stood up and hooked her tent bag over her shoulder. 'My stop's next, I'll see you tomorrow night.'

I frowned.

'Cinema, remember?' she said.

'Oh yeah, sure,' I replied and she kissed me on the lips, sending tingles through me. 'Thanks,' I said and I could tell from her eyes she knew what I meant.

'Any time.' She pressed the bell, before disappearing down the stairs. 'See ya.'

I moved to the front seat to get a better view and watched her walk off without looking back, then the bus turned a corner and she was out of sight. A warm feeling enveloped me and I felt balanced. Everything was in its right place.

It was straight roads from here back to the Pavilion and I spent the time staring into the flats at my eye level: neat, office-like homes, untidy window sills blocked with piles of books and verandas littered with brightly coloured toys. I wondered if I would be in a place like that in a few years. With Lisa.

Then I saw James walking down the street, arm in arm with Rachel, so I rang the bell and jumped off early.

'Alright mate?' James pumped fists and I nodded at Rachel, hoping she didn't still hate me after the incident with Sarah. 'Where've you been?' James asked.

'Camping.'

'What. Really? Actually camping? I meant where have you been 'cos we haven't seen you around.'

'I've been at the shop,' I said. 'There's a lot going on, so…'

'I know but we're still rehearsing Saturday night, yeah?'

'Yeah, of course,' I replied. 'No gig this week.'

'And what about that girl?' James asked and I shot Rachel a glance.

'The one you dumped Sarah for,' Rachel said, eyes narrowing.

'Lisa, yeah it's going well… not sure if that's what you want to hear?'

Rachel looked away and James gave me a wink. 'That's all good mate, the summer of love, hey?' He gave Rachel a squeeze and she put her arm around him.

'We're off to the beach if you want to come?' James said.

'Yeah, alright. I just need to dump my stuff, okay? The usual place?'

'Yeah, see you down there.'

I hung a right and headed into the lanes. Two streets later, I stopped in my tracks just like a few days earlier. A newspaper board outside a newsagents.

THE PENGUIN KILLER

'Oh, shit.' I walked straight in and bought a copy, which was adorned with the same headline. 'What a stupid bloody name,' I murmured as I read the article written by the journalist who had cornered me in my shop.

She'd connected the murders with the penguin book calling cards the killer had left and mentioned Red Books as the main source for the books. To her credit she had actually called him *The Penguin Book Killer*, but someone had changed it for the headline.

I reached my alley and walked straight for the shop, trying not to catch any of my neighbour's eyes. Shirley had her back to the window, Simon was in his dark den and I could only see the two

European beauties in Isaac's florists, building bouquets, so I slipped into my shop unnoticed.

I dumped the paper on the desk and picked up the post, which included a handwritten envelope with my name on the front. I tore it open and pulled out a note.

Luke,
We need to talk.
Contact me as soon as you can.
DS Mellor

I looked at my watch and felt torn: I needed to know what Mellor had to say about Grandad's case, so I knew I should call him straight away, but that would lead to me having to go and find him. I was feeling properly chilled for the first time in weeks, the shop was shut. It was a Thursday, my day off, and my mates were down the beach.

I thought about what Lisa would say.

'Screw it,' I said and grabbed my guitar.

Today was a day for living.

-Fighting The Urge-

This wouldn't have happened if the papers had printed the words. He'd given them everything they needed. The best sentences.

He had the idea when the body had slumped, exposing a pale underarm. White, featureless like a blank page.

Blood had been used as an ink once hadn't it?

It had been easier to carve the words than he imagined – less blood once the heart stopped pumping – but then he ran out of space and could write no more.

But they didn't print the words. So he searched for a way to print them himself.

He'd been clever this time. Nobody to argue with. Nobody to hurt. But it hadn't worked – new machines with complicated rules he didn't understand. His anger took over again. He was strong when he was angry. At least the words didn't have those other books to compete with now. Gone. Into the sky.

But now he had to hide. Hide and wait. The black hole was the only place to hide. It had been pulling at him every hour of the day and he'd fought it... but now, after this failure, its weight was too much. It had won, drawing him in. Its power over him was too strong.

If he was caught it would be over. And what then? The words would never be read.

He had to be clever.

So he waited.

The papers printed more words but none had been the words he had left behind. Didn't they realise how much energy had gone into the book? The sacrifices that had been made? Didn't they know the deaths would stop if they printed the words?

An idea came to him. He thought of someone new he could persuade.

The black hole released him and he tried again. Carrying the words with him once more.

Friday 4th August 1995

It's A Shame About Ray – The Lemonheads

Feeling rejuvenated by my time away camping and a day on the beach with my mates, I started Friday with renewed energy and rang the police station straight away. I was soon following the receptionist's directions to a terraced house in Freshfield Road, Kemptown. Another day with the shop closed, but I needed to get every bit of information out of Detective Mellor.

Two police cars were parked down the road and a forensics van was parked outside the house but that wasn't what made the house stand out. Boxes and crates were piled up in the tiny front garden: each one overflowing with newspapers and old bicycle parts, threatening to spill onto the pavement like some freeze-framed wave of rust and paper.

A strip of a clear path a foot wide led from the gate to the front door. The white house looked quite desirable, if a bit shabby, but worse was to be found inside.

'I'm looking for Detective Mellor?' I said to a guy top to toe in forensics gear as he opened the front door half way and squeezed out.

'He's in the garden,' he replied. 'If you can get through!'

He gave the front door a hard shove against whatever was inhibiting it, to reveal the most junk-filled house I have ever seen. I don't know what hit me first – the sight or the smell - but it took me a few seconds to gain the courage to enter. Stacks of boxes lined the hallway on both sides, topped with teetering piles of yellowing newspapers. The stairs were the same, as were the rooms beyond from what I could see. I took one step in and the warm, fetid odour of damp paper invaded my nostrils. There was a tang of animal as well, so I kept my eyes peeled as I tiptoed along a narrow runway of orange and green carpet, into the kitchen.

A rectangle of space had been cleared connecting the sink with the cooker but the rest of the kitchen was rammed full with even more books. For a second I felt at home and stared around in wide-eyed wonder. There was no order to the piles: non-fiction sat with fiction and, despite being in a kitchen, cookery books were absent.

A scratching sound behind me made me turn.

'Oh, Luke.' Mellor forced the back door open. 'Come with me.' He gestured through the door. 'We need to talk.'

I squeezed through the back door, still in a daze, and followed Mellor into a square of a garden, full of what I assumed were car engine parts.

'How?' I asked and stared at the front panel of a VW campervan.

'God knows,' Mellor replied. 'There's no gate, so every piece must have come through the house at some point. Years ago by the look of the stuff.' Mellor stood with his hands on his hips, eventually turning to me. 'Now listen, I'm guessing it's you who spoke to the press about the penguin books, right?'

I swallowed and avoided his gaze, fixing my eyes on what looked like the wing of an old truck. 'A journalist was asking questions,' I said, wondering why this was such an issue. Mellor had said the press would find out all the info eventually.

'Why did you tell her about the books for God's sake?' Mellor shifted his feet. 'DI Knowles is on my case as it is – he *expects* results – and if he finds out I've been giving info to the public he'll...' Mellor stopped and looked away.

'I tried not to,' I explained. 'I asked her to leave but she didn't listen. I said I had to close up the shop.'

'It doesn't matter – she found out and they've given the bastard's a bloody name – *The Penguin Killer* - like someone's going around murdering flightless birds for fuck's sake.' Mellor looked hot but kept his jacket on. 'And now this.' He gestured at the house.

'Is this related to the murders?' I asked.

'Looks like it,' Mellor said and peered through the kitchen window, then came back to me and pulled a bag from his inside pocket. 'Listen, I've got another eighth of the last stuff you had, if you want it?'

I looked at the grass-green buds in the bag and could almost smell them. I hadn't smoked the last lot yet but knew it was good stuff so couldn't refuse.

'Fifteen quid and the bag's yours.' Mellor pushed the bag into my hand and glanced up at the windows. 'Just leave the money under that tyre.'

I stuffed the weed in my pocket and stared at Mellor, bemused.

'And I'm going to ask a favour of you in a few days,' he said.

'What favour?'

'Nothing big,' Mellor replied. 'Just a little job.' He nodded at the tyre and walked back into the house, so I pulled the notes from my pocket and hid them where he said. Still, it felt odd. One minute he was berating me for not following a police procedure I knew nothing about, the next he was blatantly breaking the law.

I followed him inside, into the fug of wet paper, through the kitchen to what would have been a large dining room if it wasn't crammed with even more piles of hardback and paperback books. One corner remained book-free where a desk nestled in between crates of A4 envelopes and piles of typed pages and brown folders.

'Is the owner dead?' I asked.

'Yep,' Mellor replied without turning. He was focussed on a cardboard box of paperbacks.

'So what happens to all the books?'

Mellor laughed and glanced at me. 'You want them for your shop?'

'Well, I just wondered...' I didn't like the idea of rifling through some dead person's belongings but, other than the odd customer selling books, that was how most of the books came to the shop.

'They'll get taken away by some distributor like that warehouse that got torched last week, only they had new books,' Mellor said, then pointed to a patch of carpet near the desk. 'This is where they found him.'

'Who was he?' I asked.

'A local guy,' Mellor said, obviously holding something back.

'Who found him?'

'The neighbours. They heard the cats fighting and knew he looked after them well, so... he'd been dead for about a week.' Mellor looked at me. 'Forensics found the patterns like on the last body. Cuts on the arms and torso.'

I wondered why he was telling me this. Was it because my Grandad had been one of the victims or because he liked bouncing ideas off me? My hand brushed the bag in my pocket and my stomach sank as it dawned on me he was just humouring me so he could sell me weed.

'And they found this on him.' Mellor picked up an evidence bag off the desk and held it up for me to see.

A green penguin book. *Death in Ecstasy* by Ngaio Marsh. Number 249.

I recognised it from the shop but couldn't see how it fitted with the other books.

'Another crime book,' I said. 'But what does it mean?'

Mellor swept his hand out. 'He died in his element.'

I looked at the books and the desk. This man had been totally absorbed in his work. It had consumed his home and his life.

'So the book left behind is definitely connected to the particular person the killer has murdered,' I said.

'I think that's a given considering the murderer leaves one at each murder, don't you think?' Mellor gave me a condescending look and I noticed a smirk.

He did like bouncing ideas off me, but only to make himself feel clever. He had all the clues and felt a power trip when he held the information back. The bastard! These killings were too important for one person's ego to block. I breathed in deeply. Control it, I told myself. Maybe I could play his game and use his ego to get a few more titbits out of him?

'How old was he?' I asked, remembering the photo of Grandad lying surrounded by books and could see the obvious similarities.

'Middle-aged,' Mellor replied. 'Late fifties maybe. He owned the house outright and had an income, but we're not sure what he did.'

'Not as old as Grandad,' I said.

'None of them were,' Mellor said.

'I thought age could be a factor,' I said, testing him.

'No,' Mellor said with a laugh. 'The others weren't that old. Not young but not in good shape, so probably weaker than the killer.'

'And were the others surrounded by books?'

Mellor looked at me in a way a hawk looks at a mouse. 'I think it's time to get the cleaners in. I'll let you know when I need that favour from you.'

He'd run out of patience again and I had nothing to show for it.

'Okay,' I said, blaming myself for pushing him too hard and made my way out along the narrow path of clear carpet.

'And no more chatting to the press,' Mellor shouted. 'You can leave that to us.'

I ignored him as I walked up the hall like a tight-rope walker at the bottom of a papery ravine. Some folders were lying open on the floor and I could see the front pages of what looked like reports. Each had a title and an author's name with a few numbers underneath. A white shape loomed up suddenly on the other side of the front door, making me jump: one of the forensics guys having a cigarette.

Enough snooping. I squeezed out of the front door, through the smoke and back into the searing heat of another hot and sweaty day.

A few hours later I was feeling chilled. Literally. The air-con in the cinema was working overtime and my chocolate ice cream had given me a headache. Still, the film wasn't bad and I was with Lisa. She was my oasis in the desert of death and gloom which seemed to surround me. Any distraction from thoughts of symbols cut into bodies and titles of books was always welcome.

Lisa laughed at another Hugh Grant gaff and I couldn't keep my eyes off her. She was so natural when she laughed, I guess we all let our inhibitions go when we allow ourselves to laugh but Lisa was so infectious.

'So you liked it more than *Waterworld* then?' I asked after the film finished and we meandered down to the beachfront to grab a drink.

'Was it ever in doubt?' Lisa took my hand. 'I mean, come on – Hugh Grant!'

'And Tara Fitzgerald,' I said with a grin.

By the time we made it back to the flat I was feeling a cloud of melancholy drift over me: the evening was coming to an end, just like I knew my time with Lisa would. The end was getting nearer.

'What shall I put on?' I asked as I hovered by the record player, desperate to keep the chilled vibes going while Lisa reclined on the sofa.

'Something retro,' she said and pushed my smoking gear under the sofa.

'You don't fancy a smoke?' I asked and flicked to the LPs I'd borrowed from Dad.

'Do you know what that stuff does to you?'

I put *Low*, by David Bowie, on and was distracted by a handwritten logo on the LP sleeve. I'd seen it on some of the record sleeves at my parents' house: two ovals intertwined like planet's orbits. 'Err, yeah of course I do – it chills me out and opens my mind, man,' I put on a hippy voice, like Stephen would, but could see it hadn't impressed Lisa.

'I mean permanently,' she said.

I shrugged and sat next to her. 'I hadn't thought about it.'

'The stuff I've read would put you off... guys from the 60's with psychosis and-'

I held my hand up. 'Alright, alright, enough of the heavy stuff, I get it. Drugs are bad. But they make me feel good, okay.'

'Sometimes,' she said. 'And sometimes it winds you up and makes you paranoid.'

I looked at her and wondered how to reply. She was right, but I didn't want to admit it. The next song came on: drums and bass, then a guitar lick. *Sound and Vision*.

'This is what it's all about.' I pointed at the record player and tried to explain. 'You know how music sounds better when you've had a few drinks and you just have to dance? You feel alive.'

Lisa nodded.

'Well, weed is the same but in a different direction. It allows you to listen – not just hear the music.'

'Okay, you're getting all Doors of perception here – but it's still bad for you,' Lisa said.

'But without it… I'm not sure I'd still have that creativity. The songs would stop coming and-'

Lisa put her hand on mine to stop me.

'*You* are what creates the songs, not some drug. Without *you* there would be no music.'

I smiled and wondered if I could use what Lisa had said in the lyrics of my next song.

'Play me something,' she said and stretched out to get comfortable. 'On the guitar.'

'Okay.' I switched Bowie off, grabbed my guitar and started a Lemonheads song.

'No, play me one of yours,' Lisa said.

'Okay then,' I ran through a few in my mind before settling on a Beachhead song – something mid-set.

After a few chords I was drawn in, like being enveloped in a cloud. I played and sang without thinking. I watched Lisa as she moved a few cushions to lie down. She pulled a piece of paper from under a cushion and read it as I sat and strummed, holding the notes and happy to play the song to its natural end.

When I stopped she said, 'Is this the list of books the killer left?'

She turned it round for me and I recognised the four book titles, number and authors.

'Yep,' I said and sighed.

'There's no pattern.'

'I know.'

I put the guitar down and sat next to her.

'But the killer's saying something.' She bit her bottom lip as she thought some more.

'But why books?' I asked. 'Why not write a note or-'

'Your Grandad died surrounded by books, right?'

I nodded.

'So maybe the killer literally used what was around at the time?'

'A little convenient… but, okay, so what are they trying to say?' I asked.

'You have to remember they don't think the same as us. I mean, why kill at all?' Lisa said. 'It's almost impossible to adapt your train of thought to that of someone who was able to take another life.'

I tried to think like a guilty person hiding their tracks. 'A note would give away their handwriting.' No that wasn't enough. 'But the books had to have another purpose. A message maybe?'

'Not a message,' Lisa said. 'I know it sounds odd but what if they are describing the victim.'

I frowned and stared at the list. 'I don't know much about the other victims, so…'

'But your Grandad fought in the war, so *The Good Soldier* fits.'

I nodded and remembered the book Mellor had shown me that morning in the hoarder's house. 'There's a fifth book now.'

'Another murder?' Lisa looked at me. 'You didn't mention it?'

'I… look, we were having a good time and I didn't want to go on about it, okay?' I took the piece of paper to write the title down: *Death in Ecstasy*. 'Besides, I don't want to get you involved.'

After a few moments of silence she asked, 'Where was the murder?'

'In some cluttered up house over Kemptown way,' I replied.

'And the others?'

'I don't know.'

'But there were books? Not just the penguin book but other books?'

'Yeah,' I said, picturing the piles of hardbacks and paperbacks. 'The place was stuffed full of them and other junk.'

'Then that has to be the link.' Lisa looked serious but happy with herself at the same time. 'You need to find out where the other murders took place, or who the people were. If they are book related you will know.'

'Know what?' I asked.

'Then you'll know where the killer's going to strike next.'

Saturday 5th August 1995

Rocks – Primal Scream

Lisa left early Saturday morning and headed straight for the café, leaving me to open the shop up. Saturdays were different to weekdays. They sounded different and, I don't know why but I swear they smelt different. Weekend clientele were different to weekday customers. There were more of them for starters. Typically they were people who worked during the week and only had the weekend to fulfil their hobbies, so they hobbied hard, scooping up books by the armful.

'How much are these?' A tall, balding American tourist asked, carrying a bundle of hardback World War Two history books.

I totted them up. 'Twelve pounds fifty – call it twelve.'

'Twelve pounds, is that all? I'd get more if I could afford shipping them home.'

'I could charge you more if it made you feel better?' I said with a smile and ripped a paper bag off the wall for him.

'Ha ha, that's what I love about you guys – a great sense of humour!' He took the bag. 'Be seein' ya.'

'Cheers,' I replied.

'Ha ha, cheers...' his voice trailed away with him.

I settled into a new crossword and saved a couple of clues to research later:

Arboreal marsupial, two words.

French monkey, five letters.

Time swept me away and by the time Isaac brought me a tea and the real day set in I noticed a subtle change in the type of customers coming in. They were younger and more… I could only describe them as 'local'. It took me a while to click, but when I saw a few had yesterday's Argus paper tucked under an arm or poking out of their bag I could see my fears had become reality – the vultures had arrived.

The first one to buy a book was a guy in his twenties who arrived with a sheepish smile and placed a green penguin book on my desk: an Agatha Christie mystery.

'One pound,' I said, eyeing him up.

He passed me a pound coin, snatched the book away and jogged away with a cheeky smile like he'd just won the lottery.

The second came soon after and then more. They all bought penguin books and none of them said a word. In between each customer I sat in a quiet fume, swinging from blaming myself for telling the journalist about how the penguin books were linked to the murders and reminding myself it was good for business. But every pound coin felt blood-stained. This was profiting from Grandad's death – all the deaths – and it felt wrong. The very books the people were buying were on the shelf when Grandad died, or lying on the floor around him. Those books had witnessed his murder at close hand.

I needed to stretch my legs and thought about having a smoke but a lady not much older than my Mum came to the desk with a pile of books.

'Thank you,' she said with a smile as she handed them to me.

I totted them up and relaxed when I noticed there were no penguin books in her selection.

'It's lovely this place,' she said. 'Like a library, you must love working here.'

'It's not bad – I get to choose the music,' I replied. 'That's three pounds fifty please.'

'Thank you.' She took the books. 'Have a nice day.'

'You too,' I said and felt my shoulders relax.

It was good to have a normal customer and they did seem chatty at the weekend. I picked up my NME and flicked to the reviews but stopped mid-page as my mind wandered. Lisa had said if I could work out the killer's motives I would be able to work out where they would strike next. Every death I knew about was book related: my shop; the hoarder's house; the warehouse. They were all stuffed with books and Detective Mellor had confirmed there had been books at the other two murder sites. So what about the library? It had to be on the list of targets, assuming the killer had a list. I thought about ringing Mellor to tell him my theory but pictured his condescending face and gave up on the idea.

I huffed and pushed my chair back to stretch.

A young couple came in and disappeared into the hobbit warren, followed by another local with a paper under their arm. Locals, wanting to buy a penguin book from where the *Penguin Killer* bought their copies. It was grotesque. They searched, they bought, they giggled… I had a smoke and the rest of the day rushed away with itself. Before I knew it, it was time to close up, grab my electric guitar and head to the studio for rehearsals.

'One, two. One, two,' I tested the mic. 'Anybody out there?'
Nope.

As ever, I was the first one at the rehearsal studio. It didn't matter what day or time of day - the rest of the band were always late. I tried to relax and get into the musical mood. I wasn't seeing Lisa tonight, so had no plans, no rush. Plus I needed to run through some new lyrics for the new song we were going to try out in the next gig, so it was perfect. I had the place to myself.

The studios were just a set of sound-proofed rooms in an old warehouse near the train station where nobody would complain about the noise. One room was set up for recording and had all the decent equipment, while the other three rooms were available to rent out for twenty quid a session. They came with some half-decent amps, a few mics linked to a PA and speakers, plus a drum kit, minus the snare and cymbals. All we did was turn up, turn on and play. No lumping about amps or speakers.

I plugged in and adjusted the levels, then cracked on. After ten minutes I'd run through the new song twice, had the lyrics down and was left twiddling my thumbs. Playing and singing without the rest of the band made me feel like a bloody busker.

I picked up a copy of the paper left by an earlier band and re-read the article about the *Penguin Killer*. I had walked past the library on the way over and felt a pang of guilt, but hadn't a clue what I could do. I didn't fancy explaining my theory to them: 'Excuse me, did you know the local serial killer has a thing for books and I think you're next on his list?'

An article I had missed earlier caught my eye. It was about the graffiti artist – or vandal as the paper called them. As I read on I saw they were calling them the *Pavilion Poet* which made me think they had a specific role at the paper just for making up crap names. They hadn't touched the Royal Pavilion, I thought, but I guessed the name simply came about because most of the pieces were nearby.

According to the reporter, the *Pavilion Poet* had struck again: this time the back wall of an Indian takeaway. No picture but the words had been printed: *Salvation for the mirror blind*.

'What the...?' I mumbled to myself.

They were getting more obscure by the week.

I heard a noise and looked up. No movement at the door, so it had to be one of the other bands. Where were the guys? I asked myself. Usually one of them had turned up by now. We had the room booked for four hours and they were already half an hour late. I didn't care about the money – it was the wasted time that mattered. Rob would take ten minutes setting up his kit, James would just plug in like me, but Mike always has something to brag or talk shit about... some new pedal probably or how he'd learnt a Blur lead break – and improved it.

I heard an engine outside: a deep, spluttering rumble which sounded like Mike's campervan. What I'd give to get my hands on an old splitty like that, the lucky bastard. I heard a door slam shut then some footsteps.

'Hey Luke, how's it going?' Rob was first in with his bags of cymbals.

I nodded back.

'Alright.'

James walked in, nodded and set his gear up by the bass amp and then Mike came in with two bags of pedals and what looked like a new guitar. I turned away so I didn't give him the satisfaction of ogling. He'd been like it all through Uni: his parents were minted and gave him anything he wanted. He was singing, 'Tell me what you've seen... was it a dream?' He looked over. 'Alright, Luke? Sorry we're a bit late.'

A bit late? Cock. Mike gave the others a lift and made them all late. Thanks for the offer, I thought, remembering how far I had lugged my guitar and pedal bag.

'No worries,' I said and played an A-minor chord.

Then I realised the song he had been singing – Verve, *On Your Own*. He was pushing my buttons the posh git. Stop getting worked up, I told myself, I had to keep my head and not get arsy with him.

'Oh.' Rob looked up from his kit bags. 'I left my snare at home.'

I turned to him and could guess the look on my face by his reaction.

'It's alright.' He held his hands up. 'It won't take me five minutes to get it. You can give me a lift right, Mike?'

'Yeah sure,' Mike said and sent a smirk my way.

Thoughts were buzzing round my head like a swarm of tie-fighters: we had a gig in a few days and if we didn't rehearse the new song it would sound shite, the set will be ruined and everyone will think we were crap, which meant we wouldn't get booked again and… I took my guitar off, placed it in the stand and switched the amp off.

'I need a spliff,' I said and grabbed my bag.

Anything to stop me from shouting my mouth off.

By the time Mike and Rob had made it back, James and I were stoned and giggling away as we sang down a mic plugged into a phaser pedal set to max, turning our voices to jelly.

'Very good,' Mike said with a nod. 'We should use that on the new song.'

'Nah, the new song's sorted, shall we give it a go?' I said.

'When you're ready,' Mike replied and I pushed away a wave of anger.

Just as I had explained to Lisa, the weed – along with calming my mind - gave depth to my hearing. The music sounded good. The new song rocked and fitted well into the set, so I felt comfortable again. In control and centred.

'How about a few covers?' I asked, knowing Rob was always up for blasting a cover version.

'Alright,' James said. 'Seeing as we've got everything else nailed, let's do it.'

The old favourites came out, I explained a few chords where needed or wrote down the scales for Mike, and we had a bit of fun.

Just like the early days when we were sussing each other out along with our sound. The nerves had loosened and we laughed with each new track. This was free-playing. We all knew the songs because the originals had been set in stone, or cut in vinyl. We all had mics and sang away to our hearts' content. No pressure.

We finished *Rocks* by Primal Scream and I guzzled water to cool my raw throat.

'So we're all good for next week's gig then?' I asked, expecting to keep on a high.

Mike nodded.

'Drinks and clubs after?' Rob said.

'Of course,' I replied.

'It'd be rude not to,' James said. 'And… seeing as tonight is Saturday night… why don't we dump our gear and go out on the town and get smashed?'

I remembered what Lisa had said about seizing the moment. There were times in your life when you had to just go with the flow and get drunk.

Sunday 6th August 1995

Common People – Pulp

'People have been growing food here for generations,' Dad said, resting on his garden fork and pointing to the far off grassy hills. 'Thousands of years really.'

'You mean the Whitehawk camp? I remember Grandad telling me about it,' I said and remembered a school history field trip which, as far as I remembered, involved running over grassy hills and eating warm ham sandwiches in the sun.

There was nothing but grassy ditches up there but the archaeologists had found evidence of a Stone Age camp. Pottery and bones, the usual.

'Older than Stonehenge,' Dad said, still resting while I lugged a watering can over from the almost empty water butt and watered one of the marrow plants.

I stopped to turn a half circle and survey the housing estate which lay on the edge of the patchwork of neat and wild allotments. Grandad's plot was at the far end so hadn't been attacked by vandals, although someone had given the lock on his shed a go though, not that there was much worth nicking from in there.

'Must've been hard back then,' I said. 'Growing your own food. Not much to last through winter.'

'You sound like your Grandad.' Dad laughed and started digging again. 'He was always planning ahead to make sure there was something to eat.'

'Did he grow food when you were a kid?' I asked.

'Oh yeah!' Dad beamed. 'Sacks full of potatoes, onions as big as your head and strawberries to die for.' He took a second before he realised what he had said and his face dropped.

'Must have been great,' I said.

We'd been working the allotment all morning and there'd been a couple of moments like that, when one of us said a throw away comment, like *'that'll be the death of me'* or *'over my dead body'* and we would stop and a silence would wrap around each of us as we thought about Grandad. Dad hadn't said anything about him being murdered but something in his manner told me that, like me, he hadn't come to terms with it yet.

'We had a few beds too, when you were young. Do you remember?' Dad didn't wait for my reply. 'A few rows of carrots and some tomatoes in the greenhouse.'

I didn't remember much about the old house but let him reminisce.

'Then life got in the way.' He shook his head. 'Too busy with work and all that. We let it slide and…'

'Nana loved her roses, didn't she?' I said.

'Yeah,' Dad said. 'Nothing made her happier than seeing Grandad carrying a big bag of horse manure down the drive. Ha ha!'

I poured the last of the water out, returned the can and slumped into one of the plastic chairs in the shade.

'Another cup of tea?' I asked and shook the huge thermos flask Dad had brought, along with a huge lunchbox of sandwiches Mum had made.

Dad nodded and turned over a new lump of nettles. I had argued it was too hot for tea but after a bit of hard work it hit the spot.

'Funny how the bits Dad started this year are fine,' Dad said. 'Yet anything untouched is rampant with bloody weeds.' He wiped his brow. 'Must have been an ongoing battle keeping this place clear.'

I offered him his cup as he sat next to me.

'So what happens now, with the plot I mean?' I asked.

'If I keep paying the council I can keep it,' he said with a shrug, like he was considering it. 'It's not all hard work you know… I mean look at them marrows – Dad had them in the ground and under cloches the week he died and I've barely touched them. And as for the rhubarb and raspberries, well…'

'They look after themselves do they?' I said, remembering one of Grandad's well-used gardening phrases.

'All you do is prune the raspberries once a year according to a book I found in the shed,' Dad said.

'Oh yeah, I'd forgotten about the shed.' I peered back through the open door into the cobweb-curtained box of a room.

'Mostly old junk to be honest,' Dad said. 'Although there is a tin you might be interested in. Dad must have kept from his army days but I bet you could get a tenner for it in the shop.'

I got up for a look, feeling the warmth from the sun-baked wooden wall and the heavy scent of creosote.

'Found it,' I said, spying the brown A4-sized tin on a shelf. I gave it a shake and felt something solid beneath the rusting lid, which retained some of its original brown colour and had *Chocolate and Boiled*

Sweets emblazoned across in army font. It would make a good stash box, I thought as I took it out into the sunlight.

'Ooh, chocolate,' Dad said when he saw it and looked at his watch. 'Come on, if we get cracking and we can have half this bed done before lunch.'

An hour later, back in the chairs with our sarnies, Dad was still thinking about Grandad.

'He did well after the war because he had his head screwed on,' Dad said and nodded at the nearest houses. 'You notice anything odd about these places?'

I scanned the houses – semi-detached, dark brick, good windows. Some newer houses near the entrance were covered in red tiles, but were all standard. Nothing unusual but I knew how Dad, the policeman, thought and took a second more to ponder before answering. 'They're all council houses, so they're identical.'

Dad nodded. 'Yeah, but what about what's outside? When we parked up?'

'Well there was that new Mercedes outside one place,' I said. 'That was a bit odd.'

'Exactly!' Dad slapped his knee and took a bite out of his sandwich.

'Which means… they stole it?' I said.

Dad scowled at me. 'No,' he mumbled, finishing his mouthful. 'Just because someone doesn't have money doesn't make them a criminal. They earnt that money so they're entitled to spend it on whatever they want.'

'They'd be better off saving up to buy a house,' I said.

'That's what you think,' Dad replied. 'But to them the car is an asset.'

'But everyone knows cars lose money and houses go up in value.'

'And maybe Grandad would have been like that, who knows? He saw the world as it really was and worked hard to step out of the class trap while he could.'

'By buying a house when he married Nana?' I asked.

'Yes, but a house was just one step. Grandad learnt a lot during the war. He watched the Officers and wanted what they had. What was the one thing they all had?'

He let the question hang, so I shrugged.

'Land. That was the only true asset. The only thing you could own that had real value.'

'So why didn't he buy any then?'

'He did,' Dad said with a mix of anguish and satisfaction written across his face. 'And he left it to me.'

'Where?' I asked and sat up in my deck chair.

'Just some fields north of Hove.' Dad gestured across town. 'And one day I'll sell it to some investor wanting to build new houses. Dad knew what he was doing.'

I stayed silent, waiting for Dad to say what he was holding back.

'The trouble is… it could cause me a few issues while I'm under investigation. That's why I took Dad's file. If it got into Knowles' hands he would be after the land. He's as bloody bent as they come.'

I thought of telling Dad how Detective Mellor had sold me confiscated weed but I knew the argument that would follow and didn't have the energy for it.

'And his team would be the same?' I asked.

'Probably.' Dad sighed. 'I guess they'd have to be to keep up with him. He demands answers you see? So they do anything to get them.'

'That's a good thing really,' I said, trying to see the bright side. 'If they're after Grandad's killer.'

Dad's head snapped round when I said those words but his eyes softened when he spoke. 'Yes, I guess so. Just don't antagonise them, okay? Keep them sweet and they'll stop sniffing around.'

I nodded.

'Come on, lunch is over,' Dad said and pushed himself out of the chair. 'Let's finish this off, pack up and I'll drop you off home.'

The cool temperature of the shop was bliss after working all day in the sun. I headed straight up to the flat to check for phone messages and left Grandad's old tin on the side. Nothing from Lisa, but Rob had left a message.

'Alright mate? Just wanted to see if you're coming down the beach tomorrow? No worries if not. Mike said to say the girls are coming. Erm… otherwise, see you at the Level for that Radio One thing on Wednesday, yeah? Cheers.'

I'd forgotten about Wednesday. I was supposed to open up the shop but now I'd got into the habit of closing it I was getting used to the freedom. Plus business yesterday had been good enough to make up for a couple of average weekdays, so I could afford to close. Besides, like Lisa said, I shouldn't be stuck indoors when summer was blooming outside.

I grabbed a cold drink and was about to stick an album on the record player when I heard knocking downstairs. I stomped down to see Detective Mellor at the front door. He was wearing his off duty clothes with a bag over one shoulder, staring into the darkness of the shop and checking his watch.

'Let me in then,' he hissed through the glass pane as soon as he saw me.

I fiddled with the locks.

After what Dad had said about Inspector Knowles I decided to keep what I said to a minimum.

'Right.' He walked straight through to one of the back rooms, plonked his rucksack on a wooden chair and unzipped it. 'That favour you said you'd do for me.'

I didn't remember agreeing to anything but kept cool.

He flashed me a look, keeping his hands in the bag. 'How was that weed by the way? Good stuff?'

'Yeah, alright cheers.'

'Good, good.' He sounded like a Doctor. 'I've got something I need you to look after, okay?'

He pulled out what looked like a thick tome of a book wrapped in brown-paper and handed it to me. It weighed my arm down more than I expected.

'Just for a few days, okay?' Mellor was already zipping up his bag.

'Okay,' I said and gave it a squish to see how solid it was. Hard but it had a bit of give, like an eraser.

'Good.' Mellor slipped the bag back over his shoulder and gestured back to the front door. 'I've got to rush, so I'll see you next week to pick it up.'

'Right,' I said and followed him to the front door.

'I almost forgot.' He turned with a smile and opened his bag again to produce a few pieces of A4 paper held together with a paper clip. 'You think of yourself as some kind of amateur sleuth don't you?' He cast the paper onto my desk with a sneer.

'I'm just trying to help catch my Grandad's killer,' I replied.

Mellor squinted. 'Well, either way, I brought you something you might find interesting.' He tapped the sheets of paper with his forefinger.

I leaned over and saw a list of names. 'What are they?' I asked.

'Books,' Mellor replied.

'More books?'

'And their authors. I want to know if you can see a link.'

I was intrigued but couldn't see where this was going. 'They're linked to the murders then?' I asked.

'Of course they are.' Mellor huffed and zipped his bag up.

I picked the sheets up. 'I still don't get it.'

'They're from that hoarder's house – the last victim.' Mellor grabbed the door handle.

'What? These are the books that were lying around? How can that help?' I felt my cheeks redden as he turned the handle to leave without me knowing what it was he expected me to do.

'They're not the books in the house – not the real ones anyway. They're the books the deceased had been working on. Manuscripts. He was a reader for the agent who was killed last week.'

'What! They knew each other?' I felt my heart rush. This link was important - the earlier victim was a Literary Agent.

'He worked for him,' Mellor replied. 'So there's a chance our killer knew both of them. Maybe worked with them both or was lead from one to the other.' He glanced at the list. 'Either way, the killer could be one of the names on that list. They could be an unpublished author.'

Monday 7th August 1995

Breaking Glass – David Bowie

You don't often see the pitch-black dark of night on the south coast in summer. The dusk lingers for hours and, as I knew from taking my sunrise photos, the early morning dawn paints light across the sky long before the sun actually rises. So when I looked up through my tiny bedroom window and saw stars in the black sky, I knew it had to be two or three in the morning. I glanced at the clock to check: 3:45am. Too early for my daily photo-trip.

I didn't usually have problems but I'd been sleeping lighter than usual but since the murders, like some ancient instinct passed through the generations was keeping me alert, ready to defend myself. I reached over to Lisa's side of the bed, found the cold sheet and remembered I had gone to bed alone. I must have been getting used to her being around to miss her not being there.

I moved to a cooler part of the pillow and huffed. Just a little bit more sleep I thought and ran a Beachhead song through my head, going over the lyrics and chords. But it didn't work. My mind was too active. In those waking minutes, between sleep and full awareness, it felt like my sub-conscience busily working away. The mystery of the murders had given it a problem to solve and it wanted to use every minute available. Now I was awake, it connected to my conscious thoughts, which gravitated to the penguin books left by the killer.

There had to be a link that would show the killer's next move. I huffed again. I was too tired to think properly and too awake to go back to sleep, so I pushed myself up and switched my alarm to mute.

I may as well head out, ready for the sunrise, I thought. With a scratch and a stretch, I threw on some clothes, grabbed the camera and headed out.

It wasn't as quiet as I thought it would be down at the beach. There were a few drunk clubbers enjoying a summer Sunday night out, staggering around or dancing on the pebbles. I felt like I was intruding, so headed back into the lanes to meander and search for a good photo. I missed this. Touring with my camera, searching for a jaunty angle of a building or an object left behind by someone: a boot; a jumper; a flower. My eyes always had a frame in mind and saw everything in boxes.

That's when I saw the *Pavilion Poet*.

A movement of shadow caught my eye, which I ignored, assuming it was a homeless guy or someone taking a slash, but then I heard the unmistakeable metallic tinkle of a spray can being shaken and I stooped to hide behind a car. The shadow was in a dark corner where the road turned a right angle and the street lights didn't quite reach. The hiss of paint spray came and went in bursts and I crept forward to the next car to get deeper into the shadows. I waited to make sure I hadn't been spotted, then raised my camera, resting the lens on the car bonnet, and zoomed in. My heart pounded a deep rhythm, which vibrated the camera as the figure came into focus. They were wearing a dark hoody and tracksuit bottoms, with a rucksack on their back. Every bit of clothing was black and the shadows obscured their face.

I held my breath to steady my hand and risked a shot. The click echoed around the buildings but the Poet didn't react. I took another shot then changed focus for a third shot as they made a long sweeping spray with their arm. It was their final stroke. They took a step back for a last look as they slipped the can into their bag, turned and ran off. I tried to get a couple more shots but knew they would be blurred images.

I kept hidden as the jogging footsteps faded, then crept out to visit the wall. The smell of paint was strong and I couldn't resist taking a photo of the graffiti. Fresh.

I struggle with words way more than with music and have to pay attention to get my own lyrics in my head let alone someone else's lyrics, but there are some lyrics you can read and the melody hits you straight away. I guess that's the sign of a great songwriter.

I read the words and finally the connection became clear.

Don't look at the carpet. I drew something awful on it.

Maybe not the best lyrics Bowie ever wrote but pretty memorable. I rushed straight home and checked the sleeve notes in Dad's LP, *Low*. I knew it. Track two: *Breaking Glass*. I rushed to find the newspapers I had kept over the past few weeks and flicked through the copies to find every article about the *Pavilion Poet*. It was slow going but eventually I had every piece of graffiti written down on paper. I didn't recognise all of them but they worked as lyrics and sounded like the sort of thing Bowie would write. If only I had more albums to check some of them, or a library… then it hit me. I had my own, personal library downstairs! I ran down and headed straight for the music section where *Learn to Play the Beatles* sat next to *Piano for*

Beginners. I ran my fingers along the shelf: *80's Organ Favourites; Jazz Guitar Greats.*

Bowie's Greatest Hits.

Half an hour later I had every piece of graffiti identified by song and year. All my notes and books were spread out on the lounge floor and I lay on my back and let out a contented sigh of achievement.

It was tainted by one thing. There was no obvious correlation between when the lyrics were sprayed and when the songs had been released… was there a pattern?

My eyes drifted up to the tiny window and saw the cool blue dawn of a new day. My relaxed smile faded as I turned to my camera and the maroon photo album.

I had missed the sunrise.

I spent the rest of the day in a state halfway between contentment and annoyance. I had figured out the connection between the *Poet's* cryptic pieces of art, although I had no idea what they were trying to say, but I had missed the first sunrise since Grandad died. I knew it would have to stop one day but I thought it would end as a conscious decision, like when I filled the album up or on his birthday, not because of a mistake or being distracted.

The day plodded by in the shop, with cups of tea and customers breaking up the monotony. Lisa came round in the evening for some dinner to help me go through the sheets of paper Mellor had given me.

'So he thinks the killer's name is on this list?' Lisa asked between mouthfuls of pasta as she studied a sheet.

'Could be. He said one of the earlier victims was a Literary Agent and the guy in the house full of crap was one of their readers, so…'

Lisa nodded. 'Yeah, those guys read the first chapter of a book by new authors and tell the agent whether it's worth reading or throwing in the bin. So these are the books he was reading for the agent?'

'Yeah, I'm guessing Mellor got someone to write down all the manuscripts on the desk.'

I remembered the piles of boxes and the scattered official-looking documents in folders with names and numbers on the front. It was obvious now they were front pages of novels with the title, author and word count of the book.

'So the killer has to be an author who resents being turned down,' Lisa said.

'I guess so – that fits.' I let the idea sink in. 'Pretty bloody severe, but yeah, they're getting their revenge… but why did they leave those books on their victims?'

'Forget the penguins!' Lisa said. 'Why don't the police go through the agent's letters and work out who's been rejected in the last few months?'

'I don't know,' I replied. 'Mellor just gave me these sheets and a package to look after. Still don't know why he gives me the info 'cos every time I come up with someth-'

'Wait.' Lisa held her hand up. 'What package?'

I pointed at the brown-paper block on the kitchen sideboard and Lisa stood up to get it. She gave it a squeeze, like I had done, then smelt it.

'You don't think that's odd?' She asked, holding it away from her like it was a lump of out of date cheese.

'Why? I just thought it was a bit of give and take… he gave me information. You know how important solving this is to me. I couldn't say no, could I?'

'That's the problem,' Lisa said. 'Mellor knows how important it is to you so he's using you. Who knows if these lists are real or not? He could have made them up for all you know.'

I put my fork down and, despite having Lisa looking out for my interests, I felt unsettled. She was right.

'What is this anyway?' She said and placed the package next to my plate.

'I just guessed it was resin,' I said with a shrug. 'He sells a bit of weed on the side, so…'

'He does what?' Lisa had her hands on her hips now.

I'd never seen her get worked up like this and found her even more attractive than usual.

'This must be worth hundreds of pounds,' she said.

'Dad said it was best not to mess with anyone linked to Knowles, so I agreed to take it. Just for a few days.'

'And that doesn't seem odd to you? A policeman asking you to look after drugs?'

I shrugged as Lisa shook her head and looked into space.

Eventually she said, 'Look, I can't see any good will come from this. You have to let me take it back to my place.'

'What?' I stood up. 'I can't let you get in anything like that, you–'

'It's okay,' she said and I could read in her eyes that she had done worse before. 'Let's just open it up to check what it is, then I'll take it home in the morning and get rid of it.'

'And what do I tell Mellor when he asks for it back?' I asked.

'Nothing!' She almost screamed. 'It's bloody illegal. He can't threaten you… if anything you should be threatening him!'

'That won't help will it?' I unpeeled a corner of the paper to reveal the dark brown colour of what looked like a malt loaf. I lit my zippo and burnt the corner, watching it lighten in colour and expand before I rubbed a crumble into a rizla and smelt it.

'Definitely resin,' I said, holding back the urge to add some baccy. I hated the stuff normally, but it smelt good and I fancied a smoke after eating dinner.

'Okay.' Lisa still looked serious. 'Wrap it up and put it in a bag or something.'

I looked around and spotted Grandad's old tin from the allotment shed. 'Here you go.' I prised the rusted lid off with my fingernails, working around the edge inch by inch. 'This should be good but I need it back though, okay?'

'Sure,' Lisa replied. 'Just get it packed away and we can forget about it.'

The lid flipped open with a metallic prang and I pulled out sheets of paper, allotment plans and seed catalogues which Grandad had stuffed inside.

'Perfect,' I said as the package fitted in snuggly and I pressed the lid shut.

Lisa took it from me and slipped it into her bag. 'Right, let's get out of this bloody place and have a drink on the beach.'

'Okay,' I said, eyeing up the half-full rizla on the table.

Lisa took my hand. 'You can have a smoke when you get back if it helps you sleep, but tonight I want you as you are.'

Tuesday 8th August 1995

Paperback Writer – The Beatles

'…with a jester's hat on and Noel was behind him playing some kind of mandolin, then Damon Albarn walks up wearing a suit of armour and they start a fighting with longswords.'

Lisa looked up from her cereal and stared at me with one eyebrow raised.

'And Gaz Coombes had this crazy long guitar – more like a sitar really – and he was dressed like a minstrel.'

'Luke.' Lisa held her hand up. 'Enough now okay?'

'Yeah, but then the best bit was when Paul Weller appeared on a steam-driven moped with a crossbow–'

'Luke.' She looked me in the eyes. 'There's nothing more boring than hearing about someone else's dreams. I'm sure it's all really vivid to you but it just sounds like some crap film to me.'

I tried not to look hurt and focussed on the telly. 'I just thought it sounded like a good analogy for the evolution of music… how music hasn't really changed that much. We're all minstrels really…' my voice faded away as did the images from my dream.

'What was in that stuff you smoked last night?' Lisa asked and grimaced at the instant coffee in her mug.

I shrugged. 'Just resin I think…'

'Luke, it could have been anything.' She looked genuinely concerned. 'You smoked drugs confiscated by the police.'

I couldn't stop a smirk creep across my face when she said it like that.

'And you're still stoned now by the look of you. Seriously, Luke. You need to stop smoking so much – it screws up your brain.'

'Well I know that,' I replied. 'That's just rock and roll.'

'Not now, later,' Lisa huffed and took her bowl to the sink. 'Plus you start forgetting things... I mean, what happened to your early morning photo call today?'

'Ah,' I said and remembered my trip the morning before when I had seen the Poet. 'I turned the alarm off.' I lied.

'That's a good thing.' Lisa came over and gave me a kiss on the cheek. 'It means you're getting over losing your Grandad.'

She was probably right. Starting every day with a ritual to remember the dead wasn't the best way of getting Grandad out of my mind.

'Listen, I've got to get in early for work – get myself a decent cup of coffee, so I'll see you later, okay?'

'Okay,' I replied, gave her a kiss goodbye and let her see herself out.

My head felt slower than usual. It could have been last night's smoke, like Lisa said, but something else was clouding my thoughts. I tried to make sense of the feeling, but my head kept gravitating back to Grandad.

I cleared my breakfast stuff away and stared at the list of books Mellor had given me. I needed something to focus on. So I settled on the sofa and concentrated on the five A4 sheets of typed paper, working through the names, looking for any which rang a bell. Anyone Grandad might have known or talked about.

Twenty minutes later: nothing.

What if the writer had a pseudonym? I thought. How would I know?

I noticed the time and relocated downstairs to open the shop. I snuggled into the worn leather chair and switched to the sheets of book titles. What a load of nonsense. It was like reading through my green ledger but with zero chance of finding a book I'd actually heard of. Titles like *Machiatti's Revenge* and *A Village Of Her Own* rubbed shoulders with *A Thousand Furlongs Of Sea* and *A Diary Of A Fisherman*. But then I remembered *To Kill A Mockingbird* and *The Grapes Of Wrath* and realised it was impossible to tell a good book by its title, or its cover.

In my still-stoned-state I spent a few minutes staring into space on the revelation of not judging a book by its cover. Eventually, I returned to the list and noticed stars next to some of the titles. Without Mellor to ask, I had to assume the stars had been some kind of marking system created by the reader.

I heard the phone ringing upstairs and, without checking the shop, I closed the door and ran up to the flat, chucking the papers on the kitchen side.

'Hello?' I answered.

'Luke?' It was Detective Mellor. 'Just checking you've still got the package?'

I wasn't sure if it was running upstairs or the guilt, but I felt warm.

'Yes,' I replied. 'Of course.' I lied, remembering Lisa had put it in her bag before leaving, which meant it was at the café now.

'Good, good. It's quite valuable so I need it safe, okay? Make sure it's somewhere safe, Luke.'

'Okay, I will.' I looked around the flat trying to think of something to say and saw the sheets of paper. 'I've been going through the list of books.'

'And?'

'Nothing yet, I was just wondering about the stars.'

'What about them?' Mellor asked with a tired voice.

'Were they from the reader? The guy who died? I mean, if the killer's in the list they were probably turned down, so the stars might help.'

I could hear paper rustling at Mellor's end before he replied.

'No, the stars aren't important, they were typed up wrong. Just look for any names you recognise okay? Anyone who did business with your Grandad.'

'Yeah, sure,' I said but something in Mellor's voice made me think he was lying.

He hung up and I spent a few seconds listening to the dial tone before putting the phone down.

What could I do now? None of the names rang a bell and Grandad had never mentioned anyone writing a book. I didn't know anyone who had written a book, apart from… I took a sharp breath and tried to remember what Simon had said when I was in his antiques shop. He was working on something at his desk - what was it he'd said?

A writer's work is never done.

The room felt cold.

I stared out of the window at the perfect blue sky. The black roof tiles were already shimmering in the heat, creating mini mirages blurring my view towards the distant sea. Towards the antiques shop. I started forming a plan. One good thing about being slightly stoned was I could concentrate on one thought for a very long time. My mind was focussed: all I needed to find out was the name of the book Simon was writing.

I snapped out of my planning mode. I needed energy, so I made myself a cup of tea and went back down to reopen the shop. From the comfort of my chair, I let a plan develop, using all the local knowledge I'd taken in over the past few months: routines; gossip; opening hours; traditions. At midday, I closed up the shop and visited Shirley, with a plan to trick her into distracting Simon under the pretence of setting him up for a date with one of her hairdressers so I could creep into the shop and… none of that was needed.

As I walked past Simon's antique shop, with its bad breath of dust and polish wafting up the street from its open door mouth, I squinted into the dark depths and could see his desk was empty. I stepped tentatively into the gloom and couldn't see him anywhere. This was my chance.

I stepped past the cabinets, between the folded tables to the back of the shop where the low wooden palisade blocked off Simon's desk surrounded by pieces of furniture in various states of disrepair. I paused to listen for any movement in the back rooms, then crossed the threshold and rifled through the pieces of paper scattered across the old teak desk. Sheets covered in a scrawled handwriting, lists of names and a few pages with chapter numbers at the top. I moved a few sheets, looking for chapter one and what looked like a list of titles. Some were crossed out but one had been circled: *No Way Back*. I didn't remember it from the list but this was what I needed! Carefully, I crept back, into the shop proper and made for the door. I looked at the Penguin Donkey as I passed, which only held eight titles now, and breathed a sigh of relief as I walked out into the sun and fresh air.

'Luke?' Shirley screeched in my ear making me jump. 'What you up to?'

My heart leapt and started thumping a Chemical Brothers beat as she stared at me.

'Just been looking for Simon,' I replied and gave her a smile.

'Haven't seen you for a bit,' she said. 'How's that girl of yours?'

'She's great thanks, it's going well, yeah.'

'Good. Good to hear.'

'And you?' I asked. 'All good? Business picking up?'

'Yeah, well, you know how it is.' She shook her head, vibrating her mass of curly hair. 'Got enough regulars and a few tourists pop in, but we could always do with more.'

'Right, yeah.'

'So you heard the latest?'

I frowned. 'Latest?'

'About that *Penguin Killer*?' She whispered and I felt a shiver run down my back. Shirley was looking up and down the road. 'Sarah's uncle works in the police and he reckons they've nearly got him.'

'Really?' I said wondering how much Shirley knew about the case, she must have known the books came from my shop but did she know Grandad was the first victim?

'They got intelligence that he lives around here.' Her wide eyes fixed on me. 'Something to do with the pattern or something… so they're closing in.'

'That's good to hear,' I said without conviction because I was trying to work out if it was true. The murders were book related, not random killings, so how could the distance from the killer's home have any relevance.

Shirley's mouth was open as she stared at something happening behind me. Her eyes flicked to me, then away, then back to me and she took a step back. 'Looks like you've got visitors, Luke.' She side-stepped back to the safety of her shop.

I turned to see Detective Mellor striding down the street with a clipboard in one hand and two, larger, uniformed policeman behind. I walked towards them, wearing a look of confusion, and met them outside my shop.

'I haven't managed to-' I started but Mellor cut me off.

'Luke Redfern, please confirm you are the owner of these premises,' he said in a voice I recognised from when I saw him outside the burnt warehouse.

I glanced at the shop window then back to him. 'Yes, it's my shop.'

Mellor turned his clipboard to show me a yellow sheet of paper. 'This is a warrant to search your property for-'

'Wait a minute.' I held my hand up and pulled the keys from my pocket. 'Let's get inside, eh?' I scanned the street both ways and spotted movement through the florist's window and a gathering of heads peering from Shirley's doorway. 'Right,' I said when we got in and noticed the two officers looked confused. 'Is this to do with Grandad?'

'Luke Redfern,' Mellor started again. 'We have a warrant to search your premises. We believe you are harbouring Class B drugs with the intent to supply.'

'You what?' I said and took a step back.

This was a first for me – it wasn't the drugs - I had a bit of leftover grass from what Mellor had sold me and Lisa had taken the block of resin, so I was in the clear – it was the blatant back stabbing. Scores of thoughts rushed around my head as I thought of how to reply to Mellor who was still talking.

'If you are found to be harbouring Class B drugs you will be arrested and…'

There was no point in getting angry.

'…maximum sentence of…'

Dad had warned me about this. Well, not exactly this but he had told me to be careful. I had let Mellor into my world and now he'd set me up. What was his goal here? Was it personal? Or was he doing it to look good in front of Knowles? Maybe he was after a promotion?

Mellor turned to the two coppers and pointed at the door to my flat. 'Check upstairs first, then go through the shelves down here if you have to. It's a knackered old place, so look out for nooks and crannies, right?'

'Yes, sir,' they replied and were soon stomping up the narrow wooden steps.

Mellor's eyes met mine. He looked happy with himself and maybe a bit guarded, ready for me to attack him. His eyes tempted me to shout at him and defend myself and I knew he would enjoy that, so I kept cool and stayed silent. I had one over him – the gear was gone and I couldn't be arrested for domestic use of cannabis – so I gazed a gazeless stare and waited for what would happen next.

-Can't Go Back Now-

They were closing in on him, he could feel it.

He'd waited and watched but he knew time was running out, so he had to be quick if the words were to be read and adored just as he had adored her. The readers would adore the words.

How the words longed for readers.

But his message was still not getting through. They had seen the books he had left behind but had they read the words on the bodies?

Although the black hole made him feel safe and had given him strength when he needed it, the pressure from what he read in the papers and every time he saw the police in the streets, made him feel like a rat in a corner.

He would deal with the papers and make them understand, but there were other voices out there which needed to be quiet, or the words would never be heard. They were the voices who talked to the police and thought they could stop him.

The book was bigger than all of them, didn't they see that?

If they didn't, he would have to make them understand.

Wednesday 9th August 1995

She Said – Longpigs

There's something timeless about lying in the sun with your eyes closed, feeling the warmth soaking in across your body and the sunlight fighting to get through your eyelids. If I ignored the sounds around me as I lay on the beach, I could have been anywhere, or any time in my life. I could have been a kid again lying next to Mum and Dad on a Greek holiday, or in my Mum's parents' garden down in Eastbourne when Stephen and I stayed for a week in the summer holidays. All I had to do was lie in the sun and close my eyes and I was back in either of those care-free periods of my life.

I didn't want to open my eyes but I smelt a fresh joint had been lit and could hear Rob chatting to Mike.

'It wasn't even a live band for fuck's sake,' Mike said.

'Bloody backing tracks just like the band before them,' Rob replied.

'If you can call them a band, just a bunch of singers.'

'One of them was miming, I'm sure,' Rob said.

I could hear James breathing heavy the other side of me like he was asleep and opened my eyes a slither to let the orange sun in. Shapes came into focus: two silhouettes sitting up, facing out to sea.

'It was the same last year,' I said and Mike and Rob turned to me. 'Some girl got booed off for having her vocals on the track… her mic was on but she sounded awful.'

'Here.' Mike passed the joint over and I sat up to take it.

'We'd have done loads better,' Rob said. 'I mean, no one would know the songs but at least it would sound good.'

'We'd only get three songs though,' I said.

'We'd have to start with *Loud And Clear*,' Mike said and I knew why – it had the longest lead break of our songs.

'Yeah.' Rob agreed as ever. 'And what about *Dawn Song*?'

Mike shook his head. 'Too mellow.'

'It'd have to be *Sunmaker* then.' Rob tried again and we nodded.

'Still reckon *Avalanche* is the best song we've come up with,' James said as he sat up for a toke on the spliff.

'Really?' I said. I liked playing it but I never got the same buzz out of it like I did with some of the other songs. 'Better than *Fast track* or *Cobra*?'

'Any day, I love that song…' James took another puff, '…not your best lyrics like, but the way it builds up to the second chorus.'

'We should have done more covers,' Mike said and I wondered why he used the past tense. He looked at me. 'Just to keep the crowd happy.'

I looked out to sea. 'I know, but there're so many bands out there doing that… we need to keep true to our own stuff.'

'So we'd have *Loud And Clear*, *Sunmaker* and *Avalanche*?' Rob asked.

We all nodded and stared out to sea, daydreaming.

'So, what happened yesterday with the rozzers, Luke?' Mike asked. 'Rob said you had a visit.'

I shook my head. 'Don't remind me. The bastards.'

'I thought you were cool with them what with your Dad being high up and all that,' Rob said.

I shrugged. 'I thought so too.' I could feel the knot in my stomach retighten as I pictured Mellor's smug face. 'I was set up,' I said, being honest.

'Set up?' James asked, sitting up. 'By who?'

I stared out to sea, wondering how much I should say. Part of me wanted to let it all out and have a real cathartic moan, but another part told me to hold back – nothing bad had actually happened. Not like it had to Grandad. Still, I was always honest with my mates.

'The police.' I remembered the two uniformed officers going through all my stuff while I watched helplessly.

'What the fuck?' James said.

'The police set you up?' Mike said and gave me his one eyebrow-raised look, like I was making it up.

I pictured the clothes, books and records strewn about the flat like I'd been robbed. They knew what they were looking for.

'The Detective looking into the murders sold me some weed,' I said and noticed James and Mike looking at each other. 'Then he asked me to look after something for him and-'

'You dick,' James said and shook his head.

'But he gave me info about the killer and…'

'He played ya, mate.'

'What was it?' Rob asked. 'The package?'

'Resin,' I said. 'A decent sized block.' I made a box shape with my hands. 'Strong stuff too!'

'You tried it?' Mike asked.

'Of course. Anyway, Lisa took it, so all they found was what was left of my weed.'

'So you just got a slap on the wrists?' Mike said and I nodded.

'And you're cool with that?' James asked.

'It could have been worse,' I replied.

'No, I mean Lisa. You're cool with her having it?'

I shrugged, knowing she could take care of herself.

'Mate, you've been set up by some desperate copper busting petty criminals to get up the ladder and your girlfriend's got his dope?'

'She's not my…' I started.

'He's right,' Rob said. 'He's gonna want it back or he'll be in the shit, so I'd watch out if I was you.'

'Probably worth a few quid,' Mike said.

My head was starting to pound with the pressure, so I laid back down and closed my eyes. 'I'll figure something out,' I said, trying to play it down. 'I'll get it handed back in… might even get a reward.'

But deep down I knew they were right. I'd seen something new in Mellor's eyes when they raided the flat. I guess it had always been there – an eagerness I had thought – but when it became clear he wasn't going to find anything in the flat that look in his eyes grew stronger, like he was pained. Desperate. Like he would do anything to get what he wanted.

'It's still messed up,' James said. 'You're living in the place where your Grandad was killed and the detective trying to find the killer is planting drugs on you.'

I had talked to the guys about the *Penguin Killer* on Saturday night and I'd thought they'd been amused by the whole situation, but maybe they'd talked about it when I wasn't with them? I'd have been freaked out if the roles were reversed and they were telling me about it – but the papers were making it sound much worse than it really was, I was sure.

'Yeah, watch your back mate,' Mike said.

'Why don't you just move back to your parents while the whole thing blows over?' Rob said.

'I can't.'

To them I'd just moved house but to me my whole life had changed and reset to a new location. I had officially left home and become a proper, tax-paying adult with responsibilities. You don't just turn back on that.

'Why can't you?' James asked.

'Because they've turned my bedroom into a bloody office,' I said with a smile but felt my spirits drop another notch.

We disbanded half way through the afternoon after Rachel turned up for James, so I headed back to the shop. I felt eyes on me as I walked the cobbled street and soon heard Shirley jogging behind me.

'Luke, Luke!' she bellowed. 'What was all that business then?' she asked when she caught up.

'Oh, nothing,' I lied. 'Just helping the police, you know how it is.'

Shirley nodded. 'Right,' she said and lowered her voice. 'To do with the, err, killer?'

'Yes.' I maintained eye contact with her, daring her to mention Grandad.

Normally she was bubbly and full of energy, but now I saw her true form - she wanted information, nothing else, and in that moment I hated her for it. She was nothing more than a gossip. That was why she hadn't talked to me for those days when the murders first came to light. My shop had been the gossip and there was nothing else she wanted to talk about so how could she talk to me?

'Well,' Shirley said. 'I hope it's not been too hard for you or your Dad. It's bad enough when you lose someone, but to find out it happened like that…'

She was genuine – I could see it in her eyes – and my opinion shifted back slightly.

'Thanks, Shirley, we'll get through it… once they catch him.'

'Yeah, chin up, eh?' She said and waddled back to her shop.

I strolled to my shop, gave the silhouette in Isaac's shop a wave and opened up Red Books with a warm feeling in my chest. Then I remembered the mess in the flat that I had to clear up and the vitriol returned. I was angry at Mellor, nobody else. Myself maybe for being an idiot. How could I have been so stupid? Reeled in like a kid.

Just like a few days before, when Lisa saved me with her tent, I knew I had to get away. I was fed up with the penguin books, the vulture customers, the papers and the bloody police. But where could I go? An idea came to me and two phone calls later it was all set up.

I started to relax again, had a cup of tea, got back into my crossword book and felt the warmth returning.

Capital of Italy. *Rome.*

Original Beatles drummer. *Pete Best.*

Subterranean crops. *Potatoes.*

After a few minutes, I grimaced. This was too easy.

Maybe I should put some effort in and get the place tidied before I headed off so I wouldn't have to face it when I came back? For that, I needed some good vibe music. I bounded up to the flat and flicked through the records, focussing on the singles.

Longpigs: *She Said.*

Perfect energy music I could sing along to. Get the adrenaline pumping and release my angst!

As the heavy guitar reverberated around my flat I piled up clothes, returning them to drawers or cupboards in the bedroom and pushed the cushions back onto the sofa in the lounge. Flashbacks came to me of the police tearing my world apart, but the anger was going. It had all been temporary. I refilled the kitchen drawers, piled up the newspapers, making a mental note to throw some of the oldest ones away, and grabbed the pile of papers on the kitchen side. I paused and stared at the sheets Mellor had given me as I realised I hadn't checked the list for Simon's book, grabbing my notes to remember what it was called.

No Way Back.

I ran my finger down the first sheet, then the other side and so on, scanning the titles. It had to be there, I could feel my confidence rise as I turned to the last page and ran through the list… nothing.

I re-clipped the sheets and flicked through the papers underneath, from Grandad's allotment tin. An old Gardeners' World and an ancient seed catalogue from Grandad's shed, both of which went straight in the bin, followed by some papers I hadn't seen before: yellowing pages of typed words. Probably scrap paper from Grandad's old job for writing planting notes on, I thought as I re-arranged them. I found the front sheet and recognised the style straight away. I took a step back and everything seemed to go quiet.

The pages were a manuscript. A novel.

A Home for Memories Past by Mary Fairweather.

I grabbed Mellor's list again and ran through the titles. It had to be there, I could feel it. Not the first page or the second… there!

'Shit!'

In black and white. I checked the sheet against the manuscript – an identical match.

A Home for Memories Past   -   Mary Fairweather

My eyes went out of focus as I started piecing together what must have happened.

This is what linked Grandad to the murderer. This was why he had been killed.

Grandad must have been asked to read the novel by the author, which meant not only did Grandad know them, but the author trusted him. But I didn't recognise the name.

Who was *Mary Fairweather*?

Thursday 10th August 1995

Going Underground – The Jam

'I think you're going to love him, seriously,' I said.

'What, because he's nothing like you?' Lisa replied and poked me in the ribs.

I fought off her hands and tickled her back.

'No, seriously, he's a funny guy… your kind of sense of humour.'

'Intelligent you mean?'

'Point proven,' I replied. 'That's exactly what he would have said.'

Brighton was a long way behind us and the green and straw-brown hills of the South Downs sped past under the ubiquitous blue skies we had taken for granted all summer.

'So where was it we camped?' I asked.

'Way over that way.' Lisa pointed into the distance.

And here we were escaping again. Running away from the shop and anything to do with the *Penguin Killer*. I wrinkled my nose, realising I had started using the stupid name for the bastard who had killed my Grandad. It was ridiculous, but it did take the edge off the horrific truth of what the murderer had done. More running away from the truth, I guess.

I looked at Lisa and gave her a smile. I needed this and hadn't been to Stephen's place for months, so I didn't really need an excuse.

'So, he's cool with us turning up at his work?' Lisa asked. 'I mean, it's a recording studio, right?'

'Yeah, he's fine – said he'd take the afternoon off. And it's the office next to the recording studio,' I said, remembering what I'd brought in my bag. 'You never know though, you might see someone famous!' I beamed.

'Wow,' Lisa said sarcastically, playing it down like usual but I could tell she was secretly excited by the possibility of bumping into a celebrity.

An hour later, we were sweating in a tiny white room where a sour-faced German receptionist kept a close eye on us. She was obviously used to groupies and wannabes trying to get in and hadn't decided if we were kosher or not, even though we knew the name of an employee.

Finally, Stephen, strolled through a glass door. 'Thanks, Suzie,' he said and the lady's face transformed, knocking years off her. 'Just my brother and his girlfriend... hi, I'm Stephen.'

He went straight for Lisa, opting for a hug, and put his arm around me. 'You've been lying to me Luke - she's not a minger at all.'

'Ha ha,' I said and gave Lisa a wink. 'Come on, let's see this amazing office of yours.'

Given the stylish décor of the reception and the amount of time Stephen had spent bragging about his job, the office was a complete let down. Sure, there were gold and platinum discs on the walls next to signed tour poster by some cool bands – any of which I would have given my guitar for – but the rest of the office was... ordinary. Drab. Grey. A room full of desks with computers and phones. I wasn't sure what I was expecting: beer fountains and half naked lad's mag models lounging on sofas surrounded by piles of CDs? That's how the media had built Britpop to be – one long party - yet here I was, in one of the engine rooms and all I saw was people, computer screens and headphones.

'So, like I said the other day,' Stephen said. 'Most of our stuff gets recorded and mixed at Abbey Road or up in Manchester, then the records get pressed out in Buckinghamshire, but we're the hub of it all…'

'With the recording studio next door,' I said.

'Yeah,' he replied. 'But that's mostly for over dubs and remixing.'

He sounded different, I thought. Not like my brother but an actual professional adult who knew what he was talking about. It was like the difference between how Detective Mellor spoke to me and how he spoke to the officers: posher and with authority. It made me wonder if I could ever pull it off – or whether I would have to talk like that. It wasn't really me.

'These guys work with the indie scouts.' Stephen pointed at two long-haired guys sitting at desks covered with CD's and tapes, each wearing over-sized headphones and nodding rhythmically to their respective soundtracks.

One tapped a pen and the other had his eyes closed. I sensed my moment. Had it all come down to this? I wondered as I slipped a hand into my bag. All those years of hard work and frustration, blistered fingers and hangovers. Did it all balance on this precise moment?

'And over here…' Stephen's voice trailed off as I veered towards the two men and carefully pulled out the Beachhead demo tape from my bag.

I breathed in deeply, casually wandered past the desk where the guy had his eyes closed. If it worked, this could be the difference between me spending the rest of my life in a musty bookshop, or being a full-blooded rock star. I shot a glance at Stephen, who hadn't noticed me, swiftly picked a tape off one pile, placed mine on top and put the original back on. Not a sound made.

I re-joined Lisa and Stephen feeling like I'd just completed a Second World War spy mission, just in time to hear him say, '…and this is the place where I spend most of my waking life.' He pointed to one of the many unremarkable desks.

'Cool,' I said and pointed to the signed photo of him with Brett Anderson from Suede.

'Cheers,' he replied and looked a tad sheepish, like he wasn't used to getting praise from me.

Lisa said, 'I like the Stone Roses hat.'

I glanced over my shoulder at the demo guys as Stephen rattled off a story about meeting Ian Brown. One was still pen tapping, but the other had finished one tape and was moving searching for another to play. A surge of energy ran through me and I turned away, feeling like a school kid who had just played a prank and didn't want to get caught. I knew it wasn't a big deal, but I had an urge to get out of the office before they found me out.

I waited for Lisa to finish the conversation with one of Stephen's work mates before saying, 'Hey, shall we head out and get some lunch?'

'He did what?' Stephen was almost shouting. 'That man,' he said as he paced across his lounge while shaking his head. 'It was his own father for fuck's sake and he showed no emotion?'

'Alright, calm down,' I said, glancing at Lisa, worried this was wrecking everything I had told her about my cool older brother.

It had taken me the whole journey to Stephen's flat for me to build up the courage to update him on everything about Grandad's death. In the end I'd blurted it out as soon as we got through the door.

'Just make a cup of tea or something?' I said.

'Yeah, a cup of tea,' Stephen replied in full sarcastic mode. 'That's the answer to every bloody problem across the British Empire – trouble with the natives? Have a cuppa tea. Or something else?' He stared me in the eyes. 'Smoking dope and getting high isn't the way out of everything you know?'

I felt my cheeks redden and started to reply, but Lisa put her hand on my knee. 'How about something stronger than tea? Got any beer?'

Stephen glanced at her and his face softened. 'Yeah, sure,' he said and rubbed his forehead. 'I'll grab some.'

While he was out of the room, Lisa whispered, 'You could have taken it a bit easier – it's his Grandad too.'

'I know!' I hissed back. 'But he always prefers bad news straight.'

Stephen came back with three cold bottles of a beer. I checked the label but didn't recognise and could barely pronounce it.

'Czech beer,' he explained, noticing my face.

'Right,' I said and took a swig. 'Nice.'

Stephen drank his standing at the window surveying the road and park beyond. As flats go it was a nice one. It had big windows and high ceilings and the stairs were wide and nowhere as steep as mine. It was in an up and coming area of London apparently, so Stephen was hoping to make some money on it.

'Look.' Stephen came back to sit opposite us. 'I'm sorry, okay? I shouldn't have-'

'That's alright,' I said. 'It's a lot to take in.'

'No.' Stephen gave me the big brother look that indicated he was already three steps ahead. 'I'm sorry about having a go at you about the weed. You'll grow out of it and that's your issue, but I'm not sorry about getting angry about Dad or you not telling me anything about what was going on.'

He took a swig of beer, waiting for me to reply.

I nodded and glanced at Lisa, who was tactfully reading her beer label.

'Alright,' I said and put my hands up. 'I should have told you earlier but it's not that easy and-'

'Just pick up the bloody phone,' Stephen said and pointed to where his answer machine sat next to his CD player: a twin of my machine, courtesy of Mum at Christmas. 'I mean, why didn't you tell me when you saw me last time?'

'I only found out that night,' I replied. 'Dad had some stuff of Grandad's and I took it by accident… there was a photo…' I trailed off '…then it all kicked off with the police and the other murders.'

'And you thought it was a big puzzle you could sort out on your own?' Stephen asked.

'Well, yeah,' I said with a shrug. 'I didn't want to go running back to Mum and Dad. Plus after what Dad said about Knowles I knew he didn't want to get involved. Anyway, it was my problem – my shop.'

'But my Grandad too.' Stephen was just keeping his anger in check this time.

I looked at Lisa but knew it wasn't her place to join in.

'Sorry,' I said and placed my hand on her knee.

'It's alright,' she gave me a half-smile. 'You guys need to get this sorted. It's important. Even when they get the murderer you'll still have to deal with it.'

'Yeah,' Stephen said. He drew a breath and sighed. 'I can see why you're trying to solve this yourself.' He looked at me. 'What with all that stuff with Knowles and Bernard.'

'Dad had been angrier about Knowles finding out about Grandad's land than the fact he had been murdered,' I said.

Stephen clenched a fist.

'So you knew about the land?' I asked, ready to take my turn at getting angry.

Stephen nodded and looked away.

'What else do you know? Do you know why Dad's been kicked out of the force?'

'No,' Stephen replied. 'He's not been kicked out from what I can work out. From what Mum's said he was under investigation just like

Bernard was and Michael before him. It sounds like a set up… a sting. All goes back to Dad's promotion apparently.'

'What? When we bought the house?'

'Yeah and when we had those holidays abroad. Greece, Italy… Portugal,' Stephen said.

'But that wasn't dodgy.'

'No, but Knowles missed out and he's been after Dad ever since. Now he's got a bit of authority he's been trying to get his revenge.'

I felt Lisa staring at me, so turned to her and she said, 'You haven't told him about Mellor yet.'

'The detective?' Stephen asked.

'Yeah. Seems like he's following his boss's methods.'

'What do you mean?'

'He set me up.'

Stephen stood up again. 'Are you serious? What happened?'

'He gave me a package to look after and then…'

'He did what?' Stephen gave his fake laugh. 'He gave you a *package* to look after?'

'Well, he'd already sold me some weed, so…'

'Are you fucking serious?' Stephen shouted. 'What the fuck!' He turned away to finish his beer and stared out the window again. 'Let me guess, he came back with a search warrant, right?'

'Yeah.' I gave Lisa a look but she was staring at Stephen.

'And?' He asked.

'I'd already got rid of it.'

Stephen turned his gaze on me. 'How?'

'Lisa took it.'

Lisa raised her hands. 'Guilty.'

'Luke, you're a dick,' Stephen said without looking at me. 'Lisa, why on earth are you with my brother?'

Lisa tilted her head slightly but didn't reply.

'Look.' I had to defend myself. 'They didn't find anything and Lisa's got it sorted, haven't you?'

'Oh, yeah, dumped it straight away – it's long gone.'

'Okay, okay.' Stephen held a hand up then tapped his bottle. 'More beer and we should get some food ordered. I need to think.'

'Sure,' I replied, thankful for a break from arguing.

Half an hour later, as I devoured my Chicken Tikka Masala, Stephen had more questions.

'So, how did the killer get in and out?' He asked.

I shrugged. 'Must have had a key.'

'Or the shop was open and he stole a spare key and locked the door on the way out,' Lisa said.

'You say *he* but it could have been a woman,' I said. 'The author on the manuscript is a woman's name.'

'What manuscript?' Stephen asked with another glare. 'You need to tell me everything, okay?'

'I only found it last night, okay? And I only told Lisa about it on the train.' I dug out the sheets of A4 paper from my bag. 'I found it in Grandad's shed and it matches one of the books the hoarder read for the agent.'

Stephen wiped his fingers and took the pile for a read. He laughed. 'No wonder it didn't get published – it's a pile of drivel. *A Home for Memories Past* by Mary Fairweather? Jeez.'

I shrugged. Unlike me, Stephen had studied English A-level so probably knew what he was talking about.

'It doesn't sound like the sort of book a murderer would write,' Lisa said.

'It's full of purple prose and clichés. Listen to this.' He read the passage in his thespian voice, 'Her mind was like a velvet house with velveteen wallpaper, velvet ceilings, velvet stairs and velvet windows. Everything was soft in my head, where I could enjoy my own memories and thoughts of futures not come and be at home in my own thoughts.' He looked at me wearing an expression of derision, then to Lisa. 'Well?' He held his mouth open but didn't wait for a reply. 'It's compete dross! I mean… it's obviously over the top with metaphor and repetition but you also have the point of view changes mid-paragraph.'

I took a swig of beer.

'It's no Dickens that's for sure,' Lisa said.

'It's generally shite,' Stephen said and slapped the manuscript back on the table like it genuinely offended him.

'So, it's not a surprise it got rejected by the agent then?' I asked.

'Er, no,' Stephen replied.

'The reader must have had a few comments about it as well,' Lisa said.

'I doubt they had to read much of it,' Stephen said and turned to face me, his face turning serious. 'But how does this fit in with the murders? With Grandad?'

I sighed before explaining my thoughts, worried I would receive equal derision. 'My theory is... the writer gave a copy to Grandad to read and he didn't like it. He told them what he thought - you know what he was like - they got into a fight... and they killed him.' I said growing in confidence as I spoke. 'The book must have been sent to the agent as well, who rejected it, so the killer turned on them too. The murderer found the address of the reader – the hoarder – and killed them and...' I'd run out of steam.

'So why the others?' Lisa asked. 'And why the marks on the bodies?'

'I don't know,' I replied.

I noticed Stephen had his thinking face on as he cleared up the plates.

'What is it?' I asked.

He stopped, theatrically holding the plates in one hand. 'I... it's the detective. I just can't...' he walked off to the kitchen, leaving us hanging. He came running back. 'I get it now!'

'What?' I stood up. 'You know who the killer is?'

'No, but this Mellor fella thinks he does.'

'Who?' Lisa asked.

'It's you,' Stephen pointed at me. 'Mellor thinks you're the killer and he's trying to reel you in.'

Friday 11th August 1995

Black Steel – Tricky

'Here you go.' Stephen slammed a plate on the table I was leaning on.

'Thanks,' I said with a wince and pieced the jolted bacon butty back together.

'Still getting bad hangovers then?' He asked with a grin and ruffled my hair.

I said nothing and sunk my teeth into it the saviour food.

'Luke do you want a coffee?' Lisa called out from the kitchen.

'No thanks,' I mumbled through a full mouth.

'Your brother's got the proper stuff – I'm making a full cafetiere.'

'Alright,' I said and caught Stephen's eye.

He laughed. 'She's a keeper.'

I shrugged and attacked the bacon butty again, not wanting to get into a discussion about Lisa's travel plans or how many days until she left.

'Seriously though.' Stephen sat beside me. 'Have Mum and Dad met her yet?'

'No.' My head was only allowing one word sentences after God knows how many pints the night before.

'She's a good laugh – did you hear her put down that guy with the curly hair last night? Genius.'

I smiled, remembering the little idiot trying to chat her up.

'She can hold her drink too,' Stephen said.

'Yeah,' I replied.

I wanted to ask why it was alright for us to get drunk and feel this crap afterwards, but smoking plant buds, which didn't have any after effect, was childish. But I didn't have the energy.

'Here we go.' Lisa set a tray of mugs and the coffee jar on the table. 'You feeling better, Tiger?' She gave my leg a squeeze. 'I told you those shots were a bad idea.'

'Shots?' I said and a blurred image of lining up glasses at the bar swam before me. That would explain the chemical taste at the back of my mouth.

Stephen switched the telly on and we watched Big Breakfast in silence, giggling in unison every now and then.

'I can't believe that was the last Crystal Maze last night,' Stephen said.

I recalled images of someone getting locked in a medieval castle chamber but little else.

'Yeah,' Lisa said. 'I preferred the original presenter.'

'But it's still legendary,' my brother said. 'Well, was legendary. I'll miss it.'

I took a sip of coffee and let the flavour melt around my tongue. This wasn't coffee, I thought. This wasn't instant coffee or the evil coffee-flavoured chocolates everyone shunned at Christmas. Another sip. This was something else. Sweet, like chocolate. Rich. Slightly burnt, like a barbecue. A bigger sip. Round flavours enveloped my tongue. Another sip. It was clearing my head.

I sat up straight and looked up to see Stephen and Lisa staring at me.

'Good is it?' Stephen asked and laughed.

'What?'

'You sound like a bee,' Lisa said. 'Mmmmm.'

'Sorry.' I smirked. 'I hadn't realised… good stuff.' I relaxed into my chair and nodded at the telly. 'Not the same without Chris Evans though is it?'

'I don't know, that Aussie bloke's a good laugh,' Stephen replied.

'True.'

'Gabi's a legend,' Lisa said and topped up my coffee. 'As long as she's on it, it'll be fine.'

'Listen,' Stephen said. 'I've got to pop into work.' He looked at his watch. 'Already late but it's Friday, so… you guys are welcome to hang around a bit to wait out the crowds on the tube or you can come with me?'

'We'd better get moving,' Lisa said and looked at me. 'As long as the lame duck's alright walking? I've got a shift this afternoon.'

'I'll be alright,' I said and finished off the last mouthful of bacon butty.

'Right you are then,' Stephen said. 'I'll grab some things and we can head off.'

Ten minutes later, we were walking through an area of London that used to be hip in the 60's and I felt ten feet tall, bouncing along the pavement in my Converse. The sun was shining, again, and every colour, from the shop fronts to the clothes on the passers-by, were vivid and bright. I took Lisa's hand and gave it a squeeze.

'And I've already got the name of our first album sorted, so-' I was giving my Beachhead promotion one last go with Stephen.

He put his arm around my shoulder. 'Enough! Jeez, remind me not to give you coffee again. I promise I'll come down and see you guys play at your next gig, okay?'

'Yeah sure,' I said. 'Maybe next Friday, yeah?' I noticed a guy some twenty paces away and walking our way, 'Check this idiot out,' I said. 'He thinks he's bloody Liam Gallagher.'

He was taller than me and had the same mod haircut as Liam had in the latest NME and was wearing big shades and skinny jeans.

'Alright,' he said to Lisa with a nod as he passed.

'Twat,' I said. 'Even dresses up like him. What's the point?'

Stephen took a second to weigh me up then said, 'That's because, little brother of mine, that *was* Liam Gallagher.'

I double took and threw a glance behind me, muttering, 'But… he's not that tall.'

'Yes, he really is,' Stephen said in a way that convinced me he was telling the truth.

Back on the train, heading south, Lisa slept with her head on my shoulder. It'd been good to get some distance from Brighton again and I had expected some clarity after talking to Stephen but now it felt like I had more problems to resolve. There was the manuscript, which weighed heavy in my bag, and the killer, obviously, but now I had Mellor to worry about as well.

My mind kept coming back to Liam Gallagher as though he was the key somehow. Seeing him in the flesh had shaken me but not for the obvious reasons. He was a legend, it was true, and I would have given my right hand (not my left, chord hand obviously) to have a few beers with him and his brother. He'd been right in front of me - the clothes, the swagger, the hair - and I'd refused to accept what I'd seen. Was it the same with Mellor? Was Stephen right? Did Mellor think I was guilty of killing Grandad and the other people? Is that why he set me up with the drugs? A cold feeling ran through me. Had he been testing me by inviting me to the crime scenes to see if I would give anything away?

I stared out at the rolling hills, listening to Lisa's soft breathing moved my shoulder. She snuggled in closer and I looked down at her. Smart as she was, I shouldn't have got her involved with the drugs or let her take the package. What sort of man was I letting her do that? I looked at the fields and remembered the freedom of our camping trip and trekking across the downs. I was sure I could smell cut grass through the open carriage window. I didn't want to go home to the shop, but what choice did I have? Mellor had nothing on me and I was innocent, but I knew he would keep trying to catch me out. And what about that block of resin? Surely he'd come back for it. If it wasn't for that I would give him the manuscript and help the police get closer to catching the killer.

As we pulled into Brighton I realised I was no closer to making a decision on what to do next.

'So, I got this letter the other day,' Lisa said that evening after her shift in the café and after my uneventful day in the shop. She paused to make sure I was looking at her, moving the takeaway spag bol from under my nose.

'Oh, right?' I said.

'It was from an old boyfriend,' she said, keeping her eyes on me, looking for a reaction. 'Jim.'

I felt an eyebrow twitch and moved another fork-full to my mouth.

'He's been in prison.'

I looked at her, waiting for a smirk or another tell-tale sign she was teasing me. 'Seriously?'

'Yeah.'

'What for?' I asked and studied her face.

'It doesn't matter, he went in early spring, long after we broke up, if that's what's bothering you? Anyway, the letter's more important.'

She was telling the truth, I could tell, but why hide why he went to jail?

'Go on,' I said.

'He wrote to ask if he could stay at my place when he came out.'

'Right,' I said, not liking any of what I was hearing. I tried to keep a poker face. 'Which is when?'

'That's the problem,' Lisa said. 'The letter came through late so… he was released last week.'

'Last week?' My voice was louder than expected, so I almost whispered. 'He's already out?'

Lisa nodded. 'He doesn't know where I live and I don't want him at mine, obviously, but he knows I'm in Brighton, so he'll probably come looking for me and…'

'Brighton's a big place,' I said, feeling relieved, but I could feel my heart pounding heavily.

'Thing is… I think I saw him today, when I was at work.'

I wasn't sure how worried I should be. 'So he knows where you work?'

'And he could follow me home,' she said.

'But you didn't go home tonight,' I said and found myself looking out the window. My senses were heightened and, as ridiculous as it sounds, I felt like I was being watched. 'But that means…'

'I'm sorry,' Lisa said and reached out to take my hand.

I shook my head. Tonight was not going how I thought it would.

'What will you do if you see him again?'

Lisa shrugged. 'Nothing. He said something about writing a new book and he probably wants to see what I think of it, but I'll tell him I'm moving on and there's no point-'

I held my hand up, stopping her and whispered, 'Can you hear that?'

'What?' She mouthed back.

I knew the old building well and could distinguish between floorboard creaks and plumbing squeaks, so I held my breath to listen. It was dark outside and getting late, which might have spooked me but I had definitely heard banging downstairs, I just couldn't tell if it was in the shop or… 'Someone's at the front door,' I said and jumped out of my seat.

Lisa stood up too. 'Just go and answer it.' She didn't look concerned.

'Yeah, it's probably just Isaac wanting some milk or something.'

The knocking sounded more frantic as I came down the stairs and could see a silhouette through the front door blind as I walked through the shop.

'What is it?' I shouted as I fiddled with the lock and opened up.

I hadn't expected to see Simon, who looked gaunt and had paint on his hands.

'Luke,' he said, his eyes were wide and his mouth looked twisted. 'I need your help… it's Shirley.'

'Shirley?'

'What is it?' Lisa asked, popping her head round the door.

'She's…' Simon was panting and couldn't talk.

He pointed up the street towards his shop. The light from the streetlamp turned the wet paint on his hands red. He looked back at me. 'She's dead.'

I was going to ask him how he knew Shirley was dead but I'd never seen anyone as agitated as this. I gestured for us to go and he led us down the alley, past his shop to the hairdressers.

What we saw next will stay with me forever. It was far worse than the shock of finding the photo of Grandad. I was here. In the flesh. Adrenaline flooding my veins. All of my senses were alert and picking up every detail: the smell of the blood; the metallic taste in my mouth; the slip and squelch of our shoes on the soaked lino.

'Shirley?' I shouted and went to hold her hand.

She was as limp as a doll. I studied her face: her eyes had rolled back and her mouth was open. Then I saw the red line across her throat and everything sped up like in a film. Lisa ran off to ring the police leaving me with Simon, who stood shivering in the doorway, while I tried to stop looking at Shirley's open mouth and blood seeping from the gash which had split her neck open.

Eventually, I crawled away and joined Simon for some fresh air while he rambled on about how he was supposed to meet her friend for a drink and when she hadn't turned up he went to find Shirley…

As he spoke I couldn't tear my eyes away from Shirley's face. I'd never seen her so quiet. Her white blouse was drenched in maroon blood which had pooled around her like a moat I daren't cross again. The fingers on her outstretched hand were splayed out like she was trying to grab something. The horror and the reality of the situation took hold of me and I sobbed, leaning against the doorway, taking in gulps of air. Lisa returned and said something, but I didn't listen - a new thought came to me.

I stared around the room but couldn't see what I was after. My eyes drifted back to Shirley and I wanted to close her eyes or cover her up, but found myself held back by some invisible barrier.

'Come on.' Lisa pulled me away. 'It's not good to stay here.'

'But the book…' I whispered and she never heard, '…there must be a book.'

Friday night soon became Saturday morning as revellers from the pub on the corner were turned away by the police cordon. They'd taped the road off at either end where crowds of onlookers peered over and gossiped like school children. Ironic for Shirley, I thought. People seemed to arrive from nowhere – police, medics, neighbours - and soon the forensics guys were in charge and Lisa, Simon and I were ushered to his antiques shop where we drank tea and talked to a police woman who took our statements. I stared out into the street as I listened to Simon repeating what he had told me. Then I gave my statement and Lisa gave hers, which was practically the same.

'And you were in contact with Detective Sergeant Mellor about the incidents?' The Officer asked and I felt Simon look at me.

'Well, yes, after I helped him with his enquiries.' I glanced at Simon wondering how much I should say.

'And I understand you have a connection with one of the victims?'

'Yes, but shouldn't…' I gestured to Simon.

'What? Surely we should all know what's going on here?' Simon said, looking flustered. He ran a hand through his hair. 'What's going on here?'

'It was my Grandad,' I said and Lisa squeezed my hand.

'Eric?' Simon said and pushed his chair back.

'He was the first,' I said.

'What?' Simon looked around the shop, then back to me. 'Eric was *killed*?'

The way he said it made it sound like he was in a play. Overdramatic.

'Yes.' I stared out the door, at the lights and shadows.

Isaac walked up to the doorway and gave me a nod, but seeing we were busy, turned and left us to it.

'Well.' Simon stood up. 'I'd read about it but hadn't known it was so close, I mean…'

'Please sit down,' the Officer asked and Simon complied.

'Look, can we go now?' I asked. 'It's been a long night and you know where we are if you need us.'

'Yes, fine,' she replied.

'See you later, Simon,' I said as Lisa and I made our way out.

I paused as Detective Mellor strode past and glanced my way. It was long enough for him to sneer when he recognised me, like he was expecting to see me.

'Come on,' Lisa said and we headed back to the flat.

My head was dizzy and vacant as we floated home.

'Fuck,' I said as I collapsed on the sofa.

Lisa hugged me and whispered, 'I'm sorry.'

A tear ran down my cheek as I stared into space and shook my head. There was nothing I could say.

Saturday 12th August 1995

Paint It Black – Rolling Stones

The next morning felt heavy. It took me a few breaths to work out why I had a tight feeling around my chest, then the image of Shirley's dead, open-mouthed face came back to me and I jolted.

'You okay?' Lisa asked.

'Yeah, I…' I paused and took her in. 'Are you okay?'

'It's not something I'll forget,' she said. 'But you knew her… it was horrific.' She snuggled up beside me. 'We can talk about it if you want?'

'Yeah,' I said, knowing she was right, but I couldn't find the words.

I'd known Shirley ever since Grandad had moved in and refurbished the shop, and when I moved in she'd popped in every day, asking if there was anything I needed. She cared. It was strange to think of the street without her. She was one of the good ones: always happy and full of energy. Salt of the earth, my Grandad used to say.

She had nothing to do with books, so why had she been targeted?

'Why her?' I said.

'She doesn't fit in does she?' Lisa replied. 'Not after what you said to Stephen about the books link.'

'No,' I said, letting the cogs in my mind slowly click into place. 'And there wasn't a penguin book. No marks on her body.'

Shirley loved a good gossip but it never hurt anyone did it?

'A copycat?' Lisa asked.

'Not much of a copycat if they didn't leave any of the trademark signs are they?' I said and paused to think. 'It has to be the same person. People just don't get murdered in Brighton.'

She gave me a sympathetic smile but I could tell she was holding something back.

'What?' I asked.

'I...' She looked away. 'I think you should give the police that manuscript.'

I shook my head and sat up. 'No, not after what Mellor did. The last thing I want-'

Lisa cut me off. 'This is bigger than just you and Mellor isn't it?'

'But the police hold stuff back all the time and...' I realised how stupid I was sounding.

'What you really want is for the killer to be found, right?'

I nodded.

'Then you have to hand it in. Maybe not to Mellor but how about giving it to someone else?'

I gave a little shrug, seeing her point. The thought of getting rid of it did make me feel a touch lighter.

'I'll think about it,' I said.

Later, as we watched Zoe Ball in some kid's telly thing and ate breakfast, I still couldn't see why Shirley was targeted. I walked a circle around the sofa as my thoughts slowly condensed to form a solid realisation. I felt cold for a second. The radio was still playing in the bedroom: Sounds of the 60's on Radio 2. A familiar beat was playing and seemed to match my mood. *Paint it Black*.

'What was it Shirley was really good at?' I asked.

Lisa shrugged. 'Curling hair?'

'No, she was a gossip, yeah? So she had information – on everyone. She knew everyone's ins and outs, didn't she? I mean, she knew about you the morning after you stayed here, so-'

'Did she?' Lisa looked impressed.

'Maybe she knew something about the killer? She might not have known the link or maybe didn't realise what she knew… she must have seen something and gossiped about it without knowing it was connected to the murders. And now we've had two murders down the same street.'

'Months apart though,' Lisa said and gave me a look like when she had told me about the letter from her ex.

'Yes…' I dragged out the word as a new thought came to me.

Lisa hadn't said what her ex had been put away for but she had said he went to prison in the spring, which was around the time Grandad had died. There had been nothing since and now this new spate of killings.

'Do you-' I stopped, realising my thoughts would only upset her.

'What?'

'Err, nothing.'

Maybe I would go to the police after all, I thought. I could give them the manuscript along with some extra information.

Lisa left before ten and I decided the shop would survive another closed day, so I gave it five minutes before I left the shop, heading straight for the police station. The black and yellow tape had gone from either end of the road, but a cordon had been positioned around Shirley's shop, where the blinds had been fully drawn. A small pile of bouquets lay on the floor and I wondered if they had been bought from Isaac's shop.

The police station felt cold when I entered, cooling my sweaty back after a long walk on yet another hot day - the radio said it was going to be the longest summer for decades. I pulled at my t-shirt to waft cool air up my front and glanced around the empty waiting room before walking up to the receptionist who sat at a high desk behind a clear glass screen.

'Yes dear,' she drawled.

She looked about ten years older than my Mum and, going by the size of her back side which barely fitted on her chair, I guessed had spent her working life sitting down. An empty cake box sat to one side of her keyboard.

'I have information for an ongoing investigation,' I said, trying to sound official.

'Which investigation?' She asked, fingers hovering over her keys.

'The, err…' I couldn't remember the official name so said, '…the *Penguin Killer.*'

Her eyebrows raised as though she had heard it all before.

'What information?' She asked.

I pulled out the manuscript and raised it for her to see.

'I just need to see a junior officer about it really,' I said, hoping Mellor would still be at Shirley's shop.

'Name?' she asked.

'Luke Redfern.'

'Ah, yes, I have you on the list, I'll take you to the investigation room.' She slipped off her chair like a seal into water and disappeared from view, only to reappear at a door across the room which led to a long hall. 'This way,' she barked.

I followed, holding the folder to my chest.

'Like I was saying, I only need to drop it off with a junior offi-'

'In here.' She opened one of a dozen identical doors leading off the hall.

I stepped into a warm and windowless grey room with walls covered in sheets of paper. The centre of the room was home to four desks and one occupant, who looked at me as though he'd been waiting for me.

'Ah, Mr Redfern, please take a seat,' Detective Mellor said. 'I understand you've brought something for me?'

My feet felt stuck to the brown carpet as I took a deep breath and remembered what Lisa had said – the case was more important than anything else. 'Yes,' I said and forced one foot to move forward, then the other.

'Thanks Janine,' Mellor said and the receptionist left the room.

As soon as the door click shut, Mellor hissed, 'Just leave the package in the bin in the corner, then fuck off.'

'What?' I snapped.

My nerves were turning to anger.

'The package you conveniently lost,' said Mellor, who looked smaller sitting down. 'I'll take it back now thank you.'

'No, I brought this.' I placed the manuscript file on the table. 'I found it in my Grandad's stuff.'

Mellor's sneer spread into a more vicious than usual smile. 'I didn't think you were stupid enough to actually bring it in here. Nice decoy.' He tapped the file with his forefinger. 'I'm guessing you've written down where I can find it?' His eyes didn't leave mine.

I swallowed. 'No, I…'

Mellor stood and leaned across the desk. 'Don't play with me Luke – I want that shit back!'

Finding the killer was more important than this, I told myself again.

'I'll tell you later,' I said. 'But this.' I pushed the file over. 'Is no decoy. I think it's bloody important.'

'No.' Mellor's voice was rough and it was clear he hadn't had much sleep. 'You give me what I'm owed or-'

'No.' I was stern. 'You owe me after setting me up you…' I couldn't find the right word. 'Finding the killer is more important.' I stabbed a finger at the file. 'And this was written by the bloody killer!'

Mellor shifted his weight and stared at the file.

'Another one of your theories?' He said with a grimace but I could tell he was taking me seriously. 'Sit down,' he said and grabbed the manuscript.

'It could be the missing link,' I said, calmly now. 'This is what it's all been about, hasn't it?'

One eyebrow raised and fell as Mellor flicked through the pages.

'Where did you find it?' He asked eventually.

'My Grandad's allotment shed.'

Mellor was probably piecing together information I had no knowledge of, I thought, as he sat with a stony look on his face. He placed the file back down and asked, 'Was this book on the reader's list?'

'Yeah, I checked.'

'Right – if we confirm it, we've got the link for the five murders and possibly the arson.' He turned to look at an array of papers pinned to the nearest wall.

Five murders. I really needed to sit down, but didn't want to be here longer than necessary.

'But the killer's getting sloppy,' Mellor continued. 'We've got him trapped and he's lashing out… but we still don't know who he bloody well is, do we?'

I shook my head, feeling like a schoolboy at a teacher's desk.

'Nothing from forensics and now this new murder.'

'No penguin book this time,' I said.

'No.' Mellor moved to the map of Brighton on the wall.

Six red pins had been pushed in and I recognised the two closest together on my shop's lane. Grandad and Shirley. The warehouse was clearly marked and I could see where the hoarder's house was, so the other two pins had to be the two murders I knew nothing about. One was down Kemptown way and the other up in Hove.

Mellor downed what was left in his mug. His jaw tensed and unclenched as he ran ideas through his mind. He was clearly as invested in this case as I was: frustrated and angry.

'There's something else,' I said.

'What?' He didn't bother turning round to look.

'A potential suspect,' I said and a thought came to me. 'But first I need you to answer a question.'

He turned and squinted. 'Go on.'

'Did you really think it was me?' I asked.

Mellor stared at me and I couldn't see a single muscle move in his face.

'Am I one of the suspects?' I asked.

Mellor's face finally twitched and then, like he could hold it no more, he burst into laughter. 'You really think this is all about you, don't you?'

'What?'

'Just like your Dad.'

I sat up straight as my back tensed. 'My Dad?'

'Yeah, your Dad. *Former* Chief Inspector Redfern. Did you think I didn't know about him?'

'No,' I said. 'But my Dad's got nothing to do with the murders.'

'When I saw the connection I escalated it and was told to put pressure on but- 'Mellor shook his head and turned back to the map, muttering. 'Of course he's got nothing to do with it.'

'So am I a suspect or not?' I asked.

'No, you're not.'

'Good.'

Stephen was wrong, but Dad was right – Knowles was trying to get to him though me. I looked around the room, searching for more information, but it wasn't like on telly or in the movies: there were no photos pinned to the wall and I couldn't see a list of suspects.

'Well, I've got someone you might want to look into,' I said.

'Who?' Mellor asked and pulled out a pad and pen.

'I haven't got his full name.'

Mellor blinked and pushed his glasses up to rub the bridge of his nose.

'But I know he went to prison early spring and got out a week or so ago…'

Mellor's eyes narrowed. 'Fits with the dates.'

'…and he likes to write. From what I know he's a writer.'

'Name?'

'All I know is he's called Jim and he used to live in Brighton.'

'No surname?'

I shrugged.

'Which prison?'

'I don't know.'

Mellor scratched a few notes down then slammed the cover shut. 'Right, I'll check it out and send the manuscript for prints.' He sighed. 'Listen, I really need that block back okay? If you've already tried it you'll know it's good shit, worth at least £20 a quarter, so the whole lot's probably worth two grand.'

He let the thought sink in. Two thousand pounds?

'I'll give you a few days, but I need it back, okay?'

I didn't say anything. I didn't even nod. This bastard could have sent me to prison and his boss was trying to frame my Dad – he was getting nothing from me. I slung my bag over my shoulder and walked out the way I came, remembering what Lisa had said: catching the killer was more important.

Sunday 13th August 1995

Inbetweener – Sleeper

'Lisa…' I asked as we made breakfast.

'Yes…' she replied, mimicking my tone.

'That package you took for me.'

I watched for any signs of her face that would give away her thoughts.

'Yeah.' Her face remained relaxed.

'What happened to it? I mean, have you still got it?'

'Oh no, I got rid of it.' She looked up from her half-buttered toast. 'It's best that way. Why? Does that bent copper want it back?'

'Well, yes,' I said and carried my breakfast over to the table.

Lisa tilted her head to one side. 'Too late.'

'What did you do with it then?'

'I got rid of it,' she said, not looking at me. 'Do you mind if I put the telly on?'

'No.' I finished my mouthful. 'So, did you tie it to a brick and chuck it in the sea? Is it hidden somewhere you can get it back from? Or…'

'None of those.' Lisa gave me her serious stare. 'And you're better off without it, believe me. That stuff wrecks your concentration, did you know that? Not to mention the paranoia.'

'Okay, okay, enough with the paranoia again,' I replied. 'I just wanted to know, that's all.'

'You just have to fight fire with fire,' she said. 'If he asks for it say you'll make a charge against him.'

I had considered it but knew it would never stick. 'With what evidence?' I asked.

Lisa said nothing.

'And if I wind him up he'll just raid the flat again and plant the gear himself-' I sighed and let it go, turning to my breakfast. 'So how long do you have to work today?' I asked.

'A full day,' Lisa said and pointed at the weather map on the telly. 'Doesn't seem right on a day like this does it?'

'No, I guess not. A sunny Sunday.'

'How about you?' she asked.

'I'm meeting up with the lads down the beach this arvo, so you can join us after if you want?'

'Sure,' she answered in a way that didn't convince me she would turn up.

The lads were already on the beach when I arrived and had assumed their usual u-shape facing the sea, sitting on towels surrounding a radio tuned to Radio One.

'Alright Luke?' Rob saw me first and the others looked up to say hi.

'Alright.'

I spread my towel out to sit next to James. 'No girls?' I asked as I carefully lay my guitar on the pebbles.

'No mate, they're all off round Stacey's.'

'Right,' I said.

I had no idea who Stacey was, which made me realise how much time I'd missed with the guys this summer. Last year we'd spent day after day at the beach and most evenings playing on the PlayStation round James' place or jamming but now my time was spent with the shop - and with Lisa.

'So what's new?' James asked. 'I heard them chatting about another murder on the radio.'

I was already skinning up a joint and didn't want to say I'd come down the beach to get away from all that stress, but my sigh must have been loud because Mike sat up and looked over.

'Near your place wasn't it?' Mike asked.

'Yeah.' I concentrated on sprinkling the green bud evenly. 'A few shops down from mine,' I said matter-of-factly. 'I knew her.'

'Shit,' James said.

'That's bad mate, sorry,' Rob said.

'So are they any closer to catching him?' Mike asked.

I shrugged. 'Who knows?'

I pulled out some Golden Virginia and thought about the manuscript and the penguin books, the hoarder's house and Shirley's open mouth. The word 'him' stuck in my head and I tried to visualise the killer. Simon had found the body and was a writer, so he was still a suspect in my eyes, despite the different book title, and the police now had Lisa's ex, Jim, in their sights, but there was also that guy from Penguin who collected books.

'They'll get him,' Rob said.

'Yeah.' I licked the rizla and rolled it tight. 'It could be anyone with a grudge – a writer though by the look of it.'

'A writer?' Mike asked.

I tore a square of card from the rizla packet and rolled it to make a roach.

'Everyone killed had a link to books, so…'

'Even the new one?' Mike asked.

'Well, no…' I puffed on the joint to check it wasn't too tight.

'So how do you know it was the same killer then?' James asked.

'It just has to be doesn't it?' I said and burnt the twist off the end of the spliff.

A voice singing on the radio sounded like how I imagined Lisa would sing and I listened for a moment.

He's not a prince, he's not a king, she's not a work of art or anything…

'Light it up then big boy,' James said.

'Yeah come on,' Mike said. 'Get it moving.'

That was the end of the killer conversation. We smoked, sat back, chilled and talked music just like we'd always had done. When the news came on the radio it was all Oasis versus Blur.

'Load of shite,' James said.

'What, *Roll With It*?' Mike said.

'No, the whole fake fight thing mate, load of shite. Nothing but hype.'

'Yeah, but it's good for sales,' I said. 'And it gets everyone talking about music – decent music.'

I genuinely believed it as well. True, it was a story whipped up by the media for the media's sake, but they'd created a wave of momentum that every songwriter or guitarist wanted to ride. More people were coming to our gigs since the whole Britpop thing took off and record labels were singing up new talent like it was going out of fashion which meant Beachhead had a better chance of getting signed. I remembered Stephen's office and decided against telling the lads what I'd done.

'Both songs are crap anyway,' James said.

'Not their best, I guess, but you like Blur don't you?'

'Sure,' James said. 'It's not only northerners who buy Oasis songs you know.'

'True. But name a better band out at the moment,' I said.

'Supergrass,' Mike was first.

'Stone Roses,' James' choice didn't surprise me.

'Pearl Jam,' Rob said and we all looked at him.

'Seriously?' Mike said.

'They're both old school – Roses and Jam,' I said.

'Roses and jam…' James copied my accent and we ended up in hysterics for the next five minutes.

That was the beauty of smoking weed compared to drinking. No fights, just giggles.

'Ah, man.' My sides were hurting. 'At least we've got a name for our first album.'

'Roses and jam!' We all said.

After a pause, Mike said. 'So next week, the chart show's on the radio. Sunday.'

'Yeah?'

'Why don't you all come round mine – I'll get some beers in and we can get pizza, play some PlayStation and see who's number one.'

'Sounds good,' Rob said.

'I'm in,' James said. 'But one condition.'

'What?' I asked.

'No girls.'

Mike nodded. 'Alright.'

'Count me in,' I said and closed my sun-dazzled eyes.

A few hours later, Lisa turned up at the beach, looking weary but happy to see me. Everything felt good.

I had no idea I'd be walking home alone that night.

God knows what time I got home. I locked the door behind me and felt a cold shudder run through me as I slipped into the shadows. I had been holding a sob back since leaving the pub and it jolted me, taking me by surprise. I felt a solitary tear run down my cheek. The curve of my guitar caught my eye and I sniffed the next tear away. The guitar was always there for me and, although I needed it now more than ever, I left it hanging. My emotions were too raw. I don't know if it was the weed or the beer, the argument with Lisa or how we left things, but all I wanted to do was curl up and cry. Not manly, I know, but sometimes we revert to our strongest emotions when we're hit by change and I didn't have the energy to be angry.

I should have seen it coming, but everything seemed normal. Content.

We'd moved from the beach to a pub on the prom when it got dark and Lisa and I got chatting on the end of a table when I said, 'I wonder how long this hot weather will hold out.'

'Longer for me than you I bet,' Lisa said and gave me an impish half smile like she had a secret.

'How's that then?' I asked, not wanting to play any games.

'I bought my tickets today,' she said with happy eyes.

One simple sentence and it was the death knoll for us. I felt a pressure build at my temples and took a sharp intake of breath.

'Flight tickets?' I asked.

'Of course,' she replied. 'I just need to book my first hostel in Cairns then I'm sorted.'

'Cairns?' I asked, wondering how I had fooled myself into thinking this moment was never going to happen.

Lisa had been open from the start: our days had always been numbered.

'Yeah, the rough guide reckons I'll get more seasonal work in Queenland,' she said in an energetic voice I used to adore but now that pure happiness had the opposite effect on me. 'Then I can head south and…'

I drifted off as she talked about mates who had been to Australia and all the amazing things they had done. I didn't care. I was jealous maybe, but all I felt was I didn't want to hear about Lisa's fun future because it was a future *without* me.

One of the girls with James overheard and joined in adding to Lisa's ecstasy. I recognised her. Becka.

'My friend just came back and said Byron Bay was the place to go. There's a beach where…'

Did Lisa not realise what was happening here? I thought. Did I mean that little to her that she was happy to discard our relationship so easily?

'You're going to have such a fun time,' Becka was saying and looked at me. 'How many days till your flight?'

'Oh,' I replied. 'I'm not going.' I said with more bitterness than I had meant and Lisa gave me a look. 'Just Lisa.'

'Okay,' Becka said, looking embarrassed. 'You'll have a great time, anyway,' she said to Lisa, then turned back to her mates.

A cold silence fell on us at the end of the table.

'You did well saving up the money,' I said, trying to find something simple to say that wouldn't betray my feelings again.

'Well.' She tilted her head. 'I got a little bonus, so…'

'Right,' I said.

Something didn't add up.

'Let's go for a walk,' Lisa said and nodded to the beach.

'Okay.' I called out to James, 'Back in a few minutes.'

James raised his eyebrows. 'Okay mate, it's like that is it? Have fun.'

'Get a room!' Mike shouted out and I felt my cheeks redden.

We crunched our way across the stones with the reflected lights of the ships in the English Channel shimmering ahead of us like bridges which could lead us anywhere. We reached the last dip, where the sea sloshed and sucked at the rounded stones.

'Look,' I said. 'I just need to know what happened to that block of resin, okay?'

I looked into her beautiful, dark eyes, which I'd fallen for weeks earlier. They were happy eyes but, just as when I first saw them, they held sorrow as well. They were asking me not to push it – not to make her tell me the truth.

But I had to know.

'Did you sell the dope to pay for your tickets?'

Lisa looked out to sea and spoke softly. 'Jim found my house and he was in a bit of a state… said he still loved me and wish he hadn't done what he'd done… how he'd been weak but was fighting it.'

'Did he hurt you?' I asked.

'No,' she said quickly and looked at me. 'He wasn't like that. He was more… like you. Artistic. He needed people to like what he created and… he took drugs.'

'Oh,' I said and looked away, seeing why Lisa had such an issue with me smoking. 'He was caught dealing?'

Lisa nodded.

'And he took the resin for you? Split the profits with you?' I guessed.

'Yeah,' she whispered.

I took it in and felt betrayed. I couldn't quite put my finger on why, but that was the overriding emotion – betrayal. She'd helped me out, sure, but wasn't she contradicting herself by giving Jim the dope and asking him to sell it?

'He could have been caught again,' I said.

'I know, but he really needed the money and…'

It was the first time I'd seen Lisa get defensive. She was never out of control, yet here she was defending her actions. She knew she was in the wrong.

'Look, don't push it, Luke, okay?' Lisa had turned to walk away. 'In the end I did the right thing for two people I really care about okay? And everything worked out fine didn't it?'

'Apart from the fact I still have the police on my case!' I raised my voice more than I'd wanted. 'And your ex will come back for more.'

'I'll be gone before then,' she said.

'I wasn't talking about the dope,' I said.

She took a step forward and looked genuinely shocked. 'What? You think I would sleep with him?'

I shrugged.

'You insecure bastard.'

'You haven't said you wouldn't,' I said and regretted it instantly.

'I shouldn't have to,' Lisa said. 'Anyway, we've always been on limited time, so why should you care? It'll be over soon anyway, right?'

'Yeah,' I said, not noticing how loud we had become. 'Because *you're* leaving.'

'Well, why not save ourselves the pain and just end it now then?' Lisa said, her eyes dark.

'Alright,' I replied quickly again. 'Screw you then. Sod off round the world and…'

But she had already turned and was walking across the beach.

And that was it.

I walked home alone and, on Monday morning, I woke up alone.

Monday 14th August 1995

New Generation – Suede

I ambled down the stairs, letting my auto-pilot navigate. My feet rhythmically pressed their way down the well-worn wooden steps, my arm swung out to push the door open to the shop and I took a sip of tea. I was barely conscious of what I was doing, slightly stoned from an early morning mini-spliff. I'd slept fitfully and finally woke at 8am with a host of freaky, half-real scenarios echoing around my head. Scenes replayed of Lisa and me arguing on the beach with torrential rain lashing at us and storm waves crashing at our feet.

It felt like my world had been torn apart.

I didn't want to think because thinking about anything – the books, the bed, the carpet or what I was wearing – all thoughts either led to Lisa or the *Penguin Killer*, and thinking about either of them triggered pains in my stomach.

This was worse than any hangover.

I meandered to the front door, mug in hand, and squinted at the open sign. I didn't have the energy to turn it round because that would lead to unlocking and opening the door, which led to customers coming in and… I grunted and took another sip of tea. Was this what depression felt like? No energy. No will power. Every sense triggering off emotions and dark thoughts which drained what was left of my energy? An ever-decreasing spiral which spun and spun until there was nothing left?

With Herculean effort, I unbolted the door, hooked it to the wall, ambled round my desk and collapsed in my chair. I smelt bad and needed a shower, my mouth felt rough and tasted of cheese. I could hear laughing outside. My brain was being overloaded with messages and all I could hear was: *I'm not good enough for Lisa and my Grandad was murdered.*

A shadow moved near the doorway and I looked up to see a vision of beauty walk through the door: tall, blonde and wearing a low-cut top.

'Hi,' she said.

'Hi,' I sat up in my chair.

'I just started working at the florist next door.' She spoke in a Scandinavian accent which had me transfixed. 'But it's closed this morning. Do you know where Isaac is?'

'I…' I remembered Lisa standing in that same place and rubbed my eyes, '…sorry, I've only just opened up so…'

'Well, Claudia and I have been waiting for half an hour now and she says Isaac is always here on time.'

A second gorgeous Scandinavian joined the first and gave me a smile. 'Hi Luke,' she said and I was starting to wonder if I was still mixing dreams with reality. 'Isaac's not answering the door and nothing's laid out like usual.'

'Okay,' I said and pushed up out of my chair. 'Let's have a look. I'm Luke by the way.' I offered my hand to the first girl.

'I'm Klara.'

I followed them round to Isaac's window and had to cup my hands round my eyes to see inside. Nothing out of the ordinary as far as I could tell. The layout was similar to my shop and I could see the door to his flat was closed. Buckets of flowers lined up near the metal shelves Isaac usually put out the front of the shop.

'Maybe he slept in?' I said. 'Have you got his phone number? I could try ringing him.'

'Yeah, good idea,' Claudia said and pulled a small book from her bag.

'I'll get you a cup of tea if you want?' I said and led them upstairs to my flat. 'Grab a seat.' I gestured at the sofa and flicked the kettle on.

It felt strange ringing my neighbour and I soon realised how quiet Isaac must have been because when his phone rang it sounded as loud as if it was in my shop. The girls chatted in a language I didn't understand and looked concerned as the phone rang and rang. I don't know if it was their worried looks or my brain slowly catching up, but I was feeling edgy. Isaac was a man of habit. I pictured Shirley again and felt my heart sped up.

I slammed the phone down. 'It's no good – he's not in.'

'Then where is he?' Claudia asked. 'He always opens on Monday.'

'I know, it's fine,' I said, trying to keep my voice calm. 'I'm sure there's a perfect explanation for it. Let's go back to the shop and have another look.'

I led them out and peered into the darkness of the florists again.

'What if something happened to him?' Klara asked. 'He's quite old, right? And he lives on his own – who would know if he fell over?'

'I'm sure he's fine,' I said, but had worse fears.

Was the killer picking off everyone on our street? Suddenly the thought of moving back to my parents' place didn't seem like such a bad idea.

'Shall we break in?' Klara said.

'Or call the police?' Claudia added with a furtive look towards Shirley's closed shop.

'No.' I tried to calm them even though everything I knew about Isaac told me something major must have happened for him to miss any early sales. 'We'll give it another twenty minutes then—'

Movement down the road caught my eye: someone running, wearing a dark shell suit and a hood up. Going by their gait they were close to collapsing. The girls turned to see what I was looking at as the runner headed straight for us. He stopped with a grunt and pulled his hood back to reveal a flurry of white hair.

'Isaac?'

'Sorry… girls…' he panted as he fought to catch his breath.

'Are you okay?' I asked.

Isaac nodded and held a hand up. Once he'd caught his breath he fumbled for his key, which Claudia took to open the door and grabbed a chair from inside. 'Sit down.'

'Ah, dear.' Isaac rubbed his knees and looked up to the sky.

'What's the matter?' I asked as a host of scenarios rushed through my mind. I looked down the street to see if anyone had been chasing Isaac but all I could see were early shoppers.

'Do you want a cup of tea?' Claudia asked.

Isaac nodded then said, 'Never again.' His voice was hoarser than usual.

I looked down at his trainers and recognised the make of his shell suit. I had never seen him wear anything like this. Then it all made sense.

'Isaac, have you been jogging?' I asked with half a smile.

'Yes,' he said sheepishly.

The relief was almost euphoric and Klara joined in my laughter.

'Oh, don't make me laugh,' Isaac said, holding his side. 'Stupid idea, trying to get fit.'

'First time?' Claudia asked.

'First for a long time… I was doing okay but didn't know how far I'd gone, then I realised the time and rushed back.'

'It's okay,' Claudia replied. 'You chill out and we'll get the shop ready.'

'Are you sure?' Isaac's eyes twinkled, happy to be looked after. 'I'm not as old as I look you know,' he said and gave me a smile. He nodded at my shop. 'Go on Luke, stop ogling at my staff and get your own shop open.'

I gave a little laugh and felt my cheeks blush.

'Okay, see you later,' I said and gave Claudia a smile when I caught her eye.

Back in the shop, I fell back into my chair with a sigh and got back into my crossword:

First Emperor of Rome.

But my mind was buzzing after the excitement. Funny how everything changed, I thought. Maybe the weed wasn't helping my mood? All it did was made me mope about in a funk. What I needed to do was get out and see people. Be part of something.

My eye scoured the room and caught on the front cover of the NME. Damon Albarn's eyes. Liam Gallagher's mouth, primed to swear. I remembered seeing him in London and made my mind up. This was a pivotal moment in our country and it was happening right now. It was about time I was part of it.

I didn't bother with my usual record shop because, today, I wanted to be part of the crowd, so I headed straight to the huge, American-style, so-much-more-than-just-records shop to join the throng of young men and women buying the singles, hot off the press.

'Don't buy that it's shit,' a lad in a sports top with white lines was berating a guy in baggy jeans for picking up the Blur CD.

'You reckon?' Baggy jeans replied. 'Or is it too complicated for you 'cos it's got more than three chords?'

'At least it's not pop shite,' Sporty said.

Baggy jeans was staring him out and grabbed a second copy of *Country House*. 'We'll see in the end, won't we?'

Sporty grabbed another *Roll With It* CD and followed him off to the till, readying another attack.

'What about the b-sides, they're always…'

I shook my head. The world was going mad, but I needed to be part of it. I ignored the CD's and tapes, walked past the lines of albums to the back of the shop where the vinyl singles were kept. Now I had a big decision to make: according to the press only southerners bought Blur and I was probably middle class, although not as much as Mike, so should I rebel and opt for Oasis? They had the swagger and the tune was rock and roll, but Blur were actually saying something – slagging off the rich. Plus their songs were diverse: they didn't mind mucking around in the studio and trying something new.

'Fuck it,' I said and grabbed one of each.

I had taken part in the most important vote of my life so far… and ended up sitting on the fence. What did that say about me? The guy behind the counter gave me a look when he saw both singles and shrugged as if to say *at least he's buying vinyl*.

While he put the sales through the till I saw a girl with long blonde hair walk down one of the aisles and disappear behind a rack of CDs. Was that Lisa? I felt my stomach churn with excitement. I needed to see her. Maybe I could apologise? I paid the cashier and craned my neck to see where she had gone.

'Thanks,' I said and rushed off.

I walked past the rows of albums, gazing at the Beach Boys and Beatles with a wistful thought of seeing a Beachhead album there one day, then turned a corner to see the girl - kissing a man. I could tell it wasn't Lisa but in that split second, as I tried not to stare, my heart clenched. I was still raw. I had to steer clear of Lisa if I didn't want more emotional pain. She had gone.

I walked past Sporty on the way back and the logo on his top caught my attention. It was the same as on the shell suit Isaac had been wearing. A thought came to me. What if Isaac was lying? Sure, he was unfit and could do with losing a pound or two and he probably was younger than he looked, but the running gear had looked odd on him and… I suddenly remembered where I had seen it before. I was out of the shop in a flash.

I thought about taking the camera film to the local one hour shop but I needed to get the film developed properly and I only had half the equipment I needed, so I had to get into the Uni lab where all my old equipment sat, unused in cupboards. I rushed through the streets, concocting excuses and plans to get me inside, but as soon as I saw the building I knew none were needed – the Uni had an open day for prospective students!

I knew the place like the back of my hand, so I slipped in, eyeing up the main hall like a newbie, then slunk away through a side door, wound back into the photography wing and had the dark room to myself.

I'd forgotten how much I enjoyed the process of developing photos. That was the problem with studying something you loved, like photography for me – or music. At first you dive in headlong, but then you're tested on it and forced to do it over and over to death, until you start resenting it and eventually turn your back on it. Even Grandad's sunrise photos had been developed at Boots.

'Right then…'

I laid out tall bottles of liquid, trays and timers in groups. I set the first timer off and disappeared into the flow of the method. I poured and swished and my hands took a life of their own as they repeated movements they had carried out hundreds of times before. I hung the film up to dry, switched the light to red and set up the machine.

My thoughts returned to the reason I was developing the photos: the *Pavilion Poet*. I'd seen the logo on Isaac's jogging gear when I caught the *Pavilion Poet* in the act, so what if it was Isaac all along and he'd been running back from another spray?

As the machine warmed up I wondered what I would do if I proved Isaac was the graffiti artist? Congratulate him? I certainly wasn't going to sell him out or tell the papers. One thing didn't sit right though. The music. Isaac just didn't seem like a Bowie fan to me.

I ran through the negatives to find the best shots and paused as I came across my copy of the police photo of Grandad and put it to one side to develop later. I found the sharpest *Poet* photo and cut it for fixing onto paper. Another timer, more liquid and the image came into focus. This was my favourite part. The art. The hard work might have been done in capturing the shot but now I had to use my instinct to feel when to pull the paper out. Silhouettes of the windows in the backdrop were taking shape as the shadowed walls loomed onto the page. Smaller shapes appeared, sharpening by the second and I could make out the shape of the *Poet*: arm out stretched and I could just make out a tiny cloud leaping from the can onto the wall.

Perfect.

I hung it up to dry and worked on focussing in. I needed a close up. The same process and the image came into view. This was more like it. I had kept the fix time down to avoid over saturation. The window was in the corner now; the shadow of the wall being painted; the silhouette of the *Poet*. The hood was clear along with a wavy line. Hair maybe? A nose and chin could be seen protruding from the hood and they could have belonged to anyone. The rest of the body darkened and took shape. The logo was clear on the black jogging bottoms and something about the shape felt familiar. I pulled the photo out, shook the drips off pegged it to the string.

'Oh,' I said.

The angle of the shot wasn't perfect but the raised arm did help and left me in no doubt. Isaac wasn't the *Pavilion Poet*.

The *Poet* was a woman.

-Her Words-

It had all been about words.

Her words.

He didn't have them. He could never write. He could never explain how he felt. Not until it was too late.

And he did feel.

More than she ever knew.

She had always written but he hadn't noticed at first. Diaries mostly and then stories: short stories or snippets of real life. And then she wanted to bring it together. Like they were physical pieces of her life and by tying them together her life had meaning. So she wove them like a long carpet. Her book, she had called it.

When he had worked, she had written. That had been the agreement. After the loss and emptiness. After the pain, she had needed it and he had given her strength. He could tell when she needed to write and he'd always given her the time and space to do it.

That was how he remembered her, bent over her desk or lying in bed, with her pencil scratching away. She was always quieter afterwards, like her words had been used up. All she wanted was for him to hold her. So he did.

He had read some of her words, when she was out, but it didn't make sense until he read the whole thing as one and that was only after she had gone for good. It made him cry. Some of it made him laugh. All of it made him wish they had talked about it more.

Just one more conversation.

What he would give for that.

He had always thought himself the strong one, but now she was gone he realised how strong she had been for him. He needed her now, but at least he had her words.

And her words needed to be shared. He owed her that.

Tuesday 15th August 1995

Just When You're Thinking Things Over – Charlatans

Another heavy morning.

From my bed I stared at the ceiling, haunted by dreams of Lisa. The weight of our parting lay heavy on me again and, as the dream memories faded, I talked myself into believing nothing much had changed. I'd only known Lisa for a couple of weeks and life hadn't been that bad beforehand, had it? Before the murders kicked off, I thought, and remembered Shirley's face.

I reached for my tin and rolled a one-skin. I needed something to numb me so I could fall into the day and let it take me away like a strong tide. Smoke, shower and toast, then I was downstairs, in my chair with my cuppa, breathing in the sea air and trying to focus on a new crossword.

Antipodean bird with a taste for fish.

I looked up and scanned the room, searching for inspiration. I thought about raiding the wildlife shelves but my gaze floated back down to my desk and fixed on a green penguin book.

'Of course,' I said to myself but froze with my pen at the bottom of the 'P'.

My eyes returned to the book and gripped the pen a little tighter. Something was whirring away in my slow brain but nothing had come to fruition yet – all I felt was fear. Once again, my body knew what was happening before my mind did. My senses came into focus, fuelled by adrenaline as my fight or flight instincts kicked in.

The rainbow of book spines became vivid, the sea salt strong and seagull squawks magnified.

The book hadn't been on my desk when I went to bed. I knew that.

I looked around and felt a strange feeling of clarity wash through me. Another sharp intake of breath and I accepted what had happened – someone had broken into the shop and moved the books. The front door was untouched, so they must have come in through the back window and, for all I knew, could still be there. Hiding. Watching. It could have been the weed affecting me, but I felt a tingle across my neck.

I placed my mug on the desk and picked up my long, metal ruler.

I had to make sure the shop was empty.

The sound of footsteps on cobbles echoed outside the shop as I concentrated on every sound inside. A creak here, a drip there… any sound could betray whoever had broken in, but I knew every floorboard creak, every shadowy nook and every bookshelf wobble. This was my land. I was in control here.

I closed the front door and moved like a ghost, down the narrow corridor, glancing into the penguin alcove as I walked by. Empty. I passed the door to upstairs and entered the back rooms. Everything looked normal but it felt like something was different. I couldn't tell if it was the air, or a subtle smell triggering my sub-conscience, but I was sure something had changed. I stepped forward and felt the edges of the ruler cut into my palm. The gap behind the first row of books was empty so I crept forwards, peering at the base of each bookshelf for giveaway shadows. The space behind the next row was empty, which left a handful of remaining hiding places.

I should have taken a moment to think about what I was doing but I was so focussed on defending my shop I didn't think about what I was going to do when I found the intruder.

I took another step and peered into the next aisle.

Empty.

They had to be in the space between the final row and the wall by the joss stick holder and window, which I could see was closed. It was time to be bold, I told myself, but I was starting to sober up. An image of a cruel-mouthed murderer, hiding behind the shelf clasping a bloody knife came to mind and I shuddered. The book on the desk must have been left by the murderer - the person who had physically attacked people - and here I was cornering them like a wild animal: the person who had carved words into their victim's dead flesh.

I took a step back.

Then I pictured Grandad's dead body in the police photograph.

Was the person who killed Grandad cowering a few feet away from me? I felt the muscles in my arms tense and looked around. I grabbed a large hardback book - *Wild Alaska* - and felt its weight in my hand. A hefty tome. I took another step back and lobbed the book over the last bookshelf, into the hiding place and ran off as the crashing sound chased me up the shop.

I threw a glance back when I got to the stairs… nobody was there. No blood-thirsty killer rushing out to get me. The book had simply bounced off the wall and clattered against the floor. It hadn't hit flesh.

I shook my head and strolled to the back of the room and peered into the last, empty space between the bookshelf and back wall. I picked up the splayed out book and felt a complete twat. I made my way back to the front room and stared at the penguin book on my desk. Who had put it there? Was it the killer winding me up? Or Mellor playing tricks with me?

I growled and rubbed my forehead. Maybe Lisa was right? Maybe the weed did mess up my head and stopped me from thinking straight.

I looked at the title: *Keep it quiet*. I dug out my Polaroid photo of the penguin books and could make out number 992 to the left of the shot. It had a similar smudge on the spine, which meant it had come from my shelf. Maybe I had left it here after all? No. No way. I wouldn't forget that. Would I?

I huffed and visited the penguin alcove to study the shelf: there were no other copies of 992. What should I do? Should I tell Mellor? I meandered back to my desk, fell into my chair and downed the rest of my tea.

The more I thought about it the more I was sure the killer must have left it as a warning. They must have the same key from when they killed Grandad, which meant they'd been in the shop while I was sleeping upstairs. The thought sent a cold shiver through me. Lisa would have said it was a power trip; the killer was showing me they had control over me.

Maybe I should change the front door lock or get a lock fitted to the flat door?

I sighed and looked out the window, between the piles of books. My paranoia had subsided and the caffeine from the tea started up the cogs in my mind. I had to get to grips with this. The message was clear and I was definitely in danger now the killer knew I was on to him, which meant I was on the right trail... but how did the murderer know? Was the killer someone I knew and had told about the murders? No, I had only talked to a few people and they were trusted mates or family, so probably not. Had the killer overheard one of those conversations?

I felt like ringing Mellor but I still didn't trust him and knew he would pressure me about the missing block of resin. So what could I do? Was I next on the killer's list?

I pictured Shirley's dead body again and realised I was being a fool - there was only one thing I could do.

'Hi Luke!' Mum opened the door and beckoned me in.

'Hi Mum,' I replied as she gave me her version of a bear hug.

I dropped my bags in the hall, careful to lay the borrowed records I was returning on top, and sat at the bottom of the stairs to take off my Converse.

'Where's Dad?' I asked.

'Mowing the lawn,' Mum said and crouched next to me. 'How are you feeling?'

'Alright,' I said with a shrug. 'A bit detached from it to be honest, I mean, it's not normal is it, having a serial killer pick off your neighbours?'

'No,' Mum said and stroked my head. 'You're better off here while the police make their enquiries.'

'Yeah,' I said, trying not to sound too sceptical.

'They'll get them in the end, they always do.' Mum sounded chirpy but I could tell it was forced.

Or they'll drive them underground, I thought, and they'll re-surface months later when the papers are no longer interested.

'I'll put the kettle on,' she said, leaving me to unpack my bags in Stephen's room.

I felt down. Not because of the killer, but because the warning had worked and I'd backed down. I had run off 'home' with my tail between my legs and was risking being downgraded to being treated like a child again. At least I had the band to distract me, I thought, and spent half an hour running through a few songs on Stephen's old acoustic guitar. We had rehearsals tomorrow and it was always good to keep fresh.

Eventually, I ambled back downstairs and started sliding the borrowed LPs back in their place. Dad had it organised in alphabetical order, which Stephen took the piss out of him for, but it made sense with such a big collection. The dark-wood cupboard sat under the new sound system and had to be over two meters long and rammed full of LPs. Mum always had a habit of leaving records out or putting them back in the wrong sleeves, which sent Dad up the wall. Of course, as soon as Stephen found that out he spent every Sunday redistributing a selection of records with an evil grin on his face.

'Ah, there it is,' Dad made me jump after creeping up on me across the plush new carpet.

'Rolling Stones?' I said.

'Yeah, under-rated this one,' he ran his finger down the track listing on the back, seemingly marvelling at every other song. 'Some good stuff on here. Shall I put it on?'

'Go for it,' I replied.

It was obvious where I got my thirst for music from and watched him place and play the LP with the care and speed of a professional. I loved listening to tunes with Dad, learning a few things along the way. I mean, he was there, in the sixties, so he knew what was really going on.

'This was the year it all got going,' Dad said and relaxed on the sofa. '1971.'

'Really?' I said. 'I always thought '67 was the big year. Summer of love and all that.'

Dad tilted his head. 'It was good, but I guess I was a bit too young for a lot of what was going on, but in '71 I was at the gigs and the decent records didn't stop coming out – Simon and Garfunkel, Carole King, Led Zeppelin, T-Rex.' He nodded at the record player. 'Rolling Stones.'

'This is pretty good too,' I said and picked up the *Low* album.

Dad wrinkled his nose. 'I guess so… I've never really been into Bowie.'

'Oh,' I said. 'I thought this was yours.'

'No.' Dad took the album and flipped it over and pointed to the planet orbits logo in the top corner, drawn in felt tip pen. 'It's one of your Mum's.'

'What?' I said, genuinely taken back. I'd assumed all the records had been Dad's because Mum had never shown an interest in music.

'We liked a few similar bands of course, but she had a half-decent record collection when we met. She drew a logo on hers so they didn't get mixed up with her brother's.'

'Right,' I said and nodded, still staring at the logo.

I had seen it before but couldn't place it. Did a new band have a similar logo? Maybe I saw it on a t-shirt when I bought the singles yesterday, I thought.

'I listened to those bands you mentioned,' Dad said, reminding me of the LPs I'd lent him. 'Some good stuff there.'

'I thought you'd like it.'

'Of course, it's easy to see where they get their influences from…'

'Here we go,' I said and shook my head. 'Everything's been nicked from the sixties.'

Dad smiled but stood his ground. 'That band Blur – they've nicked everything from the Kinks to Bowie.' He held his hand up to stop me arguing back. 'But you know what?'

'What?' I said, distracted by the phone ringing in the hall.

'It's bloody good,' Dad said. 'Better than most of the crap we had back then I can tell you.'

'Luke!' Mum's voice rang out. 'Luke, it's for you!'

I raised my eyebrows at Dad to say *who's that?* and gave Mum a frown as I pulled the lounge door behind me, muffling the drums and guitar from the stereo. She gave me a shrug as if to say she didn't know who it was and handed me the receiver.

'Hello,' I said.

'Ah, Luke, I knew I'd find you eventually.'

It was Detective Mellor. I clenched my teeth and grimaced at how easily he had found me.

'Just wanted to let you know your information proved very useful.'

'Right,' I said, wondering what he was talking about.

'I managed to locate the person you drew my attention to. James Alton. We picked him up for questioning last night.'

Lisa's ex! Mellor had managed to find him. Was he the killer? I wanted to ask, but I held back.

'I'll keep you informed on future developments.' Mellor's voice lowered a notch. 'And can confirm the package has been retrieved, what was left of it. Nice work.'

'No problem,' I muttered as I felt tension sweep up from my stomach.

So Lisa *had* given her ex the resin to sell. Serves him right, I thought, but felt a touch of guilt – I'd never dobbed anyone in before.

'Any evidence for the murders?' I asked, hoping for some penguin books or a copy of *A Home for Memories Past* by Mary Fairweather in his flat.

'Nothing as yet.'

'Right,' I said and thought about what to say next. Mellor had his weed so would probably hear me out. 'Listen, I know it's probably nothing but I found another book.'

Silence.

'I think the killer was in my shop again and he left me a message,' I said.

'Go on.'

'It was more of a warning actually… it was a book called *Keep It Quiet*. Another penguin book.'

'I see.' Mellor didn't sound shocked but I guessed was taking notes.

'So I'm going to lay low for a bit.'

'Good plan,' Mellor replied. 'Just while it all clears over.'

'Okay,' I said and Mellor hung up.

I sighed and placed the phone back down. What now? I stared through the kitchen to the garden where Mum was putting out some washing. Seeing her from a distance something clicked and it all became clear. It was probably in the way she stood – a posture I'd seen all my life but hadn't recognised on that night. My weed-addled brain had been so slow… the Bowie LP, the logo and the photo I'd taken, all added up – my Mum was the *Pavilion Poet*.

But how could I prove it?

Wednesday 16th August 1995

My Generation – The Who

I was disorientated, waking up in Stephen's old bedroom and, for a change, something new was on my mind: my theory about my Mum.

I headed straight to the utility room under the pretence of washing some clothes. There had to be evidence somewhere in the house so why not start there?

'Morning Luke.' Mum popped her head around the corner. 'Let me do that,' she said, opening her arms.

'No it's fine,' I replied and held the ball of dirty t-shirts and socks away from her. 'Grandad's washing machine is okay, but it always smells better when it's washed here,' I said, trying to distract her.

'Well that's the fabric conditioner.' She tapped a tall bottle of blue liquid.

'Cool,' I said. 'I'll make sure I get some when I go shopping.'

Mum smiled, happy to pass on some wisdom. 'You just pour it in this part… that's it. Do you want any breakfast?' she asked as she left.

'No, it's alright I'll get it myself.'

I shoved the washing in, added powder and twisted the dial to a symbol I recognised, relieved when the machine leapt into action. The sound covered my movements as I rummaged through the baskets of laundry. Going through my parents' dirty laundry wasn't my idea of fun, but I was determined to find the jogging set I'd seen on the *Pavilion Poet*.

Nothing.

I gave in, had breakfast and watched telly while I mulled over where to search next.

'Right, I'm off to the allotment,' Dad said with a tinkle of his car keys. 'Luke are you up for a bit of digging?'

'Ah, no, sorry, we've got rehearsals tonight so I was hoping to go through a few songs beforehand.'

'Alright,' he said with a smile but I could tell he had wanted me to go. 'I'm taking your Mum into town along the way, so we'll see you later.'

'Okay, bye.'

Just like the old days when I needed to slink out to the garage and have a smoke, I waited for the sound of the car to fade out down the road before I ran upstairs to riffle through my Mum's wardrobes like I was a six year old kid looking for Christmas presents. There was nothing remotely sporty anywhere except some old trainers she wore in the garden but they were a dirty white colour. I paused, hands on hips, and tried to focus. If it was me, what would I do? If Mum really was the *Pavilion Poet*, Dad obviously had no idea, so where would I hide something from Dad? I had a few stashes in the past but most were in my bedroom, which had now been blitzed.

I wandered out to the landing and stared at the loft hatch. No, that was Dad's domain… same with the garage. I ambled downstairs, checking any cupboard I could find. The one under the stairs was virtually pristine with no place to hide and the cupboard under the kitchen sink was full of every cleaning liquid you could think of and had no spare room. I gravitated back to the utility room – somewhere

Dad usually avoided – but every cupboard was half full and blatantly devoid of any black running shoes.

What was I thinking? My Mum, the *Pavilion Poet!* I took a deep breath and tried to distance myself. Was this more paranoia caused by the weed like Lisa had said? Maybe this whole deal with the *Penguin Killer* was getting to me and making me think everything in the paper was connected to me. Did that make me completely self-centred? Yep. I needed to get out more.

My washing machine load was done, so I dragged it out and pushed it into the tumble drier. A button on my jeans clunked against the wooden divider between the two machines with a hollow knock and I stopped.

I stared at the white MDF strip. It was about three inches across, so you barely noticed it. I knocked it with my knuckles. Definitely hollow. My mind was working overtime. This would be a perfect stash hole. I gave it a push but it was solid, built into the unit. I ran my finger around the edge and found a metal edge just at the top. I pressed the top of the panel and, with a click, the panel popped open to reveal a narrow cupboard space.

I stared in disbelief.

Inside was a pair of black running shoes, black leggings and top, and a black rucksack. They matched the make and style from my photograph.

My Mum *was* the *Pavilion Poet!*

She'd been running around Brighton in the dead of night, spraying graffiti on walls. I reached in to feel the bag and recognised the tubular shapes of the spray cans.

'Jeez,' I said and sat on the floor. How was I going to deal with this? I studied the door and the special clasp Mum had worked into the underneath of the unit. Nice work. Better than most of Dad's DIY to be honest. I took a moment to take it all in. I was shocked but my first emotion was respect for Mum. She was a rebel! I didn't know why she was doing it, but her graffiti had people talking. I also felt a drop of sadness. I used to think I knew my parents inside out and could predict their every move but this shook everything I knew about Mum. Bowie, DIY and graffiti?

I pushed the door shut again with a satisfying click, shook my head and spent the rest of the day mulling it over but by evening I still had no idea what, if anything, I was going to do about it.

The last chord of the song hung as I let the volume drop: my fingers holding the strings tight as Rob's cymbal crash and James' final bass note faded with me. Mike was crouched by his amp, shaking his guitar to create feedback like he was Jimi bloody Hendrix. The crowd usually loved it, but it was totally over the top in the rehearsal room. Eventually, Mike stood up and the four of us shared the same satisfied look we had at the end of every set.

'Sweet,' James said and unstrapped his bass.

'Yeah,' Mike said. 'I'm loving the new lead on *Shift* – sounds awesome.'

I placed my guitar in its stand and let Rob respond to Mike's self-congratulatory remark.

'It sounds great Mike, really cool.' He was smiling. 'Gives the song an edge.'

'Cheers. It's gonna sound amazing on Friday.'

I took a seat and thought ahead. After Friday we had nothing booked and August was usually a good month for outdoor beer festivals and parties, so there was a good chance of getting a new booking.

'You know,' I said. 'After Friday we could always mix the set list up a bit. Maybe add in some summer covers? Then we could… what?'

Everyone was staring at me. It felt odd, especially as Mike was paying attention to what I was saying.

'What is it?' I asked.

'Well,' Mike said. 'You see, I've got this job in London that starts…'

Everything seemed to slow down. James was staring at his feet and Rob was wearing his serious-sad face.

'…in September but I need to head up soon to find a flat, so…' he left it hanging, waiting for me to respond.

'Well done,' I said, wondering what the big deal was.

'So I'm guessing this is my last rehearsal and Friday will be our last gig,' Mike said.

Nobody spoke. All I could hear was the buzzing of our amps and the pulse of blood rushing through my ears. My lungs needed more air.

'Why?' I eventually said. 'You can come down for rehearsals and gigs.'

Mike shook his head. 'It's a proper job so I won't have that much spare time,' he said. 'I need to impress them.'

'Right,' I said more angrily than I had wanted and looked from Rob to James who seemed unaffected by the announcement. In fact, they looked sheepish. 'You two already bloody knew, didn't you?'

'Sorry,' Rob said. 'But we thought it would be pointless saying something before we rehearsed.'

'Yeah, we know how bad vibes mess you up,' James added.

Was he talking about Lisa? I felt my shoulders sag. This was my second break up in just a few days.

'We knew it was coming mate,' James said in his calm voice and I couldn't disagree.

Just like with Lisa.

'Yeah, Uni's over now,' Mike said. 'And it wasn't like it was going to last forever.'

A hundred replies ran through my head and I searched for the least aggressive one as a dull ache started to clench my belly. I straightened up to relieve it but the pressure was still there.

Was it really over? Beachhead. My songs. Our songs. Our music. The good times. The buzz.

The pain I'd felt from splitting up with Lisa was resurfacing. I leaned on my amp and watched my knuckles turn white as Mike talked about his job, but I wasn't listening anymore. He could have said something earlier – weeks ago really. Then I could have had a say in how it ended: where our last gig would be and what song we'd play last. I just wanted to have my say… or was I being childish? Maybe it was time to accept these changes rather than fighting them. Go with the flow. Only get bothered about the things I *could* affect.

How I reacted was more important than resisting it, wasn't it?

I thought about Simon, running from his problems, hiding in the shadows, writing his book, and Dad ignoring the truth of what had happened to Grandad. We all had different ways of dealing with change and no-one had the perfect answer, but what about those people who embraced change? The way Isaac jumped at every business opportunity or how Grandad set up the shop after Nana died.

It was time to be positive.

I waited for the conversation to die down before saying, 'Friday night it is then. So we'd better make it a bloody good one.'

Mike offered me a lift back to my parents' but I felt like I needed a walk. It was still warm and some fresh evening air would do me good, I thought. The band splitting up was another earthquake in what I could now see had been my easy life. Lisa was right – I was sorted. I just didn't know how I was going to deal with this change.

I meandered through the streets, imagining I looked like a guy on some cool Bob Dylan album cover with my guitar case in one hand, and, I don't know why, I took a detour past the shop. Half way down the familiar cobbles I could see a shadow in the doorway of the shop and knew who it was by the way the streetlight lit her blonde hair. What was Lisa doing here? I felt the depression from the evening slip away in a beat and couldn't wait to see her face again. To hold her and smell her perfume again… she turned when she heard my footsteps.

'About bloody time,' she said and I stopped in my tracks, leaving a few metres between us.

There was something in her eyes I hadn't seen before and it scared me. I remembered what I had done to Jim and a surge of guilt tightened my chest.

'Hi,' was all I could say and desperately wanted to get into the shop for whatever argument was about to kick off.

'Hi?' Lisa said and stepped towards me. 'Is that all you've got to say you bloody snitch?'

'Snitch? Come on…' I said.

'You screwed Jim over you bastard. Now he'll be back in jail and he won't last it… he's not strong enough.'

'You still care for him then?' I said, feeling I had to defend myself somehow.

'Of course I bloody do! We might not be together but I loved him once.'

I placed my guitar case on the floor, ready for a long argument. 'So why did you give him drugs to sell, knowing he could get caught?'

'He needed the money,' she replied.

'And so did you,' I said and thought of the flight tickets. 'But you let him take the risk.'

Lisa was scowling. 'He had contacts and I knew the money would set him up for a bit – get him a place and out of my hair.'

I shook my head.

'This is pointless. What's done is done.'

Lisa came closer and pointed a finger at my chest. 'I took a risk for you and this is how you repay me?'

'I asked you what you did with it and you never told me,' I replied. 'I wouldn't have agreed to it - plus I genuinely thought Jim could be the killer… a former prisoner? A writer? The dates fitted and I just wanted him checked out.'

Lisa held my gaze for a few seconds then said, 'Do you really think I would go out with a murderer?'

I shrugged. 'How well did you know him? You never said why he was sent down, so how did I know if he was dangerous or not? Anyway, if he killed my Grandad I don't care who he is – he should be locked up.'

'Well he's screwed now either way isn't he?' Lisa looked away and I could see tears building in her eyes.

'I'm sorry,' I said and reached out to rub her shoulder but she shrugged my hand off. 'Listen, I'm not staying here at the moment but we can get a cup of tea if you want?'

Lisa nodded then turned to me. 'Why aren't you staying here?'

'Too dangerous,' I said with a shake of my head. 'Long story.'

I unlocked the door but it jammed halfway. I stared into the darkness of the shop and shoved the door again, hearing it knock against something solid.

'Bloody door,' I said. I squeezed in and leaned round to turn the light on. 'Shit!'

Lisa was at the window, cupping her hands to see.

On the floor, next to my desk, lay a policeman with an orange penguin book on his chest.

Thursday 17th August 1995

Sabotage – Beastie Boys

So here we were again: Lisa and I waking up in my flat. Something in my sleepy head told me this wasn't right – I should be at my parents and Lisa and I had broken up. Was this a hyper-real dream? No, it was warm and real. The events of last night came flashing back to me and I remembered how we got here. Nothing had happened between us but by the time the police had left, Lisa needed a place to stay and I was too tired to walk home, even though Dad offered to pick me up. We felt safe with two policemen on the front door, so we kipped in my bed.

I reached out to touch Lisa's long hair and stroked it trying not to wake her.

'Morning,' she said and turned to give a full body stretch.

'Morning,' I replied, not wanting to break the spell.

Lisa looked at me and I tried to read her eyes but they were a mix of worry and fear. 'I shouldn't have stayed here,' she said.

'Why?'

She looked away.

'It's not like we're back together or anything,' I said.

Lisa rolled out of bed and pulled her clothes on.

'Well?' I asked.

'It's not that,' she replied. 'It's… everything. Jim. The police.' She looked at me. 'That bloody killer on the loose.'

'I know,' I said but didn't really have a handle on it. If I thought about it too much it freaked me out.

'The killer was here,' Lisa said. 'Again.'

'I know.'

That made three times that I knew of: once for Grandad, again to leave the warning and back again with the policeman.

'That's why Mellor stationed a policeman here,' I said. 'To catch the killer. He thought he'd come back…'

'And look what happened.'

I remembered the pool of crimson blood around the copper's head. Panic had set in and, just like when we found Shirley, Lisa ran upstairs to phone for an ambulance. Then he'd groaned and opened his eyes.

'They said he'll be alright – he was just knocked out for a bit.' I tried to make it sound like an everyday event.

'And what if it's you next? That's why you moved out remember? We need to get out of here.' Lisa pulled her jumper on.

'Look, don't rush. Grab a shower and some breakie.'

She paused. 'Okay, but the police will be back and after everything with Jim…' her eyes were welling up.

I got out of bed to give her a hug.

'Look,' I said. 'If anything, this proves I was wrong about Jim, doesn't it? He's cleared because he was in the station so he can't be the killer.'

Lisa pushed me away. 'Of course he's not the killer.'

'But the police didn't *know* that did they?'

'And he'll still be done for dealing, won't he?' Lisa crossed her arms.

I looked away and the reality of what I had done weighed heavy in my chest– what my jealousy had done: lashing out at someone I didn't even know.

'Okay,' I said. 'You're right. I shouldn't have done it and–' this was my problem, I told myself, I had caused it. 'I'll sort it out.'

'How?'

'I'm not sure yet, but there must be a way. I'll have a word with Mellor and-'

'But Mellor's got what he wants,' she said. 'He'll get a conviction and a promotion and he'll probably try and set you up again if you keep smoking that stuff.'

I shook my head. 'It's not that simple. Mellor's out to impress Knowles,' I said as I felt the beginnings of a plan take shape. 'And the thing Knowles really wants is my Dad.'

It was awkward when Lisa left. Two police were on guard at the front door and she flinched when I gave her a peck on the cheek.

'See you later then,' I said in the hope I would, but she just nodded and walked off.

I faced the rows of books, which had been the wallpaper of my daily life. I drank in the view and longed for the safe and simple days of weeks before when I could just chill in my chair and work my way through a crossword. I picked up the Polaroid photo of the penguin books which had been useful last night when Mellor had asked about the book, which had been taken off the shelf:

Death of a Hero.

Number 42.

When I checked my records against the photo, two other books had been stolen.

'Is that why the killer keeps coming back?' I'd asked Mellor. 'To steal the books?'

Mellor frowned. 'Maybe,' he said without looking at me. 'But more importantly he has two more books.' The light flashed off his glasses as he turned to me. 'Which means he's planning to kill again.'

Now, as I stood in the main shop room, the thought I hadn't been able to shake came back to me: how had the killer managed to get in the shop and sneak up on the policeman? He had mumbled a few things when he came round but it was nonsense: he hadn't seen anyone and had been struck from behind.

I stared down the dark, narrow corridor to the backrooms and the penguin alcove. There were only two ways a person could have got in other than the front door: the back window, which was impossible to open or close from outside, and from the upstairs flat. But there was no way you could get in the flat unless you crossed the roof. Is that what the killer was doing?

I rushed up the steep stairs and checked every window. They either faced sheer drops which couldn't be climbed, or led out onto steep rooves of cracked ancient tiles, which would break or slip if anyone had tried to walk over them.

Once again I was at a loss. Time to get out, I thought. I left the front door unlocked and gave the two uniforms a friendly nod as I left. Three steps down the road I bumped into a face I recognised.

'Oh, hello.' It was the guy who worked for Penguin – the book collector.

'Hi,' I said, feeling awkward.

'I hope everything's okay?' He nodded at the police at my door. 'I was in town so thought I'd pop in and have a browse but...'

'We're closed I'm afraid,' I said.

'Right, oh well,' he replied and looked genuinely down. 'Maybe next time then.' He gave a little smile and walked off.

I watched him amble down the street and enter Simon's antique shop and wondered why I had that tight feeling in my stomach again. Something didn't seem right, but I couldn't put my finger on it. Just getting paranoid again, I thought and headed off in the opposite direction.

I wandered inland and found myself heading for the cemetery. Isaac had often mentioned it and offered to take flowers for Grandad when he visited his wife's grave. I'd always said no on the grounds I could tell he was trying to sell more flowers, but maybe he was just being nice?

It had been weeks since I visited Grandad's grave, I'd been so busy. I still missed him but was surrounded by so many memories of him at the shop that I didn't feel the need to visit his ashes. But I'd forgotten about Nana. As soon as I saw their names engraved in the tiny stone plaque, my eyes welled up. I wondered what it was about gravestones that triggered such strong emotions in us. It's not like Nana and Grandad were here, but something in the recesses of my mind believed that if I talked to them here, they would hear me. It was the same voice that told me I should behave in churches and then filled my head with swear words.

I rubbed the rough side of the stone and sniffed the tears back. New flowers had been put in the holder so Dad must have been here recently. I tried to remember Nana and Grandad together. Her smile and his smell. I looked at the gravestones around me and all I thought about was death. I knew everybody died. Everyone has a finite time alive and should *make the most of it* as aunts and cheesy posters usually say, but I don't think I had truly grasped the cold reality of it until I stood there, in the heat of the sun with my gaze fixed on Grandad's name carved into the stone above the years of his life. 1921 to 1995.

What would my dates be? I wondered. 1974 to 2058? And would I have a Grandson staring at my gravestone in sixty years' time pondering the meaning of life?

So far my life had been pretty meaningless. Apart from getting a degree and writing a few songs people had tapped their toes to, what had I actually achieved?

I looked at the dates. 1995. He could have easily had ten more years, but the killer had taken him away from Dad, from Stephen and from me. My eyes drifted up to Nana's name and years. She could have had more years too. I wondered if my headstone would be shared with a wife's name. Or would my name remain alone for centuries until the winds and sand had brushed the letters away? I thought of Lisa and how disappointed she'd been. Not sad in the end, just disappointed.

My resolve set in and things became clear. If I wanted to make something of my life – to have a purpose – I had to make things happen. And the first thing I needed to do was right a wrong.

The sun wasn't far off setting when Detective Mellor turned up in the corner of the street where I had seen the *Pavilion Poet*. It was out of the way of tourists and I kept in the shadows with my hood up and my back to the wall where the message Mum had sprayed gave me some kind of comfort.

'I'm glad you could make it,' I said.

'Have you got it then?' Mellor's eyes were red.

'Will you let him go?' I asked.

Mellor ran a hand through his thinning hair. 'I haven't got time for this. I could always raid your flat again and take what I want.'

'Alright, alright,' I said.

I took a matchbox out of a pocket, keeping my other hand concealed, and handed it to him.

'What's this?' He said with a scowl and handed it back.

'Oh, sorry,' I said, wrong one. 'How about this?' I offered him a twenty pound note but he just stared at me.

'Stop playing silly buggers you little shit or I'll-'

'Alright,' I said and pulled a brown envelope from my inside pocket.

Mellor grabbed it and pulled out the sheets of paper, reading them in the streetlight. 'A will and a letter from the council?' His eyes narrowed. 'You'd sell your own Dad out for that drug dealer? What's in it for you?'

I shrugged. 'Dad's already lost his job.'

'It's a girl isn't it?'

I tried not to look sheepish but it wasn't working.

Mellor laughed. 'You sad bastard.'

'Just make sure Jim is let out, alright?' I said.

'Why?' Mellor sneered.

His face in that moment made me certain I had made the right decision. This wasn't just for Lisa, or Jim, but for me. This was revenge.

'Because it's the right thing to do,' I said and pulled my hood down.

'Yeah right,' Mellor replied and stared at me. 'Actually you probably believe that shit don't you?'

I looked away, hoping he was falling for it.

'Thanks for this,' Mellor tapped the envelope. 'But I think we have the right man. Jim's going down. Nothing you can do about it.'

'No,' I pleaded.

Mellor laughed again and took a step away.

'No,' I said again, this time without emotion.

Mellor stopped.

'No,' I said once more as though reprimanding a dog.

'What?'

'Let him go or your career is over,' I said.

'What? Seriously?' Mellor took a step forward but restrained himself. 'I don't know what fucking game you think you're playing mate but, in case you've forgotten,' he stabbed a finger at his chest. 'I'm the bloody police and,' he pointed at me, 'you're a little druggy twat who's one step from getting fined for wasting police time.'

I tilted my head to one side. 'Can you threaten me again but one step to your right please? I want to make sure I got your face in the light.'

'What?'

I pulled the remote camera operator from my pocket and clicked it again.

'I might frame that one,' I said. *'Confused copper gets payback*, what do you think?'

Mellor shook his head. 'You're bullshitting me.'

'Maybe that degree came in useful after all,' I said.

Mellor looked over my shoulder and at the bins in the corner, searching for the camera.

'You'll never find it,' I said and cast a glance at the scores of dark windows behind me. 'But if you don't complete our deal and release Jim, I will send the photos of you dealing drugs.' I held up the matchbox and twenty pound note. 'And threatening a family member of one of the *Penguin Killer's* victims.'

Mellor was breathing deeply: his shoulders rising and falling with each lungful.

'Which do you think would have more impact?' I asked. 'Or you could just take the papers and let Jim go.'

Mellor sniffed and looked away. 'Fuck you,' he growled and stomped off.

I pulled my hood back up and felt my knees weaken as I walked away. That had been harder than I had thought. No camera. Just bullshit. Time to be a man. I just hoped Mellor released Jim before he realised the Will in the brown envelope was for Nana, not Grandad, and the letter wasn't the lease of land Knowles was after, but a rental reminder for Grandad's allotment plot.

-Now or Never-

The black hole was happy and still gave him strength. It was time to stop fighting it and use it. Let it give him all the strength he needed.

He didn't care what it made him do now because time was running out. Her words *needed* to be read – they needed to be shared, otherwise what had been the point of her life? Her words wouldn't be read if he was caught, so he had to be clever like her. He imagined her in the world she had created, with velvet walls and floors. Safe.

There was only one thing he could do now. He had to take her words to the papers. If he explained to them maybe they would understand? They would print the beginning and people would be hooked, like in the old days. Then they would have to print the rest or buy the book. Someone would have to print it. The readers would demand it!

A small voice told him he would still have to go to jail for what he had done, but he didn't mind. It was a price worth paying.

So he would pay the papers a visit and find the people who write the stories. He would take her book with him.

And maybe a penguin book just in case.

Friday 18th August 1995

Black Hole Sun – Soundgarden

'Oh, hi Luke,' Simon said. 'Where are you off to?' He nodded at my guitar.

'I've got a gig,' I replied, wondering why he was sitting outside his shop at a tiny table, nursing a cup of black coffee. Any thought of him being the *Penguin Killer* vanished at the sight of him: small and mole-like. 'My band…' I said as if that explained everything.

'Great.' He seemed the most content I had seen him for weeks. 'Good day?' He asked and pulled the second chair out for me to sit.

'Alright I guess.' I carefully rested my guitar against the window and joined him.

I'd spent the day pretending everything was normal and there was no murderer out to get me. Dad had brought my stuff round and argued I shouldn't move back into the flat, but I was adamant. I'd opened the shop at nine; Isaac brought me a tea; I flirted with the girls in his shop; five people bought penguin books; seven bought other books and I closed at five.

'It's hard to rely on the tourist trade,' Simon said.

'Yeah,' I said, wondering what was with Simon. His wife had left him and his neighbour had her throat slit just a couple of days ago, yet he was sitting here like the lord of the manner.

'Is it covers then?' Simon asked.

'What?' I replied automatically, lost in thought, remembering my phone conversation with Lisa. Jim had been released with a warning. My ploy with Detective Mellor had worked. At least I thought it had

– Mellor hadn't come round yet demanding the papers he really wanted. Unless there'd been something in Nana's will that helped Knowles get leverage over Dad?

'The band. Do you play covers?' Simon asked.

'No,' I said. 'We play original stuff… stuff I write.'

'Oh,' he nodded approvingly. 'The muse.'

'Yeah, something like that,' I said.

'I've just finished some work actually,' Simon said and looked away. 'Well, it was Polly's work as well but I took it over when she left.'

I stared at Simon, wondering what to say. Should I console him because his wife had deserted him or congratulate him on completing his book?

'It must have been hard,' I said, finding the middle road.

Simon's eyes lit up, like he was desperate to talk to someone about it. 'It's hard enough working creatively with a partner but this was like writing with someone who wasn't there… they'd already delivered their input and left it as their final word. No discussion.'

'I've never really written with anyone,' I said. 'Just brought my melody and lyrics to the band and we work on it together.'

'Collectively.'

'Yes,' I said and let Simon rattle on about the writing process.

Soon my thoughts wandered. I was weighing Simon up, like Lisa would, and forced myself to consider him as the killer again. If I had the chance to sit with the killer like this, what would I say or do to entrap him?

'What's the book about?' I asked.

'Oh, I guess it boils down to the usual I'm afraid – unrequited love and the inner workings of the human soul.'

'Ahh, deep,' I said.

'Yes,' Simon let out a little laugh. 'You could say that.'

'Any plans to get it published?'

Simon gave a solid nod. 'Yes, that's my next step. I'll send it off to some publishers but mostly agents. It's getting the synopsis right you see…'

He set off again and five minutes later I pushed the chair back to stand.

'I'll have to make a move, sorry,' I said.

'Sure, no problem.' Simon stood and shook my hand. 'It was good to chat. Good luck tonight. With the gig.'

'Thanks,' I said, holding back from telling him it was our last one. 'See you soon.'

Five hours later I was drunk and angry. Not a good mix.

The gig had gone well, one of the best if I was honest, but Beachhead was dead now. After a few beers everything seemed to weigh down on me: my relationship with Lisa was over and the *Penguin Killer* was watching me, so I was in actual danger. In my drunk, dazzled mind, I dealt with it the only way I could – through anger.

Mike had set me off when he tried to clear things up but his comments about the band just made it worse.

'It was never going to take off, mate,' he'd said. 'Some songs just don't cut it.'

'Which ones?' I asked.

'I don't know,' Mike looked at James then back to me. '*Strike?*'

'Really?' I looked to James who said nothing and turned away.

It was one of our oldest songs but I'd always thought it was a standard tune. Solid. Not overly exciting but solid.

'Why didn't you say anything before?' I asked, but knew it was too late.

This boat had sailed.

'I'm just saying in case you guys carry it on,' Mike said. 'Look I'm going out for a smoke.' He left.

And that was how it was for the rest of the evening. I wanted answers and nobody wanted to talk – they just wanted to have fun. We ended up at a club down the seafront with the girls from the beach, so, after a failed attempt at pulling a blonde at the bar and a few drunken dances, Rob and I were left mournfully watching James and Mike with their girlfriends. I downed a few shots and felt the need for a spliff, so I left.

The fresh sea air sobered me up a bit as I stumbled along the prom, past the pub and strip of beach where Lisa and I had argued, bringing it back to me again.

'You need to let go and get out there,' she'd said.

'Out where?' I asked, taking her literally.

'I don't know, just… anywhere away from Brighton. You've spent your whole bloody life here!'

I wished I could turn it off somehow, or remove the memories so it didn't hurt as much. Or maybe I could go back to the beginning of the week and change what I'd said to her… who was I kidding? This was always going to happen. Lisa said she was going travelling at the end of the summer, so we had a use-by-date stamped on us from the beginning. Our relationship had to be thrown away before it turned sour.

But it had felt so good.

My eyes focussed on a crumpled beer can ahead of me and ran a few steps to boot it onto the beach, only I missed and spun away, stumbling into a wall.

'Fuck it!' I growled and meandered away.

I sucked in a lungful of salty air and ventured onto the pebbles, squinting at the sea which glinted with lights from the pier and ships in the Channel. No, I thought, I needed to get home, so stumbled back onto the promenade. As I tried to get my bearings, I looked up and spotted a silhouette skulking around one of the large, four-wheeled bins left out by the beachside clubs and pubs. Probably some homeless guy looking for scraps, I thought, and deviated towards him, keeping in the shadows which shaded my eyes from the streetlights. The dark made me feel safe, so I crept nearer and, about twenty paces away, the person became clear. It was a man wearing a hat and with his collar turned up and rather than taking stuff out of the bin, he was putting bags *in*. Normally that wouldn't be so odd, but at three in the morning? Very strange.

Somewhere in my beer-addled and slightly paranoid mind, alarm bells rang. I crouched low and tried to focus on the man. Two bags had gone in and a third lay at his feet. Black bin bags. He pushed the third in, followed by a tinkle of clinks as its weight pressed down on the empty bottles inside. He closed the lid and walked off with a cursory glance over his shoulder.

I followed.

I kept close to the wall, in the shadows and focussed on where the nearest steps were so I knew my nearest escape route. My mind felt tighter now, like some fight or flight hormones had sobered me up.

The man was a quick walker and I let him get some distance away before checking the bin. I pushed the lid back far enough to stick my hand in and grope for the nearest bag while I kept one eye on the man. I yanked the bag out but it snagged on something.

'Damn it!' I hissed under my breath and I felt the contents fall out.

I grabbed at them but they felt wet and slipped through my fingers. Clothes, I guessed by the feel, and gave up with a sigh. What was I doing?

I pictured myself half-drunk with my hand in a bin and shook my head. Time for bed, I said to myself and continued my route home. I wiped my wet hand on my jeans and tried to focus on the man way down the prom. He turned to walk up a set of steps, so I followed, jogging to catch up. I wiped my hand on my jeans again and stared at them in the orange glow of the next streetlight. It felt like beer but smelt syrupy and the light gave it a red tinge.

Blood?

'Oh, fuck,' I frantically rubbed my hand on the ridge of a hem on my jeans to scrape the taint off.

I caught sight of the man's trailing leg as he stepped away and my drunk brain fought for reason. Blood. Grandad. Murderer. That was what alcohol does to us – it breaks us down to our basic instincts. I wanted to sleep and I wanted to run. My head couldn't decide what to do, but my body did.

I ran.

Anger burned in my chest, fuelling my legs as they pattered a beat along the prom, getting lighter as I sped up. I was determined to catch the man because, in my deluded state, I believed this was the man who'd killed my Grandad and I needed information from him. Details. Something I could give to Mellor so the police could do their job.

I reached the steps and took them two at a time and when I got to the top I caught sight of a shadow slipping into the alley on the other side of the road. I dashed across, running across the path of a lone taxi, and headed into the darkness of the narrow lane. I had no fear because this was home territory. I knew this way: the way back to the shop.

My lungs started burning as my beer invincibility started to wear off. A tightness under my ribs made me think I would throw up soon, so I slowed to a walk and caught my breath.

Where was the man? I zig-zagged through the alleys and looked down every open street but found them empty. I'd lost him. I was so tired I couldn't even swear. I meandered the cobbled ways back to my street, scuffing my shoes on the stones. It was silent. Not a footstep could be heard as I turned into my empty lane just in time to hear the echoing click of a closing door. I saw the glass of the door shake as it closed and that was when I knew – I was certain – the *Penguin Killer* was Simon.

Saturday 19th August 1995
Polly – Nirvana

The first thing I did was call Mellor. Obviously not at three in the morning when I was still drunk, but when I finally crawled out of bed at ten o'clock on Saturday morning with a pounding head. I would have slept in longer but my nagging sub-conscience had filled my head with freaky dreams and I woke thinking I was on a raft sailing down a wild river of blood.

'Detective Sergeant Mellor,' he answered the call, sounding like he hadn't had a day off in weeks.

'It's Luke Redfern,' I said and waited for the barrage of abuse.

I heard a sigh but nothing else. Was that a sign he knew I had fooled him with the papers the other night?

'Listen I-' I started.

'The suspect has been released from custody,' Mellor said matter-of-factly.

'Okay, cool,' I said. 'Thanks, but there's something else… I think I found some evidence.'

Another sigh.

'Forgive me for not jumping out of my seat Mr. Redfern, but the last piece of evidence you gave me proved to be sub-standard.'

Shit. He had worked out Nana's Will was useless, which meant he hadn't impressed his boss, Knowles, and would need more persuading. Still, he sounded posh today, which meant someone else was in the office with him. Time to be a man again.

'Yes, well let's say that was payback for screwing my flat over,' I said, trying not to get angry. 'You set me up, so having no-one to send down is your issue.'

Silence.

'Catching the *Penguin Killer* is more important,' I continued, 'and last night I saw a man throw items into a wheelie bin.'

'What time?' Mellor asked.

'Three in the morning.'

'Where?'

'Down the seafront.'

'Did you check the items?'

I paused then said. 'Yes, I… clothes I think. There was blood and I got some on my jeans so…'

'Right,' Mellor sounded alert now. 'I'll send someone round to pick up the jeans and you can show them the bin. It shouldn't have been collected yet.'

'Cool, okay,' I replied. 'Listen, I followed the guy.'

'What?'

'I followed him after he dumped the stuff and-'

'Did you see him?' Mellor asked.

'Well, no… but I saw where he went – I heard the door shut. It was the antiques shop on my street.'

'Mr Jackson?'

The line muffled as though Mellor had placed his hand over the phone. I could hear voices mumbling then he came back.

'Right, stay where you are and we'll be round in ten.'

Mellor hung up, leaving me staring at my empty flat. My jeans lay on the floor with the red stain smeared down one leg and I ran to the toilet to throw up.

'You were drunk?' Mellor's blue eyes were boring into me like so many times before.

'It was three a.m. on Friday night after a gig, so yes I was drunk,' I replied.

'This changes everything.' Mellor turned away and ran his hand through his hair.

I sat in my brown chair and Mellor paced the floor by the front door just like the first time we met.

'You have the clothes,' I said, happy I'd been able to relocate the bin and it hadn't been emptied. 'And the blood tests will match the blood on my jeans.'

'But no court would take your word you saw Mr Jackson if you were drunk,' Mellor said. 'You need something else – hard evidence which links him to a murder, or…'

'Or what?' I asked.

Mellor stared at me. 'Or you will become our main suspect.'

'What?' I practically shrieked. 'Fuck off.' This is what I get for helping out?

'If that blood proves to be from one of the victims, the only person linked to it is you.'

Shit. He was right.

'Taking us to the bin means nothing,' Mellor said. 'It could be a cover up and you simply made up the connection with Mr Jackson.'

My head was spinning. It was nearly lunch time and I was starving.

'But Simon's a writer,' I said. 'So he fits the profile and…' I struggled to think about what he'd said yesterday before the gig. I'm sure there was something important.

'The author of the book was female,' Mellor said. 'And you already checked the title of Mr. Jackson's manuscript against the list from the deceased reader – it wasn't found.'

'Yes, but Simon mentioned his book had been worked on by his wife, Polly. Doesn't that connect up?' I said, desperate to make this stick. 'Can't you at least question him about it?'

I could see Mellor was tempted but something was stopping him.

'Before someone else is killed,' I added.

Mellor huffed and resumed his thinking walk. Eventually he opened the front door. 'Let's see what the blood analysis comes back with.'

So all I could do was wait. Simon, the killer, was probably sitting in his shop with the same smug look he was wearing last night, thinking he had got away with it all. The man who killed Grandad was just a few doors away and there was nothing I could do about it! I wanted to grab him and make him confess: make him tell me what he had done. And why.

Why had Simon killed Grandad? Had he just been in the way or had his response to reading the book been so bad? In the end it didn't matter. Nobody deserved to die. Apart from Simon maybe. No, he had to be dealt with officially and would have what was coming to him – he would spend the rest of his life rotting behind bars and his precious book would never see the light of day.

    I put a record on. I needed a classic, so went for Nirvana, *Nevermind*, grabbed the crossword book and turned to a fresh page. The simple clues kept my mind distracted: Argentina; wax; microphone; orange; Jagger. Then I started piecing together the not so obvious answers, using the letters now in place, but my mind started drifting. What if the blood was from a victim and they didn't arrest Simon? Would they wait to trap him? They could at least raid his house, like they had done to my flat, in case they found some incriminating evidence.

    A customer came in and I looked up to see a familiar face. The last time I had seen him I thought he might be the killer, but now I knew it was Simon I felt relaxed.

    'Hi,' the penguin collector said and I tried to remember his name. Smith wasn't it?

    'Alright,' I replied.

    'Good to see you're open again.'

    'Yes… thanks. We haven't had any new penguins in I'm afraid,' I said.

    'Okay,' his eyes dropped. 'I'll have a look anyway. You never know, I might have missed one.'

    He padded away to the penguin alcove as Isaac appeared at the door with his wild, white hair.

'Good to see you're open again!' He said with his usual half-smile. 'No trouble I hope?'

I pictured the policeman sprawled on the floor with a halo of blood around his head and looked at the floor. In the end I had just thrown the blood-stained rug away and replaced it with a cheap one from *Evolution*.

'No, no trouble,' I said. 'Just some time off, you know.'

'Well, I don't know what I'd do if the ladies weren't here to help,' Isaac said and looked concerned.

I wanted to tell him the police knew who the killer was and they would arrest him soon. I wanted to tell him it was okay and he could feel safe now. But I couldn't. Not until the blood results had come back.

'So how's the jogging going?' I asked.

'Oh, so-so.' He looked sheepish. 'I'm not expecting much.'

'Grandad used to walk a lot,' I said. 'Kept him healthy.'

'Yes, that's the idea. Oh, you've made a sale,' Isaac said with a nod at the collector, who was coming back with a penguin book in his hand.

'I found one on my list after all,' he said with a grin.

'Do you want a cuppa?' Isaac asked me.

'Yeah sure, thanks,' I replied and he disappeared, leaving me with Mr. Smith. 'That's one pound please.'

He handed me the coin. 'Looks like the other collectors found the books in the antiques shop.'

'Why?' I asked.

'They've all gone by the look of it. Probably people buying them up after those murders I read about in the local paper. Terrible business.'

'Yes,' I replied, ripping a paper bag off the nail behind me. 'But I'm sure the police will get him soon.' And I thought about what Simon's face would look like when Mellor turned up to arrest him.

'Why's that then?' he asked, taking the book back.

'Oh nothing in particular,' I said and could hear the phone ringing upstairs. 'Just the way it normally goes – can't go on forever.' I stood up and pointed upstairs. 'Sorry, I need to get that.'

'Oh, okay, thanks,' he said as I ushered him out the door and locked it.

I gave a quick look down the back rooms and tore upstairs, grabbing the phone in time.

'Luke?' It was Mellor.

'Yeah.'

'We got the results back – the blood is a match with Shirley Wincomb and the clothes appear to be Mr. Jackson's size.'

'So…' I was expecting more.

'So, we still can't connect it to Mr. Jackson no matter what you saw.'

I pictured Simon on the night Shirley had died. His face was rigid with shock and his clothes had been dark with blood. He said he had slipped over when he tried to resuscitate her. I let the idea he was innocent swim round my head for a moment, but one thing didn't make sense.

'Why three in the morning?' I said.

'Sorry?'

'If he's innocent, why did Simon get rid of his bloody clothes at three in the morning?'

'I don't know.' I could hear muffled voices behind Mellor before he said, 'Look, I've got to go, something's come up.' And he hung up.

I put the receiver down and heard knocking on the door downstairs so ran back down to see Isaac at the door with my tea.

'Oh, sorry Isaac, I just had a phone call.'

'No problem,' he said. 'Here you go.'

I took my tea, hooked the door open as Isaac headed back to his shop. Pity, I thought, I could have done with a chat about the old times to take my mind of everything. The music was still playing so I resumed my position in the worn chair and reminisced about when I'd first heard this album. A favourite for smoking to with my mates as our musical tastes sharpened.

I tried the crossword - *Town of twisted spire* - but my mind flicked back to Simon and his story about his book. Why would he be working on a book he wrote with a woman who had just left him? And why was he up at three in the morning dumping clothes that he could have just shoved in his bin? It didn't make sense.

I listened to the song. *Polly wants a cracker.* Didn't Simon say his wife was called Polly? I'd seen a book about names and their origins in the shop but couldn't be bothered to find it. I looked at my watch. Hours until I was supposed to shut up shop but I was hungover, tired and could do with a smoke with my tea.

'Fuck it,' I said to myself and closed up. 'I'm my own boss anyway.'

Ten minutes later, half way through my spliff, the phone rang and turned my chilled vibe into a rollercoaster of paranoia. I couldn't pluck the courage up to pick it up, so left it to the answer machine.

'Luke? Luke, are you there? It's Detective Sergeant Mellor. Pick up.'

I sat up straight and wide-eyed.

'Listen, I need you to double check the books. Number 363, *Dialogue with Death*. I know it was one of the books stolen the other night, but I need you to check there were no other copies.' He sounded out of breath as he waited for me to pick up but I remained frozen to the sofa. 'Look, it's important okay. The book was found with a body… there's been another murder.'

-The End-

He had run out of ideas now and all he had was the solace of the black hole. It lay in the centre of his chest like a hungry octopus: sucking at him from all angles and spreading its filthy ink when it wasn't satisfied.

That stupid lady hadn't understood, just like the rest of them.

Her words needed to be read, he'd told the lady, but just like the others, she had sneered at the sheets of paper. She couldn't speak for herself, so *he* had to speak for *her*. It was important. The most important thing to him because that was all he had left of her and, to him, the novel was just like her. Perfect.

He had seen the fear in the lady's eyes when he pulled the penguin book from his pocket. She knew what would happen and had tried to fob him off with false promises, but it was too late. The black hole needed pain. Pain kept it alive and he needed the black hole.

He left the book with her broken body and wondered what would happen next. Where would he go next with her words? Maybe there was another way?

If he could deal with the black hole, maybe he could stop.

Stop and wait.

Stop and start again when it had blown over.

It would be hard – he would have to be strong – but he was sure he could stop. He could send the book out to agents again. Do it the correct way. Maybe this time someone would listen.

Like she said at the end of her book: endings always bring new beginnings.

Sunday 20th August 1995

Country House – Blur vs *Roll With It* – Oasis

I gazed up from my bed at the same rectangle of blue summer sky that greeted me every morning. It was another sunny day. No hangover today I thought as I stretched, which made a refreshing change.

I rolled over to check the time, remembered it was Sunday and felt myself relax. Ten past ten.

Yesterday's conversation with Mellor came back to me. Someone connected to the Argus paper had been found in their flat, stabbed and beaten. A copy of the *A Home for Memories Past* manuscript had been left at the scene, along with the penguin book: number 363, *Dialogue with Death*, which was one of the three books stolen when the policeman had been attacked. There was nothing for me to check.

'No markings on the body this time and it looked violent, so my guess is the killer knows he's running out of time,' Mellor had said.

'Shit,' was my only response and Shirley's dead face came back to haunt me again: her open eyes and mouth; the gaping wound in her neck like a second mouth.

I looked around the flat and wondered if I should head back to Mum and Dad's but, like before, the thought was soon followed by the desire to stand on my own two feet and be an adult.

'I need you to keep the shop open and act like normal,' Mellor had said. 'If you do anything out of the ordinary, the killer will know you're receiving information from me and could turn on you.'

'Right,' I'd replied, remembering the warning book left on my desk. 'Will do.'

It made sense, but I couldn't help feel paranoid. I had to act normal to avoid attracting attention, which would be odd if I didn't know who the killer was but I was certain it was Simon. I thought about laying a trap for him – offering him some penguin books for his shop or suggesting I read his new book – but it was too obvious, so I'd spent the rest of the day sat in my chair, filling out crosswords. A rock and roll Saturday.

I ambled out of bed and saw the light flashing on my answer machine and vaguely remembered the phone ringing last night.

'Hey Luke, it's Rob. Just ringing to see if you're still coming to Mike's surprise party Sunday afternoon?'

Shit, I'd forgotten all about it.

'I know you were pretty upset about the whole Beachhead thing but it would be good to see you mate.'

I groaned, wondering what I had said in my angry, drunk state on Friday night. I thought I'd just stormed off, but knowing me I'd probably thrown some comment at Mike and darted off before he could reply.

'Plus Mike's got your guitar… and we'll be listening to Radio One for the big showdown! See ya.'

I pressed delete and physically slumped an inch. Meeting up with the guys – especially Mike – was the last thing I wanted to do. I looked longingly at my tin of weed and took a deep breath. I thought about what Lisa had said about me hiding behind the drugs and how it blocked out the real me.

Enough, I thought. It was time to deal with reality.

'Twenty-one today, twenty-one today!' the crowd sang as Rob carried Mike through the room on his shoulders.

Mike was high-fiving friends as Rob carried him through the patio doors and into the garden. He looked genuinely surprised and was making the most of it. The singing was almost in key and gave me an idea for a chorus I'd been struggling with, but I remembered there was no Beachhead anymore. Mike was leaving so we had no lead guitarist and the dynamic had changed. He hadn't seen me yet but I knew an awkward apology was coming.

'In the pool!' James shouted and I could make out Rob's grin half-hidden by Mike's top.

'In. The. Pool.' Everyone chanted and I joined in. 'In. The. Pool!'

'No, no!' Mike was struggling to get free. 'Not in this shirt!' But Rob had a good grip of his legs and the pair of them tumbled into the baby-blue water with an enormous splash.

We cheered and some of the crowd jumped in, or were pushed in, to the obvious horror of Mike's parents who stood at the back of the party, whispering behind their hands.

'Cheers.' I handed James a bottle of beer.

'Cheers,' James replied. 'Mike had no idea mate. He seriously thought we were just going to listen to Radio One.'

I looked at Mike who was trying to dunk Rob's head under the water.

'It's been a while since we got together without rehearsing,' I said, remembering the parties we'd had at Uni. 'Good times.'

'We'll still have good times, mate,' James said and waited until I looked at him. 'There's no reason not to jam either. Keep fresh. Maybe we can get another lead player to fill in here and there?'

I turned back to Mike who was splashing two girls now. 'They wouldn't be as good though would they?'

It was the first time I'd openly admitted how good Mike was.

'Maybe,' James said. 'We can try though.' He took a swig of beer. 'It's Rob I worry about more than the band.'

'You what? He'll miss Mike but…'

'More than miss him, man, he loves him. And I mean *loves* him.'

I'd always been aware of Rob's affection for Mike – how he hung of his every word and seemed to glow every time Mike entered the room - but hadn't realised how serious it was. Now, I could see Rob couldn't keep his eyes off him, and it all fitted together.

'You think Rob'll leave too then?' I asked and felt my stomach clench.

Replacing a guitarist was one thing but good drummers were like hen's teeth.

'Nah, he won't leave,' James said. 'But he'll think about it. He'll need the band to keep him going.'

Mike climbed out of the pool and dried his hair with a towel from his Mum.

'So you knew about this party then?' I overheard Mike say to her.

'Of course,' she replied. 'It was Rob's idea, but we helped out. We thought you deserved it after graduating and getting your job.'

Mike gave her a hug and I saw him in a completely different light. No longer the cool cat who only cared about how he looked, Mike had let his guard down in front of his parents and all I could see was a genuine, kind person. Maybe everything he'd said about the band was true but I was too afraid of criticism to listen?

I looked around at the well-manicured garden surrounding the sprawling house and wondered what was so wrong with his parents giving him everything he wanted? I would do the same if I had children wouldn't I? If I had the money.

Mike turned to the crowd and shouted, 'It's official! I can now legally drink in the USA!' He held his hands up like he'd won a race. 'Let's get drunk!'

One of the girls kissed his cheek and I saw Rob look away. I wondered if Mike even knew how Rob felt about him. If he did, he was the old, insensitive Mike I had loathed. A moment later I caught a glimpse of Sarah and remembered what I'd done the night I saw Lisa in the club. Glass houses, I thought.

'Right.' I patted James on the shoulder. 'Time for a smoke?' I gestured to the summer house which had been host to many a band rehearsal, piss-up and smoking sesh.

'Sure, I'll be there in five,' James replied.

I shimmied through the crowd, avoiding the edge of the pool and meandered down the path to the large wood-panelled building that was easily as big as Mum and Dad's double garage. I already felt relaxed at the thought of inhaling some sweet, heady weed, but Lisa entered my thoughts again. I turned to look back at the swarm of people around the pool, drinking and dancing. Every single one was smiling or laughing, yet here I was walking away. Was I escaping reality? Or running away from something? I just wanted my mates together in a safe place where we could have a laugh and feel relaxed, but, in reality, I was taking them away from the party. Maybe it was time for something different?

A distant chord from the CD player rang out and I knew exactly what to do.

'The next song is called *Roamer*,' I said through the mic and glanced at Mike to my right, who was smiling.

The crowd were cheering, bottles in hand and I felt the buzz coursing through my body. This was definitely the right decision. The drums were already set up in the summer house, so all I had to do was line up the amps, set up the PA and get out the guitars. The look on the lad's faces said it all.

'One last gig?' I'd said.

Mike clinked his beer with mine and flung open the doors. 'Let's do it.'

And so Beachhead rocked the wealthiest neighbourhood in Brighton. The sound wasn't perfect but the atmosphere was awesome. Everyone was dancing – even Mike's parents – and every song went down a storm. Mike did his longest show-off leads, James hit his bass-breaks, my vocals were spot on and Rob added a few rolls in for fun. Whether it was the party or the emotion of being Beachhead's last true gig, the energy lit us all up and we **rocked**.

'That was great lads,' Mike's Dad said when we finished and closed the summer house back up. 'You guys should keep it up.' He looked at Mike. 'More reason for you to come home, eh?'

Mike gave me a nod. 'If the boys will have me.'

'Anytime mate,' I said and shook his hand.

There was some shouting up by the pool and we all turned.

'…to number five,' Sarah called out. 'Come on!'

The crowd had meandered back up to the pool and were beckoned us back up.

'Oh yeah,' Rob said, pointing at his watch. 'It's nearly time for the number one.'

'Who's it going to be, eh?' James said. 'North vee south.'

'Shut up,' Mike said. 'I bought Oasis and you can't get more south than Brighton.'

'True.' James nodded. 'How 'bout you Luke?'

'I…' I paused before replying and looked down.

'You didn't buy one did you?' Mike said. 'Biggest moment of the year so far and-'

'No, I did buy them… on vinyl.'

'You and your vinyl,' Rob said with a shake of his head as we reached the pool.

'Wait a minute,' James held a hand out to stop us. 'What d'ya mean you bought *them*?'

I shrugged and wrinkled my nose. 'I bought more than one, that's all.'

'Which one?' Mike asked, stepping forward with genuine amusement on his face.

'Blur, it has to be Blur,' Rob said.

'No, Oasis,' James said. 'Luke definitely bought *Roll With It*.'

There was no way I'd live down buying one of each, so I decided to lie. 'Well.' I tilted my head and said, 'I thought I'd stir it up a bit… so I bought two copies of The Charlatans.'

'Nutter,' Mike said.

The boys laughed and James punched me in the shoulder.

'You never do anything normal do you mate?'

We moved through the crowd to the radio, where Mike took his pride of place. I took in the crowd, smiling at how we all faced the radio like it was the telly. There we all were: energetic young things; the next generation in our prime. We were about to live through a moment, just like we'd heard our parents harp on about our entire lives, only this was ours. This was our moment. Uni was done. This was the next big step for us - after this we would be released into the world and we were ready for it. The best was yet to come.

At least that's what it felt like while I was still buzzing from the gig and beers.

In the end, Blur were number one.

Oasis fans groaned, but got to hear their song first. Blur fans cheered and threw themselves into the pool. In the end it didn't matter because we all sang through both songs with wide grins and shining eyes.

Good times.

It was dark by the time I stomped back to the shop, cursing at the ever-increasing weight of my electric guitar. I was in a good, fulfilled mood until I turned the corner to my cobbled street. I slowed as I passed Shirley's closed shop and peered into the darkness of Simon's antique shop, catching my sneer in the reflection.

The sorrow came back. I thought of Lisa and the pain of losing her amplified my sadness. Who was this killer to think they could keep taking from innocent people like this? Stealing people away from me.

I realised how drunk I was when I fumbled my keys into the lock and shoved the door open. With my dulled senses everything felt normal but when I sat my guitar on the rug and locked the door behind me, I had the unshakeable feeling that someone had been in the shop. Whether it was the smell or an animal instinct, I didn't know, but my senses were alerted and I was on edge. Nothing was out of place and there wasn't a warning book on my desk this time, so after a quick scout around the shop and half an hour mulling around the flat, I shook it off as paranoia, had a smoke and went to bed.

When I woke up it still felt like something was up, so I headed straight down to the shop. Mellor hadn't bothered leaving a policeman on guard because the killer had enough books, but apparently not. The penguin shelf had been rifled through. The killer had come back for more books and this time they'd been sloppy. They'd made a big mistake.

I felt a cool breeze wash over me as I stood in the penguin alcove. I had discovered how my Grandad's murderer had got in and out of the shop.

And that meant I finally knew who the *Penguin Killer* really was.

Monday 21st August 1995

Wandering Star – Portishead

I used to think all modern photographs were cliché. That there were only ten examples of a good shot and every other photo was a poor imitation of those great images of the twentieth century. Good composure had defined rules after all, so there was only so much you could do with that, and the subject was usually human, animal or landscape – just the emotional message differed.

Half way through my degree I thought I knew it all and felt a depression take hold of me as I realised I would never break into photography because every great shot had already been made. I was surrounded by other like-minded photographers who were looking for the same thing as me - the iconic shot that would make our name. Then I thought about the other Universities and the hundreds of photography students in the same position as me – and the graduates from last year… and the students in other countries. I was overwhelmed. I lost my art.

Everything had changed now.

I can't say whether it was my Grandad's death, living in the real world rather than in the Uni bubble, spending time with Lisa or what the *Penguin Killer* had done, but now I know that every single moment, every facial expression, every leaf, every glint of light is temporary and will never be repeated. Sure, that person might smile again and the tree will grow new leaves; the sun might even be at the same angle tomorrow or this time next year – but it will never be that exact, specific moment. And if you don't capture it, it's gone forever.

So there I was, standing in my boxers and a Beastie Boys t-shirt at eight o'clock in the morning, staring at the shelves of penguin books, which had been the centre of so much pain, finally realising how these shelves had been central to the whole *Penguin Killer* investigation all along. I gripped the brown envelope with my Polaroid photos and could see from the latest snap that two books had been taken but that wasn't what had me entranced.

I took out the other photo – the copy I had taken of the police photo of Grandad's body – and I saw what I had missed before. I'd been so focussed on Grandad's face, the mark on his head and the book under his arm that I hadn't spent time looking at the clear patch of carpet in front of the book shelves. Or the way the fallen books had piled up against Grandad's arm.

I held the picture up to compare it against the book shelves in front of me. The shelves looked different even from the same view because now they angled out slightly at one end as though they had been pulled out. But these were not free-standing shelves: Grandad had built them by hand when he renovated the shop. He had built them with his friendly neighbour, Isaac. These were bespoke shelves, fixed to the wall.

I kneeled close and gave them a soft push. They gave a little, so I pinched the middle shelf and pulled lightly until the whole unit swung opened to reveal a dark space behind. I breathed in sharply, realising I had been holding my breath and bent down to peer into the gap.

Nothing.

Pure black without a chink of light. It was hard to tell if I was looking at a black wall or into a cavernous space but the feel of the air made me assume it was a cupboard-sized space. I felt a soft breeze move past me. In the distance I could hear something heavy being dragged along a concrete floor – plant pots being set up for the front of the flower shop I guessed. I leaned away and pushed the shelf door back an inch, careful not to close it, then sat back and let my head drop as the consequences of my discovery took hold.

Isaac.

Isaac was the *Penguin Killer*.

My Grandad had been killed by his neighbour and friend.

My initial instinct told me I was wrong, but I'd been wrong before hadn't I? I had thought that guy who collected penguin books was the most likely suspect, then Jim because his jail dates matched and then onto pretty much anyone who had a link to writing books, so, up until yesterday, Simon had been the most likely suspect. Was there something the police knew and hadn't told me? I wondered. Is that why they hadn't arrested Simon? Were the police watching Isaac?

I pictured Isaac with his wild, wispy, white hair and couldn't see him as a murderer. Plus he had no connection with writing as far as I knew. He'd never bought a book from the shop as far as I could remember and had never mentioned books or reading.

A thought came to me - what if Simon had a key to Isaac's place and knew about the door? Or one of the girls in his shop? No, it couldn't be the girls because they changed so often I doubt any of them had been there long enough to span the killer's spree. Simon then. But how did he know about the false door? Had Shirley known too? Is that why she had been killed? Maybe it was just Isaac after all?

I sighed and stared at the shelf a little longer. What I really needed was a cup of tea to wash away last night's party and get my brain working. I tried to think logically. Had the door always been here? A meat store from when the shop was a butchers? Grandad never mentioned the secret door, so it was possible he didn't know about it. What if Isaac had built the shelves and door when he helped renovate the shop? Looking at how the alcove sat it may have been in Isaac's shop so the door could have been there for decades and Isaac had wanted to hide it? Grandad had said Isaac had been very helpful but know I knew why.

I sighed again and wondered what to do next. Calling Mellor was the obvious course of action but he was probably still dealing with the last murder. I cast my mind back to his call on Saturday night: he'd said the victim was someone at the Argus, and he insisted I carry on like normal to avoid the killer turning on me. Mellor had never taken the bloody clothes thing seriously, which implicated Simon but after I nicked his drugs and had the showdown to get Jim out of custody, there was little chance Mellor would listen to my theory about a new suspect.

What I needed was proof. Something that linked Isaac to the murders or the manuscript. I needed advice.

I rushed upstairs and dialled the phone. I let it ring and ring but I was too late – Stephen must have already left for work. I tried Lisa's phone but got the same echoing ring. I thought about ringing Mum and Dad. They would know what to do but I needed to stand on my own two feet and sort this out myself. I switched on the kettle and put a record on. Something with mood. Something low. Portishead. A few deep bars and heavy beats later I had made my mind up: I would stand my ground. This was my territory. I would act like normal and, after closing and when Isaac had gone out, I would use the door to find the evidence I needed.

By the time five o'clock came around it felt like the day had taken twice as long as normal to pass. I had kept an ear out for goings on next door but heard nothing out of the ordinary. The girls had been busy and even though I heard Isaac a couple of times he hadn't turned up with his usual tea offering.

I couldn't tell if it was the victory of solving how the killer had got into my shop, or the thought that I was so close to capturing the murderer, but I was completely calm. Bored, but calm. Calm enough to spend the whole day spinning thoughts around my head and always coming back to one question – what could I find next door that would prove Isaac was the *Penguin Killer*? The remaining stolen penguin books would be a giveaway. But how could I find his motive for the killings? The manuscript by Mary Fairweather? I considered it again and again with a cool head. He wasn't a writer, but what about his wife who had died years ago? But if she was dead and the victims hadn't liked her book, why did he kill them?

Finally, it was time to find out.

I was up in my flat eating dinner when I heard the florist's front door close and I ran downstairs in time to catch a glimpse of Isaac jogging down our street. Quick as a flash, I was in the penguin alcove with my torch and Polaroid camera. I carefully swung the bookshelf door open and crept into the darkness beyond. The torchlight didn't have far to travel, revealing an under stairs cupboard smaller than the alcove. I ducked under the sloped ceiling and checked the floor – nothing apart from a few scraps of paper – then turned my torch to the door to Isaac's shop. I had to be quick. I located a handle, took a deep breath, and turned it.

It was locked.

'For fuck's sake,' I hissed and felt a wave of suppressed stress rise from my stomach.

I had to be quick before Isaac came home. I leaned on the back wall of the door to think and knocked something with my knuckle.

A key.

I grabbed it and tried it in the door behind me. With a click, it turned and the door silently swung open. I was surrounded by cascades of flowers in buckets: their vibrant colour and heady scent I paused and listened, watching the room for any sign of a shadow or movement.

Nothing.

I could feel my heart pounding against the inside of my rib cage and held myself back. It felt very real now. Something about the spare key and the one-way lock on the secret door told me what I already knew about the killer – he planned for everything. With every step I took, I was linking the *Penguin Killer* with Isaac and that freaked me out completely.

I pushed the thought out of my mind and stepped out onto the tiled floor of the florists and concentrated on looking for evidence. My Converse trainers squeaked on the floor as I tip-toed and stepped through the towers of buckets and plants, then down a narrow path left between the rows of flowers. Nothing strange here, just tools, scissors and paper. The layout was similar to my shop, a mirror-image, so I wound my way to the door to upstairs and pulled it open. The stairs were the same as mine and, with a last glance out the front window, I stepped up into Isaac's flat.

The narrow staircase filled me with dread – the last thing I needed was to be caught in a tight space – and every step creaked, giving my presence away. I peeked around the corner when I reached the top and found an almost empty flat. I didn't have much in the way of furniture, but Isaac's flat just had the basics. I went through the rooms, staring at the plain, empty walls and the old, worn furniture. No books, no records… nothing to play music on! There was an old black and white telly but that was it.

I sighed. I had checked every room and found nothing. No penguin books, no bloody knife… but there was one door left, which I recognised as a landing cupboard identical to mine. I opened it expecting to see an airing cupboard full of sheets. But this was it.

A shrine.

I had to fight my instincts to flick through the piles of papers and photos. I raised my camera to take a few shots for the police. This was the evidence I needed. Click. The flash was too powerful and left me blinking at the photo of Isaac's dead wife. She looked sweet, sitting at a desk, pen in hand. He had loved her and, as far as I knew, they never had children. Was this what she had done? Had writing become her work? I checked each pile of hand-scribbled notes and typed paper but couldn't see any sign of Mary Fairweather or *A Home for Memories Past*.

I started doubting myself.

Was this really why Isaac had gone on his killing spree? All those lives lost over one book? It was hard for me to accept but a tight feeling in my chest understood it. I could tell by the way she ignored the camera that she was absorbed in her work - she had a purpose. My songs were my purpose, weren't they? I'd spent years writing lyrics and chords on scraps of paper, hours a day wrecking my fingertips on steel strings and paid a fortune on rehearsal space and demo tapes to get gigs, which took up my weekends. But I loved it. It was my world and was all I wanted to do. I craved success. Recognition. Anything that told me music was the right path for me. What would I sacrifice to have a song in the charts? To be adored by fans? Wasn't that my version of a writer having a book published?

A noise made me turn. It was hard to tell where it was coming from but it sounded like a bang downstairs.

'Shit,' I muttered and closed the cupboard.

Had I left the door open in the shop? I couldn't remember.

I rushed down the stairs, treading as quietly as possible and stuck my head round the corner. Nobody was there and everything looked the same as before – towers of flowers and the front door was closed. The banging sound started again. Someone was knocking at a door. My door!

I crept towards the front window of the shop and could just make out a bag I recognised.

'Lisa,' I whispered. 'No…'

I rushed back into the cupboard, careful not to knock any of the pots or buckets over, closed the door behind me, remembering to turn the key and remove it. I ducked and stepped through the false wall door, back into the penguin alcove in my shop. I hesitated for a second, but the frantic banging started up again and I swung the shelf door back in place, pushing it until I heard the click.

I strolled into the main room of the shop, trying to act normal, placed the torch and Polaroid camera on the desk and slipped the photos and key in my back pocket.

'Alright, alright,' I said and opened the door. 'Oh, Lisa,' I said, feigning surprise.

'You took your time,' she said and gave me a disapproving look.

'I had some music on,' I lied. 'Good to see you. You alright?'

'Yeah, I… look I was just on my way out and wondered-'

A shape loomed up behind her and she turned.

'Oh, hi,' she said.

I leaned out of the door to see who it was.

'Hi,' Isaac panted as he caught his breath. 'Hi Luke.'

'Hi Isaac.' I tried to sound as relaxed but heard a strain in my voice. 'Good run?

'Not bad, not bad,' he said as he leaned against the wall to stretch. 'It's getting easier.'

'Yeah,' I replied, wondering where he'd been. Had he just killed someone? Or out looking for his next victim? I desperately thought of something to say. 'I'll have to try it one day.'

Lisa gave me a quizzical look and I said, 'Come inside then. See you later Isaac.'

I ushered Lisa in, who remained quiet until I shut the door behind us.

'So, you were saying?' I asked Lisa but kept my eyes on Isaac's shadow outside and listened for his door to open.

'Right,' Lisa replied. 'I was just heading out for a drink, with Jim…'

I looked at her, trying to read her expression.

'He's heading off to London, got a place at St. Martin's in a few weeks and, well, I just wanted to say thank you.'

She looked me in the eyes and all I could think about was kissing her.

'Thank you?' I said.

'For getting him out. I mean, you didn't have to and I don't know how you did it, but thanks all the same.'

I heard Isaac's door close, followed by a few tin buckets being dragged around and my neck tensed.

'No problem, seriously,' I replied and looked at Lisa's beautiful, if somewhat mischievous, face and knew I had to get her out of the shop. She wasn't safe here. 'Look, it's fine. I had to do it… it was my fault telling Mellor about Jim.'

'Well, you thought he might be the killer, so I get it-'

'Brilliant,' I cut her off. 'Well it was good to see you.' I opened the front door again. 'I hope Jim gets on well and…' I ran out of things to say.

Another bang next door took my attention.

'Yeah, sure, okay.' Lisa said. 'Well, thanks and no hard feelings, right?'

She was trying to mend her bridges before she headed off on her travels. Probably some psycho-analytical house cleaning, I thought.

'No, no hard feelings. Have a good night.'

I almost had to push her out the door and gave her a little wave as I closed it.

'Jeez,' I said as I leaned against the wall and took a moment to take it all in.

I gave my guitar a glance but ignored it, as much as I wanted to settle my nerves, I needed to call Mellor and show him the photos. I reached into my pocket and pulled them out… along with the key from inside Isaac's cupboard.

'Shit.'

There was no way to get the key back and if Isaac spotted it was missing he would know I'd been in his shop.

Tuesday 22nd August 1995

Army of Me – Bjork

I spent the rest of Monday evening in a state of anxiety. I sat in my armchair toying with a crossword while I listened to the dull sounds from next door and occasionally stared at the penguin alcove, waiting for Isaac to come bursting through the hidden door. I didn't know what I would do if he did, but knew I had to be alert, so I waited as the light outside faded.

I studied my Polaroids of the Isaac's cupboard shrine for anything I'd missed and cursing my reluctance to look through the piles of paper. The photos were fuzzy around the edges. Due to the flash I guessed. I knew what was in the pictures, but would anyone else be able to see it? What if Isaac destroyed the evidence and all the police had to go on were these two snaps? All you would see was some keepsakes on a shelf next to a photo and a pile of paper.

Whether I was frozen out of fear, or lack of direction, I remained glued to my chair. My safe place. I told myself I just had to ring the police and all of this would be over, but I daren't move. What if Isaac came through and trapped me when I was in the flat? I could leave and go to the phone box on the corner, but what if he was in here when I got back? Or followed me?

I was scared, I finally admitted it to myself. I'd never been tested like this and had no idea how to react. This was real and my fear had me trapped.

Sometime after dark, when the amber streetlamps outside had flickered into life, I heard Isaac's door shut and glimpsed his silhouette move into the street and disappear down the road. I sat up in my chair. What was he up to?

With him gone, I felt a release and regained the impetus to act. I had to do something. I had to stop being a wimp and needed to make a decision. All I wanted was to shut myself upstairs and have a smoke… but what if Isaac came back while I was upstairs? There was only one way Isaac could come in, so if I blocked the door in the penguin room I'd be safe. I rushed to the alcove, following the disc of light from my torch, and could see what I needed to do – I cleared one of the shelves on the opposite wall to the secret door, prised the long bookshelf out and wedged it across the width of the alcove, to hold the secret door shut.

'That'll do,' I whispered to myself and rubbed my hands. There was no way it would open now.

I wandered around and looked at the front door. It looked weak – brittle glass and old wood – so I grabbed the desk and dragged it over, crumpling the rug under its thick feet, until it blocked the door with its bulk.

I nodded to myself, and felt secure.

Now I could do what I should have done hours ago and ran upstairs to the flat.

I stood there, hand on hip and one ear listening for any sounds from next door, as the line rang and rang.

'Come on,' I said to no-one.

Surely someone had to be in the incident room, I thought. But no answer. I tried the main station number and got through to the reception.

'Yeah, I'd like to speak with Mellor? Erm... Detective Sergeant Mellor, please.'

'Okay dear, it's out of hours now but I can take a message,' a lady replied and I pictured the receptionist with the huge arse, teetering on her stool.

'It's Luke Redfern,' I said. 'Owner of Red Books... and it's about the *Penguin Killer*.'

I looked around the flat as a thought came to me and my cheeks warmed: what if Isaac had been spying into my flat or had some way of listening to me?

'Yes?'

'I've got some new evidence, so...'

'And the nature of this evidence?' she asked.

'Photographic,' I said automatically.

I wanted to say more: to say I knew who the killer was, but something held me back. I'd been wrong before...

'Right then, I'll pass your message on. Thank you.'

She hung up.

I slowly replaced the receiver and felt a pressure release from my shoulders. I had done it. I'd done the right thing. I looked around and felt safe. I was hungry too. When did I last eat? I made a quick dinner, collapsed on the sofa, switched the telly on and slipped into my usual routine. One little smoke to calm my nerves...

A loud bang woke me up. The telly was still on and I had fallen asleep on the sofa. I could hear a voice as well – was that someone shouting?

'Shit!' I whispered and stood up, wide-eyed and heart thumping: the clock on the cooker said two a.m.

There was the bang again. My front door by the sound of it. I checked the answer machine: no messages from Mellor. I thought about taking a knife with me as a series of scenarios ran through my head – was Isaac trying to lure me out of the flat? I was too tired to think properly and settled for the solid torch and tip-toed down the stairs.

The banging started up again when I reached the door at the bottom of the stairs. I pushed it open carefully and slowly peeked around. Everything looked the same as I'd left it, with the desk wedged against the front door. A silhouette was at the door, peering in.

'Luke!' a voice shouted, followed by another bang on the glass.

'Lisa?' I stepped into the shop room. What was she doing here? She could be in danger now.

I tensed as I passed the penguin alcove. My torch sent shadows into the tiny room where I could see the plank still in place.

'Wait a minute,' I said and dragged the desk back to its original place.

I opened the door and studied Lisa to see if she was alright.

'For fuck's sake, Luke,' the words came out in one long mumble. 'Let me in.'

'You're drunk,' I said with a scowl.

Normally I would have found it amusing, but this wasn't the time.

'Yesss,' she replied and pushed past me. 'Ahh… I love the smell of old books.'

She sat on the edge of the desk.

'Do you want some water?' I asked and poked my head out to look down the street.

Everywhere was dark apart from Simon's shop which emitted a faint glow.

'Water?' Lisa's voice raised a notch.

'Shh,' I said and closed the door, making sure the lock was in place. 'It's late.'

'I know… but I'm not tired.' She leaned back on the desk. 'Do you want to take me to bed or give me one here big boy?'

'What?' I wasn't sure how to deal with this. 'You need to go home, Lisa. Do you want me to call a taxi?'

'Too late for that,' she sat up and stared at me. 'I knew something was wrong. I know you Luke Redfern,' she pointed at me and gave me a drunk smile. 'I've got a secret…'

'What?' I asked.

'I can stay here tonight can't I?'

For a moment I was entranced, just like the first time I had seen her, here in the shop. She was perfect. Her eyes, her mouth and the way her nose wrinkled just before she smiled.

'What is it Luke?' she asked. 'What's wrong?'

'I think I…' I started but didn't know where to begin. I cast a look behind me towards the penguin alcove and back at Lisa. 'I think I know who the *Penguin Killer* is,' I said.

She gasped and edged forward. 'Really?'

I pulled the Polaroid photos from my pocket to show her but a noise made me turn. 'What was that?'

'What?'

'A sound.' I turned the torch on and shadows leapt up across the room, making me feel edgy. 'Just wait there a minute.' I crept towards the penguin alcove.

I heard the noise again: a muffled bump and a groan, definitely coming from the alcove. Was Isaac trying to get through the door?

'What's that bit of wood for?' Lisa was beside me and made me jump.

'It's to keep the door shut,' I whispered and put a finger to my lips.

'What door?' She whispered back.

The sound started up again and this time I could hear one word clearly.

'Help…'

'Who's that?' Lisa asked.

I shrugged.

'Is it Isaac?' she asked and the moaning started up again.

I wondered if it was one of Isaac's victims and pictured someone tied up in that pitch black cubby hole behind the shelves. Had he stashed them there to finish off later?

'We should call the police,' Lisa said and tugged on my sleeve.

'No,' I replied.

Another moan came from next door and Lisa grabbed the wedged shelf. 'Whoever it is, they need help, so we'll have to open it up ourselves won't we?' she said as she struggled to move it.

I hesitated. Another cry for help, louder this time and I knew she was right. I placed the torch on a shelf and helped her prise the plank out. The shelves on the concealed door moved forwards as soon as the plank was released.

'The door's open!' I said and grabbed the torch as the door swung out into the room.

I pulled Lisa back into the main room as a loud moan erupted from the doorway followed by a thud. I pushed Lisa into my chair and stood guard in front of her with my torch pointed at the alcove.

Silence.

I waited for what felt like minutes until Lisa whispered, 'Go on then.' And gave me a shove.

'Wait by the front door, keep it open,' I whispered back and tiptoed towards the alcove.

I shone the torch light on the shelf-door, which was jutting into the room, fully open. Something white was on the floor… white hair. A head and red blood.

'Isaac?'

I rushed forward. He was lying in a foetal position on the floor with an open gash on his forehead, just like in Grandad's police photo.

'Isaac, are you okay?' I leaned down to check he was breathing.

'What's happened?' Lisa asked, standing behind me.

'I don't know,' I replied. 'He's been attacked… he's breathing.'

Isaac was muttering something but it was too quiet to hear.

'Who did this, Isaac?' I asked. 'Who hurt you?'

He muttered again so I handed the torch to Lisa and leaned in closer. I'd already put two and two together and guessed who'd done it and remembered the light coming from Simon's shop.

'Make sure the door's locked,' I said to Lisa and she disappeared, taking the light with her.

'Hoe…' Issac muttered.

'Was it Simon?' I asked.

Was Simon's wife Mary Fairweather? I thought, trying to pieces the clues together.

'Simon…' Isaac said, followed by, '…hoe…' again.

'Home?' I asked.

Lisa came back shone the light on us, glinting off something in Isaac's hand.

'Hole…' he said, becoming clearer.

'Lisa, go and call the police,' I said. 'We need an ambulance by the look of it.'

She turned and the room went dark.

'Black…' Isaac said.

'Hey, turn the lights on will you!' I shouted and leaned back.

'Black hole…' Isaac was moving now but I couldn't see him.

'Onleee… mmm...'

'What's that?' I asked.

'Only me,' he said, clearer this time.

The lights flashed on and I clamped my hands over my eyes as Lisa called out, 'How's that?'

I peeled my fingers back to see Isaac sitting up and staring at me with wild eyes.

'I want my key back,' he growled and raised the knife in his fist.

Then he lunged at me.

'Fuck!' I shouted and rolled away, kicking out, struggling to get to my feet.

'Run!' I shouted and pulled at the shelves to get up.

I must have kicked the knife out of Isaac's hand because he was grabbing and thumping at my legs like a madman. I thrashed my legs about and could see Lisa mouthing words I couldn't hear. We were all shouting and Isaac had managed to get on me – a heavy weight. I heard a crack, which I guessed was Lisa hitting him with the torch and the weight lifted, as he turned on her.

'No!' I shouted and leapt on him.

I was too late.

He had shoulder barged her and sent her flying into the bookshelves in the main room, smacking her head and falling limp like a doll.

'Bastard,' I screamed and scrambled to throw myself at him.

My mouth tasted of blood and my lungs were pure fire as he turned to fight. We grappled and struggled against each other. Fists and elbows and knees. He was way stronger than he looked and was pummelling my belly with granite fists. My whole body felt like it was calling out in pain as we pulled and thumped: crashing into the next bookshelf, towards my desk. I didn't think. I just fought to get him off me and away from Lisa.

His footing slipped and I pushed him against the wall, crashing into the shelf with Grandad's camera, which smashed into pieces on the floor. I watched in despair at the mess and the lens rolling under the desk.

What happened next stayed with me as a series of images: Isaac's crazed face of pure anger; flashes of pain; red blood; blue lights. He was breathing heavily and losing his strength as we struggled and so was I, but I thought of Grandad and how he had died like this in this shop. Isaac had killed him.

With a surge of energy, I shoved Isaac against the desk and he toppled backwards onto it: his feet lashing out, sending me backwards. I smacked my head on the guitar hanging on the wall. Without thinking, I grabbed it by the neck and swung the body at Isaac. Too slow - he kicked it away. I swung again, missed and an almighty crash erupted as the guitar punched through the brittle glass of the door, sending shards into the street.

Isaac pushed himself back up and I jumped at him with my fists, punching and pushing until he gave way and fell over the back of the desk.

I glanced at Lisa, who was still lying limp, and picked the guitar up, ready to smash Isaac.

Isaac rose from behind the desk with a sneer.

I don't know what I was expecting from him. A tirade of abuse or a confession? I wanted answers but couldn't think straight. This was survival. This was animal: blood, bone and death. I heard him mumble something which sounded like 'her words', then he raised his hand for me to see he'd found his knife and took a step forward. I raised my guitar.

'Don't do it Luke,' a voice came from through the broken door, which made me turn.

In that second, Isaac lunged and I swung. He stepped on the lens from Grandad's camera, lost his footing and fell back, smacking his head against the wall. My swing missed and I lost my footing, collapsing on the floor. I scrambled back up and lifted my guitar high again, waiting for Isaac's attack.

But it never came.

Isaac did nothing.

He stood motionless against the wall, staring into space with an odd look in his eyes as a flood of crimson soaked the wall behind him.

I heard someone speaking and a crunch of broken glass but still didn't know what had happened.

'It's alright, Luke,' a familiar voice said. 'You can put the guitar down now.'

I turned to see Mellor and blinked.

'It's all over now mate,' he said and I believed him.

My arms went limp and the guitar crashed on the floor. I stared at Isaac and the blood. The paper bags behind his head which shared the nail which had killed him.

Then I turned to Lisa and rushed to her side.

Sunday 3rd September 1995
The Changingman – Paul Weller

It was Simon who had called the police. He'd crossed paths with Isaac at the wrong time and clashed.

'It looks like Isaac was heading out to kill again,' Mellor said as I sat on the ambulance step while Lisa was checked over. 'We found an address of another employee at the Argus in his pocket.'

'Right.' I nodded and stared into space as I tried to take it all in.

Apparently, as they'd chatted in the street, Simon had bragged about his new book and how an agent was interested and he was just one step away from being published. According to Simon, Isaac had leapt at him, punching and kicking. A silent fury which I knew well and could still feel in my bruised face and cracked ribs. Simon had managed to get into his shop and grab a poker in defence but Isaac followed him, crazed: throwing vases and chairs. Simon took a swing at Isaac and managed to clip his temple, but it hadn't slowed him. Isaac had thrown more furniture and ended up pulling a huge mahogany dresser down on Simon and left him for dead.

'My guess is he heard Lisa banging and shouting at your door and decided to come for you.'

'You said he was getting sloppy,' I said.

Mellor nodded and looked down the street which had been taped off like when Shirley had died.

'Is Simon alright?' I asked.

'Yeah, just a few cuts and bruises,' Mellor replied. 'He phoned us straight away and they paged me so…' he left it hanging.

I didn't want to say it, but it was a good thing Mellor had been there. I was still going to have to write a statement but I didn't need to go through everything in minute detail because he'd seen exactly how it had finished: Isaac had slipped and impaled his lower skull on the long nail, killing him instantly.

A far quicker death than any of his victims, I thought.

'Listen.' Mellor held out a blood-stained manuscript held together with a bulldog clip. 'We're still going through the papers in the upstairs cupboard you mentioned, but I think you should see this. We found it in the little room connected to your shop... along with the missing penguin books.'

I had to concentrate to focus on the typed words on the front sheet but knew them already. Title and author: *A Home for Memories Past* by Mary Fairweather. I looked Mellor in the eyes and saw what he saw in mine: tiredness, fear and victory.

'We got him,' he said and breathed in deeply. 'We got him Luke.'

More info came out after Mellor's team searched Isaac's flat and, now the investigation was over and he was being lined up for promotion, he was happy to share everything with me. Isaac's wife had died before Grandad had moved into the shop so I never knew her but, from what Mellor had gleaned, Isaac and Mary, had tried to have kids for years and she'd spent decades pouring her energies into writing novels.

'My guess is her books were her substitute for children,' Mellor said. 'And Isaac supported her through the shop as best he could.'

'To give her time to write?' I asked.

Mellor nodded and flicked his notebook open. 'We interviewed some of their old friends who said there had been a change in Isaac after Mary died… one said *he regretted not giving her a full life* and another said *he always felt like he wasn't worthy of her*. So when she died he took it upon himself to get Mary's book published.'

'Maybe he promised it on her deathbed?' I said.

'Who knows?' Mellor replied. 'Some of the friends had copies of the manuscript and hadn't read it, others didn't know how to give feedback.'

'It's lucky they didn't,' I said and thought about Grandad.

'The point is her death affected him more than anyone realised and set him off on his mission. It consumed him and - had he lived - I'm sure a team of psychoanalysts would have had years of study devoted to him, working out what led him to kill.'

I looked at the ground and wondered if Lisa would like that type of work. Then I thought about my Grandad and Shirley. If someone had read the changes in Isaac and given him support, maybe he wouldn't have gone off the rails and Grandad would still be here. Along with Shirley and the other people Isaac had killed. The thought dissolved away as Lisa's laugh came from the ambulance. A medic came out.

'She's fine,' he said with a smile. 'A little bit drunk… just needs some rest and recuperation.'

That was nearly two weeks ago. It's odd how things seem different when you look back. I still wonder if I would have done things differently. Was there a way I could have found out Isaac's secret earlier? Could I have set a trap or got him to confess without fighting? I've been round and round it a hundred times but I don't think I would have acted differently.

When I went round my parents' house my Dad said, 'There's no way you could know you were living next to a murderer, Luke.'

'That's right,' Mum said as she laid a tray of teas and coffees on the dining table. 'There were no signs.'

'Plus, he was Grandad's mate wasn't he?' Stephen added.

Dad nodded but stared into his mug. All eyes were on him.

'And there's nothing you could have done, Dad,' I said and put my hand on his arm.

I could see tears welling up in his eyes but he coughed to cover it up and took a big sip from his drink.

'We can't all be heroes,' Stephen said and gave me a look that confused me for a second before I realised it was respect.

I looked at Mum, who was staring at Dad, with the kind of look I wanted Lisa to give me: devoted love. Then I remembered I didn't really know what was going on in my Mum's head did I?

A thought came to me and I replied to Stephen, 'I don't know about being a hero... it was just for one day.'

She gave an almost imperceptible flinch, looked me in the eyes and I held her gaze. In that moment I told her I knew about who she really was: the *Pavilion Poet*. And I was proud of her.

'Your Dad's been a hero many times,' she said and turned back to Dad. 'The police don't get half the credit they deserve sometimes.'

'Too right,' Dad said. 'The law is there for a reason…' he paused for a sip then said, '…to live outside the law you must be honest.'

We were silent for a few moments before Stephen said, 'Hey, isn't that from a Bob Dylan song?'

I looked at Stephen and to Dad, who had a sly smile on his face.

'Might be.' He glanced at Mum, who smiled back.

'I missed that one,' I said and poured my coffee. 'Since when did you get so knowledgeable about lyrics?' I asked Stephen.

'Remember young Jedi,' he replied. 'Obi-Brian has been teaching me in the ways of vinyl for many more years than you. Besides, I work for a record company – I should know this stuff.'

'True,' I said and went on to tell them the news about Lisa and me.

In the days after the Isaac incident, as I call it, I started seeing life differently. Things had changed forever. I threw away the rest of my weed. The summer faded away. The tourists went home and the children went back to school.

Eventually I bit the bullet. I bought a Discman, a portable CD player, and bought a load of my favourite albums – and a few new ones – on Compact Disc.

Life is Sweet – Chemical Brothers

The real reason I changed wasn't because everything was changing around me, or because I had a life-threatening incident… it was because I had something to change for. *Someone* to change for.

The reason Lisa had come round to the shop that night was to give me a present.

'I missed you,' she said.

'I missed you too,' I said, holding her hand and hoping the doctors were right and they just wanted a couple of check-ups after the concussion.

'It's more than that, Luke,' she looked me in the eyes as she spoke. 'We've got something… I realised that when I saw Jim again.'

I nodded, knowing she had more to say.

'It's not like we'll be together forever or anything, but I like being with you… you make me smile.'

I grinned and squeezed her hand.

'Plus that money should have been half yours really, so…' she nodded at her handbag, '…have a look.'

It felt odd going through her handbag, but I searched through lip balms and purses to find a white envelope with two flight tickets inside. One had my name on it.

'What the? Wow… but, how?' I asked.

'I knew you wanted to come really – you just needed a kick up the arse.'

I checked the date. 'Jeez, we haven't got long!'

Love Spreads – The Stone Roses
Stay With Me – Faces
Welcome To Paradise – Green Day
Don't Stop Me Now – Queen

The flight had been fine – I don't know what people whinge about. I listened to music, watched films, read books and slept. All with Lisa by my side. And as the plane descended into the tropics, over azure waters and green reefs, I gave Lisa a smile. Everything had fallen into place.

Mum and Dad had agreed to look after the shop and the Argus had printed a six page special which centred on 'the shop where the *Penguin Killer* was killed', so they had another surge of vulture tourists buying more penguin classics.

Dad had the false wall bricked up so nobody would be drawn in to see the killer's door, but still they came. His review at work was finally going through, which meant early retirement or re-joining the force, so he was happy.

Detective Sergeant Mellor got the promotion he'd been after all along. And the *Pavilion Poet* stopped writing Bowie lyrics… and moved on to Bob Dylan quotes instead.

Tuesday 10th October 1995

The Return of the Space Cowboy – Jamiroquai

'Luke!' Lisa shouted into the men's shower room. 'Luke, you've got a message!'

It was my second shower of the day, which had become a standard thing in the tropics.

'A message?' I quickly rubbed myself dry and threw my shorts on.

We'd spent the morning snorkelling the reef just off the beach and were planning a trek inland to spot some wildlife after lunch.

Lisa had that wild light in her eyes.

'What message?' I asked. 'Has Mum been trying to ring me in the middle of the night again?'

'No, it's a telegram.' Lisa was a bubble of energy waiting to burst as she handed me the envelope.

'A telegram?' I said. 'Who sends bloody telegrams these days?'

'Go on – open it! It must be important.'

I ran a finger through the envelope and pulled out the single sheet of paper inside. 'It's from Stephen,' I said as I absorbed the sparse message. 'Shit.'

Lisa's face dropped. 'Oh, bad news?'

'No,' I said and handed her the strip.

YOU'VE REALLY DONE IT THIS TIME YOU TWAT. COME BACK TO BLIGHTY IMMEDIATELY.
MY BOSS HEARD THE TAPE. HE WANTS TO SIGN BEACHHEAD.

THE END

Printed in Great Britain
by Amazon